Sinbad and the

Argonauts

Kevin Candela

Other Books by Kevin Candela

The Dragon's Game Trilogy:
Mushroom Summer
The Ballad Of Chalice Rayne
Dragon's Game
***

A Year In The Borderlands
***

Weedeaters: The Complete Acropalypse

Cover and Interior Art by Kendall R. Hart

© Kevin Candela 2016

Acknowledgements

Ray Harryhausen. Let's just start there. This book does not exist without the genius behind (among many other cinematic triumphs) Jason and the Argonauts and the Sinbad Cinemascope/Dynamation Trilogy: The 7th Voyage of Sinbad, The Golden Voyage of Sinbad and Sinbad and the Eye of the Tiger. Between Mr. Harryhausen and his visionary film partner Charles Schneer a grand screen mythology evolved from the classic mythos of the Eastern Mediterranean. If you grew up in the age of stop motion animation you saw things on the big screen that many, if not in fact most, of today's sf/fantasy fans prefer to computer graphic wizardry. I hear it a lot, anyway: "CGI just doesn't seem as real." Why? Was it the sunshine on the backs of Sakhoura's big green guard dragon and its opponent, the cyclops, as they tumbled around on the polished pebbles of Majorca's stunning La Calobra ravine beach? And the animation of the incredible Mr. H., who made something that never happened look and feel so real you could almost sense the vibrations of the great beasts' footfalls through the theater floor? Whatever it was, those movies were defining theater events of their eras and the biggest thing in the entertainment world in the years they were released. For me, anyway, Golden Voyage of Sinbad was THE movie of the Seventies. The perfect adventure. And for this book

I decided to begin with that movie – and Jason and the Argonauts – as anchor points.

Here's something you should know right off: Sinbad is not a proper name. It's not the Arabic Fred. It means "greatest of sages," so in that sense it is a title. So there can be more than one. And in this book there is: Sinbad in this tale is the son of Sinbad and Margiana of Golden Voyage. I hope that's not disappointing, but I wanted a "free and clear" Sinbad – not a happily married man – for this adventure. Would Sinbad and Margiana not be quite likely to raise a wise and good child much like themselves? And would he not still have to earn the title? I also felt it vital to connect to Harryhausen's epics, so I made this Sinbad the son of the Golden Voyage hero while keeping the Argo's crew – the survivors, anyway (not counting Argus, who "retired") – pretty much intact. Yes, I could have more accurately called it Son of Sinbad and the Argonauts but let's face it, that sounds like some kind of weird adult tale and this is not that story.

After the cinematic references come the literary ones. This time I have to credit Jason and the Argonauts and 7th Voyage because Golden Voyage wasn't out yet when, as an eight or nine year old hanging out at my grandparents' house, I got into their encyclopedias and read everything I could find on Greek and Roman mythology. Yes, while other boys my age were watching the Cardinals I was reading up on Cronus/Kronos chowing down on his kids to keep the throne much like he figured his dad should have. Greco-Roman mythology – indeed, mythos in general – are all the crazy/wild/funny soap opera any bored kid (or adult) should ever need.

I ended up putting in quite a few characters. Why? The plot evolved. Organically. In fact, I discovered as the plot continued to escalate on its own, with a tale of world-spanning conflict and conquest it's kind of tricky *not* to have more than one or two celestial high rollers in on the action.

So that's where this "ancient superhero story" has its roots: mythology and a pair of cinematic giants who realized said mythology didn't "belong" to anyone who could sue you for writing about it. Inspiring stuff for writers, really, and I hope this starts something of a trend. Stop motion could even come back if enough people demand it.

On to the thanks: First and always my wife Jackie. I can't say enough so I won't try. Next – well – it's all pretty much explained above. Harryhausen, Schneer and Company, for creating wondrously bright, colorful and magical worlds that in the end made me want to mash them up together and see how much fun I could have with them. And it was fun. Probably too much fun. Hope you feel that way reading it. Kendall R. Hart, you're one amazing multi-media artist, and your cover for this book – which you had in process before I'd typed the novel's first letter – drove me on to try to make S and the As the tightest, funniest, most action-stuffed extravaganza possible. A thousand thank yous, sir. Finally, gotta thank Don Noble (I do that a lot, it seems) for the "usual over-and-above" stuff he did to help me get the book out for sale" work.

Fair winds, friends. May the seas treat you as a gentle ally and may this adventure give you the excitement and entertainment you seek as occasional diversion to your peace.

Foreword by
A. Lee Martínez

Let's be honest. Sinbad is a lousy sailor. In every one of his seven voyages, he loses his crew and his ship and nearly dies. Given his track record, it's a wonder anyone would board a ship with Sinbad. Yet they do.

Adventure is like that.

Sinbad might be a rotten seaman, but he does have a knack for getting into (and out of) trouble, and that's what we love about him and his ilk. Sinbad, like Jason, like Odysseus, like so many great adventurers who set off in search of danger and fortune, are the embodiment of adventure.

It's easy to forget now, but there was a time the world was full of wonder. Oh, it still is, but the sort of wonder I refer to is a more fantastical, incredible variety. The Great Pyramids are amazing, true, and this planet is a vast playground of different cultures and unexpected experiences.

But where are the giants? The rocs? The diamond-filled valleys? The terrifying monsters and magical lands on the other side of the sea? While I'm loathe to dismiss the possibility out of turn, it's a safe bet that if there was an island of dragons and skeleton warriors, we'd have probably found it by now.

Sinbad's world isn't our world, but the world we dream about when we're young, before things become codified and concrete, before adults have to break the news to us that, no, there isn't an enchanted palace of gold guarded by a riddle-obsessed sphinx just over the next horizon.

Tomorrow might be filled with possibilities, but it's unlikely to ever have a man-eating cyclops in it. That's probably a good thing, but it's still a disappointment.

What kid hasn't dreamt of setting off on some wild adventure, discovering the unimaginable, triumphing through courage, wits, and perhaps a little luck? Mythology is full of such stories, and, honestly, most of them do seem to end badly. Hercules gets to fight the hydra, but he also has bouts of madness and is dumb as a bag of rocks. Jason gets the Golden Fleece, but let's not dwell on what happens afterwards. The ancient world was full of glory, but danger and tragedy as well.

But not for Sinbad, nor most of the classic films that bear his name. In those tales, Sinbad faces all these trials, and he comes out ahead. He's a joyful adventurer who faces down monsters, sorcerers, and pirates. Confronted with a life of boredom, he gladly sets sail into uncharted waters, and that's something we can all relate to.

Common sense tells us otherwise. Most of us will never risk our fortunes or our lives in an exploration of the unknown. Nor should we. We are not Sinbad. We're not even Sinbad's crew, who usually doesn't make it off the first random island they come across, but they go anyway because we all want to be Sinbad at some point in our lives.

I've accepted I'll never get into a swordfight with a magical skeleton or discover a land of harpies. It's better that way. I've no illusions that I could come out on top when tangling with an animated statue or a giant scorpion.

And yet . . .

If tomorrow Sinbad or Jason or Atalanta showed up on my doorstep, sharing wild promises of riches to be found and a dragon or two to be conquered, I'd be tempted to pack my bags and set sail, even knowing I'd never make it back.

Adventure is like that.

Once Upon a Time... Chapter One

"As islands go I think we've seen worse."

Rashid turned to Sinbad with an eyebrow cocked in that way that his captain had joked it might one day get stuck.

"Aye," he said. "Sheer cliffs, a dead strip of a beach, rough breakers, barely submerged rocks with jagged edges: what's not to like?"

"Those are hardly our enemies, Rashid. You see hazards, I see the potential for some fine crab fishing. And a little food is better than the *none* that we have now."

His gaze wandered right as Rashid questioned whether such boons could realistically be expected from the dubious-looking shore that lay about a half mile dead ahead. Sinbad brought his spyglass up and leveled it at the vague irregularity he'd spotted marring the western horizon.

Rashid eventually noticed and stopped nitpicking the desolate tan and gray terra firma.

"What is it?" he said. "Another island? A BETTER island?"

Sinbad shook his head slowly, still taking the distant

11

sight in.

"Another vessel," he said at last. "Their mainsail bears a great ram's head."

"Good," Rashid said dryly. "Sheep are not predators."

Sinbad chuckled but kept his gaze fixed on the slowly approaching ship.

"It *would* be a pleasant change to meet a truly friendly stranger," he said. "I'll admit that even the friendliest would have to bear up to quite a scrutiny from the likes of us by now."

The strange island, lifeless except for a few gulls swirling over the pale sand, drew nearer with each passing moment; Rashid's nerves were obviously fraying as he split his attention between it, his captain and that swelling dot on the horizon.

"Which way are they going?" he said.

"The same way we are," Sinbad said. He lowered the spyglass and turned to his longtime best friend. "Perhaps *they* know something about what would seem to be our common goal."

"We have a goal? Since the storm hurled us about like a wine cork I thought we'd just been out on a sightseeing tour."

"Yes we have a goal. Survival. Even the rainwater is almost gone. The men are weakening."

"Good time to meet another ship, eh?"

Sinbad considered that for a moment.

"Your point is well made my friend," he said at last. "Do we risk anchoring and sit as a target for potential pirates? Or do we trust that pirates would have little reason to sail boasting the head of a male sheep? For my part I'd think such might invoke the derision of other pirate vessels."

Rashid glanced around quickly to make sure none of the crew were near.

"With all respect, Captain," he said, "this is hardly the time for mirth."

Sinbad laughed heartily. The crew ignored it, being used to such.

"Ah but my friend, in the end is our appreciation of the ironies handed us by The Fates not one of the finest and most effective defenses we have?"

"You wax poetic. I think today I'll stick with mundane and say 'what shall we do, oh Captain?'"

Sinbad took the spyglass to his eye and scanned the approaching ship again.

His brow furrowed.

"They have a most unusual figurehead," he said softly. "She overlooks the wrong end."

He lowered the glass and handed it to his first mate, who put it up to his eye right away.

"Doesn't look like a warship necessarily," Rashid said. "Strongly built though. Ready for a battle if not actually out looking for one." He watched it a little more. "Full sail. Toward the island, as you said."

Before Sinbad could respond the crow's nest lookout finally noticed the approaching vessel.

"Ship!" the hulking Havar boomed down at the deck. "Rear starboard side! Ship!"

Rashid lowered the spyglass and he and Sinbad exchanged knowing grins.

"Let's just assume Havar has been distracted by the island up to this point," Sinbad said.

Rashid rolled his eyes. "We have better people for that job," he said. "You know Makili and Nall are both superior climbers. MOST lookouts aren't heavy enough to bend the mast."

"Havar likes being left alone," Sinbad said as the warning shouts went on (more or less needlessly at this point.) "Solitude becomes him. He's not here to chat. But he is a strong and sure hand when push comes to shove, as you know it often does."

By now almost everyone on deck without a vital job was over at the starboard rail gawking and/or jabbering about the still-distant ship with the ram's head sail. Havar finally shut up and that just left the ominous hiss of the wind and the mocking cackle of gulls to compete with the deck chatter.

Sinbad stared across the sullen jade waters. The approaching vessel was impressive, and though it displayed hints of gold here and there they hardly sparkled.

"The ship is well-traveled," Sinbad said. "One wonders if it has seen more than a single captain."

Rashid had no time for such conjectures. He was eyeing that bleak approaching shoreline too nervously. "With due respect Captain," he said. "The men are no doubt waiting for your word."

"My word?" Sinbad was still studying the other vessel.

"Yes of course," Rashid said. "Do we make for shore or stand off and meet that ship?"

That was enough to bring Sinbad around to face his first mate. "What was our last sounding?"

"Seven fathoms."

"Take another."

Rashid called Jahanda over and ordered him to use the knotted rope. Then he looked back to Sinbad as the second mate hustled off. "You're not thinking of taking the ship all the way to the beach?" he said. "Even if we get a fair sounding here it's madness to think there will not be obstacles just beneath those murky waters ahead, jagged boulders cast down when this forsaken place erupted up from the bowels of..."

"Five fathoms!"

Sinbad smiled at the obvious concern Jahanda's declaration stirred behind Rashid's eyes.

"See?" the captain said, his smile breaking into a grin. "Nothing to worry about. Nice smooth incline leading up to a volcanic ring atoll. Any boulders in the waters here have doubtless been worn down by the waves and sunken by their own weight deep into the fine sand. Nothing to worry about."

He slapped Rashid on the shoulder and strode off to address his crew, leaving his friend shaking his head for the umpteenth time in their long alliance.

"Doubtless," Rashid muttered in his wake. "There's never anything to worry about it...until there is."

Sinbad's sharp ears caught his sarcasm. He didn't look back, merely called back over his shoulder.

"Trust in the Fates, Rashid," he said. "They brought us here for a reason!"

Lowering his voice even further, Rashid eyed his best friend.

"I don't question that, captain mine," he said. "But keep in mind it might not be a *good* one."

***

"Their flag bears a monster. Let us assume that means they are prepared to deal with such things."

First mate by captain's decree Pentelus had Jason of Thessaly up at the figurehead rise in a deliberately private conversation. He was keeping his hardly ship-fit form between the captain and the rest of the Argonauts in order to block them out of the conversation.

"I think we should warn them of the danger whether the guardians still defend this place or not," Jason said. "With our firepower added to theirs we will much more easily attain the island's heart...and the temple."

"You know nothing of their motives. What if they are pirates? What if they are monsters like the one they display for all the world to see?"

Jason raised his telescope and scrutinized the faraway deck rail.

"They look like men to me."

Jason didn't see Pentelus' smile, which was both knowing and unnerving. "Appearances can be deceiving, Jason." He glanced off across the waters. "They could be monsters on the inside anyway."

"No more so than any of us, Pentelus. Remember that. Remember Acastus."

"I can hardly forget the tales you and the men tell of him, as I still hear them."

Jason lowered the lens and looked at the man he'd come to trust most over the past couple of months, a man he'd come to think of as a sort of benevolent family elder. He smiled into those twinkly blue eyes, icy as they always seemed to be.

"Ah," he said, smiling. "But I myself forget in turn that you joined us later, after the Fleece had been delivered to Thessaly." At that, most unexpectedly, his cheery mood failed him. He was morose in an instant. "How quickly triumph turned to ..."

Pentelus' brow furrowed. "Sinbad?"

"I'm all right my friend," Sinbad said, and just as quickly as he'd plunged he indeed appeared to have stabilized. "But thank you for doing all you have. Without you and your help – and your wondrous map, of course – I don't know where I would be at this point, if indeed anywhere. And even now you keep me to my senses."

"Then you trust my judgement still, my captain?"

"Of course."

Pentelus seemed to be holding back a smile.

"I could not be more honored," he said, bowing respectfully. His head came back up and he looked right into Sinbad's dark eyes. "Then you will take my advice with regards to that vessel?"

Sinbad scrutinized him for a few seconds.

"Aye," he finally said. "I will."

"Then hold back," Pentelus said. "They are making for the shore anyway."

Jason looked the ship over without the aid of the hand telescope. Indeed she was sailing on, making for the island. "She gives us her back," he said softly, "hardly the move of a pirate."

"Yes," Pentelus said. "But if we continue in and she comes about in the shallows she'll have the shore to her back and the positional edge on us."

Jason turned to him and smiled. "I must admit I had questions about your seaworthiness, my friend. But you have learned much already."

Pentelus beamed. "I am honored," he said, and gave a quick bow. "May I take that compliment to suggest you are willing to trust my judgement on this uncertain situation?"

"Very well," Jason said after a moment's silent deliberation. "Give the order."

Pentelus turned and yelled "Easy oar!" to the crew, who'd been at it a while and were more than happy to oblige. Most of them wanted to get a look at what was going on with the ship off to the east and the island dead ahead but Pentelus made sure to hold them to their rowing stations.

Once he had them all calmed and resting he turned back to Jason and they studied the other ship's approach to the island side by side.

Nothing was happening.

"Perhaps the talk is true," Pentelus said as the other ship closed to within a couple hundred feet of the strip of tan-gray beach sand. "This place has been forgotten so long that its defenses have fallen."

Not quite, as it turned out.

***

Two great swells rose up before Sinbad's beloved vessel, the Chimera. The water cascaded aside at both spots and up through the foam and froth rose a pair of incredibly huge, vaguely man-shaped creatures, each of them sporting five great arms on each side of its torso. Covered in olive green scales fringed with barnacles and sea slime, the sixty foot tall humanoids bore a man-sized rock in each of their cumulative total of twenty hands. The revolting creatures thrust their mammoth chests out at the approaching ship and – as one – let loose thundering roars that sent great shivers rippling out across the waves.

"Take cover!" Sinbad hollered at his crew as the beast-men unleashed a barrage of potentially deadly boulders. "Protect yourselves!"

He and Rashid dropped together behind the Chimera's prow walls. Boulders hit around the ship, sending back-splash waves crashing across the deck. One tore a great hole in the foresail, snagged there and ripped the sail in half as the bundled-up rock crashed to the deck. Another took out a section of the aft port rail and Gabil, a chronic griper but reliable deckhand, sending him flying off into the churning waters like a ragdoll hit by a club.

More boulders were still incoming. The creatures were hurling them a couple at a time. One tore off the crow's nest and uppermost ten feet of the mainsail mast, shearing through it only four feet or so below the head of the quickly descending Havar, whose pace down the mast handholds instantly doubled.

Rashid and Sinbad exchanged desperate looks.

"If you have any miracles left at all, Captain," Rashid said, "this might be the time."

Sinbad was already fingering the fiery orange jacinth that hung on the silver chain about his neck.

"I suppose you're right," he said. "As it is we have no chance at all."

Rising up off his knees, he peeked over the top of the rail. A boulder was coming right at him so he dropped and shoved Rashid back to keep him clear of the impact. The rock smashed into the bow dead center, turning the sheltering walls the pair had just left behind into sprays of fragmented wood that rained across them. Sinbad opened his eyes to a clear view of the angry guardians.

He stood boldly and faced them. He ripped the amulet off, threw it to the deck and smashed the beautiful crystal with his boot.

A whirlwind of fire and ash rose up from the crystal and consumed Sinbad. He was lost almost instantly within its twisting, roiling confines. Then the entire vortex lifted from the deck, leaving behind only the broken silver chain, and – morphing form as it went – rose up into the air over the bow.

***

Jason didn't follow his first mate's advice long.

"Advance on the battle!" he hollered to his crew as Pentelus stood helplessly beside him, his face a mask of disappointment and concern. "Ready the javelin cannon for those decacheires and open fire the moment we're in range!"

"But Jason," Pentelus said, seizing his captain's elbow to get him to turn his way. "Those beasts can throw farther than we can shoot. We'll be as vulnerable as that ship if…"

"Then we'll share their fate," Jason said, cutting him off. "Courage Pentelus, we have the advantage."

"We do?"

"Certainly. Those beasts are brute force and ignorance. I'll take wit and determination over that anytime."

"Yes of course, wit," Pentelus said with dejected sarcasm thick in his voice. "Perhaps if we can get in close enough you can simply challenge them to a board game as an alternative to bloodshed."

"You never know," Jason said, smiling grimly. "Their half-brothers are the Titans and some of them like Prometheus are pretty sharp."

"You're thinking of the hecatoncheires. These have ten hands, not a hundred."

"Right. And so this particular pair should be that much

easier to defeat."

Pentelus realized he wasn't going to win the argument and was conceding to that point when he spied the ball of flames rising up over the other vessel. He pointed it out to Jason.

"What can it be?" Jason said, studying it through his scope. "It's taking some kind of form."

Indeed it was, although the shape it was taking was hardly that of any "normal" entity.

It became a great bird. But not a creature of feather and flesh by any means; rather, it had manifested into the rough and irregular shape of a bird made of orange flames.

And riding atop its neck, seemingly undamaged by the fires about him…a man.

"Perhaps you were right," Jason said. "Maybe they don't need our help that badly."

"So we're backing off?" Pentelus said, his tone leaving no doubt that would have been his choice.

"No, we attack as well. Between our heavy weaponry and whatever *that* is I'm thinking the odds are leaning our way now."

"What if it attacks *us*?"

"I can't imagine its rider would be so foolish as to not only turn down assistance but attempt to fight two battles at once instead," Sinbad said. "Full speed ahead."

Chapter Two

Battered as she was already the Chimera and her crew were extremely fortunate that Sinbad's "miracle" had come when it did. Now the decacheires had a much more worthy foe at which to aim their shoreline boulders, and as this newcomer swirled and streaked above them the Chimera's crew fell to cheering from the shattered rails.

Sinbad and his phoenix mount left trails of ash and sparks that descended in their wake as they distracted the great monsters and led their volleys away from Sinbad's ship. At first he'd merely steered the magical mount away from the ship, arbitrarily arcing off to the port side, but at this point a plan was coming to him.

He wasn't sure how he was controlling the fiery steed: it was merely going wherever he willed it, as though his mind were in fact its...which, he fully knew, might just have been the case.

Magic, you know.

He willed the phoenix to take him higher...and closer.

The decacheires were virtually impossible to defeat even mounted atop this strange semi-creature, whose flesh appeared to be constantly shearing off in red-edged flakes as though its form were made up entirely of layers of flaming black tree bark.

But Sinbad had a plan.

He dodged, circled and twisted his fiery mount,

spinning the daylight specter in ever-tightening rings as he deftly kept it – and himself – clear of boulders streaking up at them from below. Often *just* clear, but that was good enough.

At last he made his move. He dove in toward the misshapen head of the one on the left as three of its arms, having just scooped up fresh rocks, cocked back to throw. But he wasn't coming in at full speed; rather, he was saving that extra kick for a last second pull-up maneuver, and when he willed the magical mount to do just that he did so in the sincere hope that no deity was at that moment bearing him ill will.

Startled by the sudden acceleration and inexplicable rocket-like rise directly over its head the titan-kin nevertheless let loose on the enemy anyway, launching all three boulders after Sinbad and the phoenix with as much force as its arms could muster (which was plenty considering the size of those arms.) The rocks, each weighing hundreds of pounds, closed in momentarily on the phoenix. But the fiery red and black phantom outraced them.

The other decacheire had fired as well, so over the beasts' heads a total of five boulders were rapidly decelerating. These came to a halt with the dull-witted creatures staring up at them – and through their midst at the soaring target they'd all failed to catch.

Gravity took over.

The boulders came streaking back down. The decacheire on the right got a clue and backed away, but the other one just stared, fascinated, at the onrushing rocks.

One came down squarely on its forehead. A thundering crash echoed out to the two approaching vessels and their crews watched with wonder as the titan fell back into the waters and lay still; its counterpart, not quite comprehending yet, stared down and saw the left one's blank-eyed face slip slowly beneath suddenly crimson water. At that point it caught on.

Wrenching about abruptly, it searched the skies for Sinbad and the phoenix. Quickly spotting them, the decacheire roared deafeningly up at the pair as they circled above its head, taunting it, trying to prod it into repeating the mistake. But this creature wasn't quite that stupid from the look of it. Kneeling down instead, it kept a close eye on Sinbad and the firebird as it sent its arms out scouring beneath the knee deep (to it, anyway) water in search of more rocks.

Sinbad stayed well aloft though he knew the tactic wouldn't work again by that point. But when the decacheire came up and opened fire on the Chimera instead, battering it once more but from much nearer as it had quietly continued its advance in hopes of getting in harpoon range, the ship's captain was compelled to go on the offensive.

He directed the flaming mount to dive straight down at the remaining monster.

Little did he realize the decacheire was anticipating the move even as it continued to decimate the Chimera's forward hull and deck: at the last moment, as Sinbad prepared to dismount and send the phoenix slamming into the decacheire, the titanic guardian – which had in fact been in sort of a crouch – leapt up and swatted the stunned captain right off his mount.

The phoenix hit the water beside the decacheire, flashed brilliantly and then vanished, leaving behind nothing more than a patch of charred bark-like fragments bobbing in the froth. Sinbad tumbled, skipped across the as yet not quite submerged torso of the other guardian monster and plunged semi-conscious into the water under the beast's great five-socketed armpit. Choking and sputtering he came up and grabbed hold of the first thing his hand came across, which he thought at first to be seaweed.

When he finally managed to get the saltwater out of his

eyes he saw he was clinging tightly to a long twist of armpit hair. Revolted, Sinbad pushed himself off and backstroked away, only to see a shadow falling across him. Reacting instantly, he grabbed a deep breath and forced himself beneath the waters just ahead of the crash of a huge boulder.

The rock didn't sink after him though. Sinbad looked up and saw through the bubbles of his own breath that it had jammed tightly in between the presumably dead decacheire's upper arms and torso. Finding himself under the titan's bulk, he knew he didn't have a lot of breath left but just as surely realized that he needed to use this cover while he had it. He forced himself deeper to get beneath the giant's back.

The live decacheire was doing just what Sinbad figured at that moment: it was circling around to get to the far side of its fallen ally so that it could search for Sinbad there.

***

"Up one degree!" Pentelus hollered at the Argo's javelin gun crew, checking the position of the decacheire as it waded around its fallen partner. The four men operating the slow-pivoting great gun obeyed, adjusting the weapon's aim with cranks. Pentelus saw them steady it and signal him that it was set, whereupon he turned and looked to where his captain stood at the very tip of the prow. "Jason!" he yelled. "On your command we stand ready."

Jason measured the shot from where he stood, which was more or less directly beneath its intended trajectory. He felt the wind on his cheek and watched the decacheire, which had reached its destination and, kneeling, was feeling around beneath its fallen comrade.

"Wait..." he called back to the chief gunman, Dimitrius, who stared back at him with steely resolve in his black eyes and nodded ever so faintly. "Hang on," Jason said. "On my signal."

He put an arm into the air. Akhin (and everyone else on board) watched that arm.

It came down sharply the instant the decacheire rose from its crouch.

The javelin gun fired its three hundred pound missile.

Jason watched it slice through the air over his head.

The decacheire had come up in a frustrated flourish, rising and flipping its ally's body over in one great splashing move. Caught by surprise, Sinbad had struggled back up to the surface for much needed air only to find himself with nothing close by to hide behind. For an instant he was eye to eye with the decacheire, which was grinning down triumphantly at him.

Then the huge javelin struck the decacheire dead center in the chest.

Pierced to the heart the monster staggered back, clawing at the air in front of it.

It looked down at Sinbad, who was still bobbing helplessly out in the open before him...but now far out of reach nonetheless.

The beast fell over. Having reeled back far enough toward land, it collapsed partially atop the beach with a massive rumble that resonated off the atoll rim and echoed back out to the two vessels.

Cheering erupted aboard both ships, which in the interim had drawn to within a hundred yards or so of each other. Jason worked his way up onto the first fallen titan's forearm, rose there and waved to his ship.

"Might as well swim to shore, Captain," Rashid yelled at him from the Chimera's smashed bow, and their shipmates nodded their concurrence from beneath the ship's shredded sails and shattered masts. "You'll get there before we do!"

Chapter Three

Sinbad dove into the opaque, oddly warm emerald water and chanced the swim back over to the Chimera instead. Meanwhile the Argo was approaching the battered vessel slowly, under easy oar.

Jason wanted their pace slowed even further. "We don't want to appear challenging."

From his spot at the prow he watched Sinbad's crew hauling their captain back up on board. The moment the heroic magician was back on his feet, he saw, the man's gaze was coming right back his way.

Jason held up one hand and waved gently. "No my friends," he said under his breath. "We mean you no harm and I can only hope you feel the same."

"I still don't think we should approach them," Pentelus said. "We aided them and saved their magician. That should be enough."

"If they're going where we are I don't see how avoiding them can be seen as anything but a suspicious move," Jason said. "As you say we just aided them. They should be somewhat welcoming, or at least not blindly hostile."

"But Jason, with all due respect, we have no idea what their intentions might be. What if they are coming to raid the temple?"

"You mean as we are? Then we'll have good company.

***

The Argo's stores were in actuality already half depleted, and what was left was none too fresh; nevertheless the feast that began shortly before the lava-colored sun melted into the ocean was a hearty and boisterous one. The two crews were mingling well, with stories and jokes all around. Spread across both ships, the spur of the moment party was soon running shorter on wine than Jason had hoped. Pentelus brought him the word that an entire cask had already been consumed, leaving only two.

"Then break open another, Pentelus!" a slightly drunken Jason told his first mate. "Surely we will find something to replace them on Kryptos."

"Kryptos?" Sinbad said. "You know the name of this place? I thought you said you were beyond the range of Thessaly's maps."

"We are," Jason said. "The map we're using is not from Thessaly."

Both of them – and Rashid, Havar and a couple of others nearby – shared a laugh at that.

"Semantics," Sinbad said, eyeing his counterpart with equal parts mirth and wariness. "I'll have to remember you're the type who enjoys playing with words."

Jason toasted him with his sloshing goblet.

"Perhaps," he said. "But the word of any Argonaut is to be taken to heart."

"What's here?" Rashid said to Jason, turning everyone's gaze his way. Seeing all the eyes upon him he quickly explained. "We're here by the whims of a great storm," he said. "You've come to a place whose name you in fact know, an island apparently far from your home, leading one to wonder why."

When he saw that this had taken Jason slightly aback Sinbad intervened.

"Their business here is none of our concern, Rashid,"

he said. "It is their choice whether or not to share it with us."

"Of course, Captain," Rashid said, looking a little sheepish. "My apologies, Jason."

"Not necessary Rashid," Jason said. "You are here and we are friends and as such I will not hold back such information. I will tell you what I know about this place."

A few of the others aboard the Chimera were close enough to be picking up on some of their conversation; to a man they were all inching closer one way or another at the moment, trying to get more of it.

"Kryptos is the vault of the gods," Jason said. "Those great monsters lying out there in the surf are no doubt only one of numerous safeguards against mortal intruders." He turned a little so he could point off toward the island's encircling cliff, glowing like gold-trimmed obsidian in the fading rays of the fiery sunset. "Beyond that ridge lies a broad sunken valley, and at its center stands a great vault, a temple of impervious crystal."

"Strange," Sinbad said. "From the shape of its perimeter I had this place figured as an atoll. What's in this vault that draws you with such dauntless intent beyond the edge of your – of *your peoples'* – maps?"

"Let me put it this way, my friend: In your long travels I presume you've come across treasure?"

"Yes," Sinbad said without hesitation, "and rarely has it proven worth the cost."

"Ah, but you no doubt speak in terms of wealth. Riches. Gold."

"As I thought were you."

"Tell me Sinbad, what use have the gods for gold and gems? Are they not beyond the material?"

Sinbad caught his drift though he appeared to be the only one. He smiled.

"I see. What would a god consider valuable enough to store in a temple of impervious crystal on an island beyond most maps?"

"What exactly."

"And what makes you think they'd just assign some material guards to their care and forget about them?" Sinbad said. "Might they not keep watch on such greatest of wonders themselves?"

"The realm of the gods is said to be a neutral ground shared by encampments. In such a place no common safekeeping is truly possible. So they sent them down here, where only weak mortals such as ourselves might be tempted by them. The gods don't bring their armies to our world; they work through men like us."

"A game."

"I've played them before," Jason said. "Apparently the one thing few of them can resist is a game. Almost childlike in a way."

Sinbad thought about it for a moment as half of both crews looked on.

"This has been a most fascinating day," he said at last, "at the end of which I find myself indebted not once but twice to a stranger...an honorable man, apparently, yet one bent on stealing from the gods' most prized vault."

"I seek to steal nothing," Jason said. "I've been a thief as well, but that's in the past."

"Then what is it you DO want, Jason?" Sinbad said. "I mean, if you're willing to say."

"I have come here seeking only one thing: answers. Answers to questions that have driven me here. Answers that can only be found here, if indeed there are answers at all."

"Yes," Sinbad said. "And to such a vague – yet agreeable – fellow I am now indebted for two favors rendered."

"Two favors," Jason said, and he nodded. "Indeed. And you can repay them both with but a single one."

"Let me guess. You wish us to accompany you to this temple and assist you in getting the answers you desire?"

"I ask nothing of you and your crew," Jason said.

"Merely your friendship. However, I would certainly consider such a great favor to even things between us."

Sinbad looked around, focusing on the surrounding faces that belonged to his own crew.

"What say you?" he said to them.

"Aye," Rashid said once he'd scanned his subordinates' expressions as well. "If that's the deal we're in. But wasn't there something in there a little ways back about their crew helping to repair our ship first?"

"Aye," Havar said. "And there was talk of treasure as well."

Chapter Four

The next day dawned quietly behind thick clouds and with it the crews of both ships were at work on the Chimera. Sinbad and Jason took in the stem to stern cacophony of hammering, sawing and chatter from the ship's still rail-less bow.

"Your craft should be seaworthy in short order at this rate," Jason said. "I thank you for changing your mind and allowing my men to help. The favor I ask is challenging enough, I may split away some of my crew to form a landing party soon."

"We will hold to our word and accompany you," Sinbad said. "I'll have Rashid put together some of our best as well."

"You do not in fact owe us anything, so this is greatly appreciated."

"I never let a man walk away owing him my life. A woman either."

"You've owed a woman your life as well?"

"Yes, but not until yesterday," Sinbad said. "That conjuration you saw me riding came from a rather unique one."

"Wouldn't have any other such wondrous surprises, would you? We may need them."

Sinbad shook his head. He chuckled. "No," he said. "That one alone was hard enough to earn."

***

Shortly after midday a twelve person landing party rowed in to the beach in one of the Argo's two lifeboats. The captains were aboard, along with five of their crew apiece. As they passed between the dead titan-kin their talk sent waves of scavenging gulls scattering off both of the hulks.

"Those will be pleasant in a couple of days," Makili, one of Sinbad's newer crew members, said.

"If we're not careful we'll end up like that too," his ever-edgy close friend Nall said. "If these are the servants of the gods imagine the gods themselves."

"The gods are nothing to fear," Jason said. "I've met some of them. They're just as frail, weak and fallible as we mortals."

"That may be true," Havar said. "But *we* can't hurl lightning bolts!"

The broad rowboat erupted in laughter, nervous as a lot of it might have been.

After what seemed considerably longer than the few minutes that actually passed they were through the channel between dead monster torsos and nearing the gray sand of the shore. Having left Pollux, the second mate, in charge of the Argo Pentelus was one of the few not smiling. And despite being near the front he was not all that eager to jump out into the presumed shallows and help drag the landing vessel in the last few yards to ground it on the beach.

Others did, however, and soon they were splashing and slogging as they pulled the rowboat up and drove its shallow keel into the saturated sand.

Jason and Sinbad stood together moments later, their team at their backs as they scrutinized the rough rise ahead of them.

"The ascent won't be too bad," Jason said, glancing

down at the map in his hands. "It's the other side that's steep. I hope we have enough rope."

"How much could we possibly need?" Sinbad said. "We brought a dozen hundred foot bundles."

Jason turned to him.

"I *hope* we have enough rope," he said. He wasn't smiling.

Sinbad gestured for the map and Jason handed it over so he could look at it.

"Strange," he said, looking over the details of Kryptos. "The valley is far below sea level. A volcanic crater whose lava pool receded after pushing the rim we see here up from the ocean floor."

"Does that matter?" Belaricus, one of Jason's crew, said.

"Probably not but it's fascinating."

"Apparently we have different definitions of fascination, Captain Sinbad," Helius, another of Jason's men, said. "Land us on the island of the nude sirens and we'll be much more fascinated, I assure you."

Despite the uncertain land ahead of them the group was actually laughing.

It was the last such break they'd have for quite a while.

***

For the first hour or so they worked their way up a modest to occasionally severe incline of as much as forty degrees at times, working hard to negotiate a deeply rutted, badly eroded slope that was strewn across its mile expanse from top to bottom with loose rock ranging from ridges of treacherously loose gravel to huge, often precariously perched boulders. Beneath and between all this sharp and brittle volcanic rubble lay potentially deadly crevices, many wide enough to fit a man, and too many of these were proving to be virtually hidden by the piled obstacles until the daring adventurers were right upon them. They had already experienced two near disasters, one involving the Chimera's captain himself, no less, when a reappraising Sinbad suggested everyone stay within a step or two of at least one other person, a move Jason readily seconded. This ended up keeping a couple of people, including Makili, from significant injury or worse since someone was close enough to help them out when they ended up in bad locations. Havar lost his footing and took a tumble, but his broad girth saved him when the edges of the two foot wide crevice he'd stumbled upon caught him by his broad shoulders and halted his belly flop into it.

They reached the summit of the island-encircling ridge just as the sun was setting. The view was staggering. They found themselves standing at the rim of the huge valley depicted on Jason's map. Far below them lay a great expanse of dark green dotted with some light patches and many nearly black ones.

Far off across this primeval swampland a bluish-white light gleamed. That distant again beyond the light the far wall of the sunken crater rose. The shimmering construct, quite starkly alone at the center of the expansive crater, had a recognizable shape even from such a distance as the landing party was viewing it: they were all looking at the largest gem they'd ever seen, in form if in fact nothing more a blue-white diamond of immense size half-buried in the distant landscape far below.

"Okay," Nall said, his voice filled with awe. "I admit I had reservations about this one, but I'm a little more behind it now."

"How in the name of the Seven Seas are we supposed to haul *that* up here?" Havar said. Hearing no response, he turned and saw the rest all staring at him. He got it then. "Oh."

***

Despite the late hour no time was wasted. Several men set about tying the ropes together.

"I'm not crazy about that descent," Raoul said, his legs trembling as he leaned over the precipice that loomed before them all. "The canyon rim here is so eroded we can't even get a look at what's beyond its edge."

Glancing over at him from where he was testing knots, Jason chuckled.

"Relax my friend," he said. "Look upon the rim to either side, bright in the light of the moon, and you can easily see what to expect beyond this convex slope before us. Nothing to fear. Besides, enjoy this breather – this, after all, is the easy part."

Havar eyed him uncertainly. "Easy?"

"Absolutely," Sinbad said. "Gravity will do most of the work. Much easier than the way back."

A few groans suggested some of the party hadn't thought of that yet.

"Fear not, my friends," Sinbad said, raising a palm high over his head to quell the grumbling. "We have yet to journey to a place where the reward failed to justify the effort."

"Tell that to Rashid," Raoul said. "With due respect, Captain," he quickly added, and bowed.

"Even Rashid admits his own haste cost him that hand," Makili said. "And you, Raoul, as well as the rest of us heard Sinbad pledge that he would atone for Rashid's loss even at the cost of giving him his own right hand if need be and opportunity is presented."

"But of course I was only jesting Captain," Raoul said. "Rashid has accepted his loss. We all know that. The lack of one hand disappears when he sees the great glitter and sparkle that lies beneath the deck of..."

Seeing the look in his captain's eyes he trailed off.

"Treasure is the word you meant to finish with, I assume," Jason said. "If you have come upon a great fortune I bow to you, for you obviously deserve it. And rest assured neither I nor any of my men will touch a single coin or gem that we have not earned as reward nor won in combat against a deserving enemy."

"Your word is good enough," Sinbad said, and they shook by gripping forearms. "And I would not burden you with the spoils we have acquired, for they come at a price I would not share with you or your men."

Jason cocked his head slightly. "A curse?"

"Perhaps," Sinbad said. "For never before have the stars themselves failed to guide us, nor the seas drawn us into that great storm that cast us to this strange place."

"Maybe it's not a curse," Jason said. "Maybe it sent you where you needed to go."

"Now that you mention it, we *are* in the market to acquire a large number of well-armed and trained mercenaries. There are rumors of trouble in the lands beyond Aderadad's western border, and despite Queen Margiana's talents she has not been able to verify or dismiss them. And despite her overwrought concerns for the safety of our ship and crew I have pledged to bring her the defenses she believes Aderadad will need. And in truth that's quite a challenge considering how rarely the urge for aggression and the wisdom to know when not to use it can be found in the same individual."

"If your home needs defending, surely my men and I will add our swords to yours."

"Well met, and appreciated. But first we'd have to know how to get there. Still the stars lie to us, you see? We study them and they confuse us."

"We can lead you home with our instruments," Jason said. "Assuming the curse that has afflicted you has not yet spread to us, that is."

"I most certainly hope it has not," Sinbad said. "Unfortunately, hope is all I can do."

Chapter Five

Dardan of the Argo was the best climber in the party. Lean and strong, he rappelled down the eroded inner rim of the crater until he'd vanished completely behind its edge, some thirty yards distant. But he wasn't out of sight long.

He worked his way quickly back up to where the others stood watching.

"There's a decent ledge a little past halfway down, Jason," he said, reporting immediately to his captain. "We can regroup there, drop the ropes down and use them a second time. With that we're assured of reaching the valley floor."

Jason shook his head.

"That would mean leaving men behind," he said. "We aren't going to do that in such a potentially dangerous place."

"Then what?" Raoul said. "We have to go back to the ships and get more rope?"

A general murmur of disapproval arose.

"Not necessarily," Sinbad said. "A few of us will descend to the ledge and check it out. Perhaps there's a solution below that will present itself to us then."

Makili, Dardan and Sinbad took the joined ropes down to the ledge, a distance of several hundred feet over which for the most part they found themselves dangling in the open air because the cliff fell away beneath its rim. At last, just as all three were losing hand strength, the slightly downward-sloping ledge came up beneath Dardan's sandals. He jumped clear, steadied himself like the Billy goat his shipmates said he might as well be and grabbed the flailing end of the rope to steady it for Sinbad. The captain alit, though not quite as steadily, and as he finally found solid footing he did so just in time to stabilize Makili as he dropped down. Once all three of them had their feet on reliable ground Dardan gave the rope three hard tugs.

The trio examined their surroundings. The ledge was dangerous but negotiable as long as footing was checked carefully step by step along the way. Sinbad led the others and together they crept up as close to the next drop-off as they dared. Fortunately that proved close enough to reveal to them what was more or less directly beneath them, which turned out to be another sheer drop. This one was also a few hundred feet down, and at its base sat a large lagoon whose dark, only faintly moving waters weren't exactly beckoning.

"If it's decently deep the ropes we have might get us close enough to it to drop the rest of the way," Makili said. "But I don't like the look of that water."

"It *is* odd that it looks different than the rest we can see from here," Sinbad said, scanning the many murky jade-green ponds visible over the first mile or so of swampy canyon floor. "And of course even if we can safely drop into it and survive its depths, there will be the question of getting back up here afterwards."

"This is my first voyage with Jason," Dardan said. "He is a legend in our lands, and when the word went out that he was seeking trustworthy allies to help him I hastened to volunteer. After all, it is Medea's army that we all have to fear…foe and friend alike. And Jason is the only one who can stop her, the only one she'd even allow near her. So when I found him and he explained that this voyage was the only chance to end her campaign of annihilation…well, all I can say is he won't see this campaign fall short of its goal for lack of a few yards of hemp."

Both Makili and Sinbad were staring fixedly at him.

Dardan looked a bit surprised at his own unsolicited admission.

"Forgive me," he said. "Perhaps it was not my place to say such things."

"Maybe not," Sinbad said. "But now that I've heard them I may later call on you for more."

They spent an uncomfortable hour or so perched together there on the ledge, a little in from its rim for safety, knotting the ends of their bundles of rope together. When they were done they anchored it with a regrettably large loop around a solid-looking rock protrusion and Dardan quickly zipped down it far enough to verify upon his return that a drop of about sixty feet remained to the pond.

"The waters are easier to see through when you're nearer to them," he told Sinbad and Makili. "I saw a few rounded boulders but they should be easy to avoid. And nothing large swimming around."

"Yes," Makili said. "In the few seconds you were looking."

Dardan smiled and gestured toward the rope.

"Your skills approach mine," he said to Makili. "Be my guest. See for yourself."

Sinbad liked the idea so Makili went over, boldly going one-handed at first so he could carry a fist-sized rock down with him. Using a piece of leather to save his palm he quickly dropped to the point where he could pause, balance himself, aim and then fling the rock down at a choice spot in the water.

He returned to the others warily hopeful after an admirable five minutes or so spent hanging and watching.

"I'm not going first, that's for sure," he told Sinbad and

Dardan. "And there'd better not be any damned eels. Or snakes."

Dardan chuckled. "Same thing. They just breathe different stuff."

They brought their report back up to Jason and the rest and – as Dardan had suggested – Jason readily accepted the situation as viable. And he had an idea of his own

"That swamp no doubt has many strong vines," he said. "The first down will fetch some and bring them back to extend our rope. With Makili's tenacity he can drop down, catch a weighted vine tossed up to him and attach it to our rope."

"Simple as that," Makili said, and he chuckled. "But please pick a decent aim so I don't have to hang there all day."

Dardan voiced the question on everyone's mind.

"Who's going to test the waters, Captain?"

"None but I," Jason said. "Should I not survive you'll still have a worthy captain in your midst."

He looked over at Sinbad, who bowed.

And that's exactly how it went. The morning survey culminated in an early afternoon descent featuring the entire party. Eventually everyone was down from above, though much of the rope – hundreds of feet of it, in fact – had to be left there for the return. At that point Makili, rested up having been one of the first down, followed in Jason's wake and slipped down the lower rope.

Coming down slowly enough to keep himself well above the Argo's captain, he guessed at where he had to be, paused to look down and saw Jason smiling up at him.

Makili clenched the rope with his already aching hands. He'd stopped about thirty feet above the end of the rope, about which Jason was slowly pirouetting.

"May the Fates smile upon you, Captain Jason," he said.

"That would be a nice change," Jason said, and he let

go of the rope.

Makili watched him splash in. For a second or two he was out of sight but then he burst up through the froth he'd just made, spitting and coughing. He looked severely distressed.

But the choking semi-panic only lasted a second or two. Recovering quickly, he dogpaddled over to the bank and crawled up onto it.

"Are you all right, Captain Jason?"

Jason rose to his feet and checked himself over. He turned to look up at the dangling Makili.

"It would seem so," he said. "I suppose I shouldn't have been that surprised at it being salt water."

***

Jason worked with amazing speed, his gladius providing him with plenty of sturdy-looking vine within a couple of minutes. In one more he had the fibrous coil's end threaded through a sizeable conch shell and was hurling it up at the flagging Makili.

Jason missed his first two tosses, the second one just teasingly close enough to entice Makili to lunge for it… and nearly lose his fading grip in the process. But the third throw did the job. Makili tied the vine off and, exhausted, dropped into the pool.

Jason was pulling the vine-rope assemblage taut by the time Makili made it to shore. Makili added his efforts to Jason's and the two drew the rope back around a broad-trunked coconut palm and secured it there so that the rest of the party could make it down without a dip in the admittedly not unpleasant pond.

By twilight – which came much sooner on the canyon floor – the entire landing party had completed its descent. Ahmad and Nall were making a fire as Jason and Sinbad stood side by side studying the pond from its edge.

"This is an odd place indeed," Sinbad said. "If that is

water from the ocean I wonder how it got in? I see no waterfall as one might expect."

"Perhaps there is a channel at its bottom that leads through the canyon wall."

"But the pressure so deep beneath the surface would be great. If this pond were being fed by the ocean from so far down water would be gushing up as through a hole gouged in a ship's keel."

Jason nodded. "You're right," he said. "An isolated saltwater pond here seems strange."

"Everything about this place is strange," Sinbad said. "I'm just glad we made it down intact."

The strangeness continued, and in fact stepped up quite a bit, for Sinbad later that night.

The campfire had peaked, been used for a bit of cooking and was smoldering embers when Sinbad was awakened by one of the many strange sounds they'd all been hearing from the foreboding jungle terrain. The screech only woke him for some reason, not the rest, and he quickly found he was not able to drift back into sleep. So he rose, dusted the sand off himself and quietly went over to the pond's banks.

The moon was virtually full and as such dazzled him like a great glowing coin as he looked down into the nearly still water. Once his eyes adjusted he found himself fascinated by the clarity with which the orb was being reflected up at him; that is, until it dissolved into a shapeless mass atop a series of ripples.

Sinbad's chin came up and his gaze quickly found the source of the ripples.

Someone was swimming out there just beyond that reflected moon. Making no noise despite the ripples she was generating.

Yes, she.

Sinbad was seeing enough of her silhouette – head, shoulders, upper arms – to tell he was looking at a female upper torso.

"Please don't speak."

He'd heard that, true enough; but he'd heard it in his head, not with his ears.

"What?" he said aloud, almost involuntarily, and he heard Belaricus stop snoring, grumble, shift…and resume snoring.

"Please," the voice in his head – decidedly feminine as well – said. "We don't need to speak. Hear my words and concentrate on the responses you would give them, but do not say them aloud."

Curious, attracted as well as fascinated by the bobbing mystery, Sinbad decided to play along.

"I'll try to do as you say," he thought. "Do you understand me?"

"Yes. Thank you for your trust."

"I hope it's not misplaced. May I ask your name?"

"I am Vrona. And you are known as Sinbad."

"Sinbad, son of Sinbad," Sinbad thought. "Yes. And of Margiana, regent of Aderadad. But how can you know…?"

"I am a daughter of the oceans. Little is beyond my capacity to know it if I should desire."

"I hope you're not a siren. I've met sirens. Not as nice as they look."

"I am no siren. I am a guardian of this place."

"A guardian? Like those monsters that assaulted my ship without provocation?"

"Those half-titans were here to keep you from the greater dangers that you are seeking."

"By smashing our ship and drowning our crews?"

"They are blunt instruments, admittedly. Incidental casualties are sometimes unavoidable, I'm afraid. The decacheires merely intended to disable your craft short of reaching the island so that you would have to repair yourselves and leave instead, but you forced them into mortal conflict. And now the shores of Kryptos are unprotected against any other foolish mortals that would

45

seek their fortunes here."

"I seek nothing but to repay a debt to a fellow captain."

"Noble words, Sinbad. Let us both hope your faith is not misplaced. For surely you know your new ally is seeking great danger here?"

"He hasn't told me what he's seeking beyond that gem-shaped temple we saw from above."

"Exactly, Sinbad-Son-of-Sinbad."

"Of course it's not like I've told him about my problems either."

"All of you are here in search of something. Beware the one amongst you who searches with the most devotion."

"I get it. Keep an eye on Jason. How does that…wait!"

The fetching silhouette was sinking slowly.

"We shall meet again soon, Sinbad Son of Sinbad. Until then may the Fates smile upon you."

With that she was gone, leaving only a series of expanding oval ripples to mark her disappearance.

Chapter Six

From the outset it was obvious that the trek through the swampland that lay between the party and its goal would be extremely dangerous. Realizing this only a few hundred feet in, knee deep in murky, virtually still water (bearing not a hint of salt), Sinbad and Jason both turned around and told their respective men that none would be held accountable if they didn't want to go any farther.

Not everyone declined the offer right away, but eventually even the most uncertain – Dardan, Raoul and Makili, notably – decided to go on.

The tropical sun turned the swampy water to vapor, forming a stifling fog by mid-morning that made the party even more miserable as it negotiated the slender channels between great tangled islands of mangrove roots. Makili was so paranoid about inching his sandals forward through the uncertain muck that he decided to try walking on the roots. He had no more than climbed up onto a thick mangrove tendril near the edge of the channel when a large boa constrictor drooped down virtually into his face. Yelping, he fell back and made a big splash in the channel.

Still in the lead and side by side, Jason and Sinbad turned to see him pop up gasping, his face covered in a slime of lime green algae.

"Are you all right?" Jason called back to him, and he

nodded.

Sinbad grinned. "Makili, you should know better than trying to find shortcuts," he hollered, seeing the thick whitish-yellow boa still dangling not far from his crewman. "Or do you not recall that very desire to avoid extra effort was what led us here in the first place?"

His other crewmen chuckled. He saw Jason looking at him quizzically, so he explained as the party continued on.

"We had just purged a neighboring land of the scourge of a powerful wizard," he said. "And having sent him to his just rewards – at the cost of several of my men, the wizard's own daughter and poor Rashid's hand – we felt entitled to a portion of his great accumulated wealth. The sovereign agreed and gave us a respectable share, but in our great haste to bring that wealth back to our home – to where it is desperately needed – well, it appears our decision to 'find a shortcut' in fact has led us here."

"You speak of desperation," Jason said. "Last night you spoke only of rumors."

They'd sloshed a bit ahead of the rest, scimitar and gladius at the ready. Behind them only Pentelus seemed determined to keep up, though even he hadn't the boldness to be moving on as Jason and Sinbad were. Nevertheless, Pentelus was doing his best to catch what he could of their conversation. Taking note of the odd on-and-off pace Pentelus was setting, Sinbad turned and saw Jason's first mate – who'd momentarily stopped to listen – immediately resume his slogging through the (at the moment) shin-deep, approximately body temperature water.

Jason looked back as well. Everyone was in motion.

"I hope there's a reward for them at the end of this," he said softly. "I can guarantee nothing."

"The repayment of debt is reward enough," Sinbad said. "May you find what you desire here."

"Should the Fates decree it," Jason said, "may it be

so."

They continued on, finding occasional patches of solid ground to cross that at least did a little to improve the slow going; that is, until a viper bit Ahmad.

Hearing his crewman scream Sinbad turned and rushed back to him over the muddy ground. In an instant his turban was off and unwound and he was wrapping it around Ahmad's ankle a few inches above the two already reddening holes in his crewman's skin. He grabbed an inch thick piece of broken tree limb and made a tourniquet that he quickly twisted tight and held there.

"AAHH!" Ahmad said, wincing. "That hurts worse than the bite!"

"Perhaps, but it's a lot less deadly," Sinbad said calmly. "Distract yourself momentarily now. Hold it like that yourself. And do NOT release the pressure. Increase it, if anything."

Ahmad's pain didn't override his common sense and stop him from doing as his captain ordered.

"Viper," Raoul muttered loudly enough for all to hear. He had killed the snake and was studying the slit eyes in its severed head. "He's a dead man."

"Quiet, fool!" Jason snapped.

Sinbad carried only two things besides his scimitar and its sheath, one being a wineskin and the other a pouch about large enough to hold one of his own fists. Pulling the latter from his sash, he undid its drawstrings and reached inside. He withdrew a little bamboo tube that featured a plunger handle sticking out of one end. The other end was open. The whole assembly was no more than three inches long and not half an inch in diameter.

"Hold still," he told Ahmad. "Don't make Raoul right."

Ahmad was shuddering and wide-eyed, but rational enough to listen to his captain. He did as requested. Sinbad pressed the open end into his shipmate's instep centered on the more noticeable of the two little fang marks, held it firm there and pulled out the plunger.

When he finally withdrew the device blood ran freely from the wound. Sinbad squeezed out the venom-saturated blood that he'd sucked up into the tube and, not pausing for a second, went after the second fang mark. He didn't get quite as much fluid from that one.

He looked up at Ahmad.

"How are you feeling?" he said.

"Other than you draining all my blood, not bad."

"You'd rather I leave the venom in?"

Ahmad didn't have to think about it long.

"Drain away."

He got a little ill in the end, especially when – assuring himself that he'd removed enough venom – Sinbad decided to cauterize the wound to keep out infection from the stagnant water. But soon Ahmad was hobbling along on a makeshift crutch and the trek had resumed.

***

As the shadow of the western crater rim crawled over their path once again the party was finding itself on dry land more and more often. Odd land, though, for it was split here and there with fissures and many of these gurgled, hissed and even emitted steam.

"I smell brimstone," Havar said. "I hope we do not have to deal with Hades' servants."

"You smell sulfur," Sinbad said, glancing back at him. "This is a volcanic crater," he said, turning back and moving on and speaking loudly as he slogged along so that all could hear. "We are approaching the center, where the shell over the ancient magma is no doubt at its thinnest. We must watch our step here even more."

"At least we CAN watch our step now," Makili said. "I will trade a few hot cracks in the ground for the misery it appears we may finally leaving behind."

"Not to worry, friend," Belaricus said. "You'll get another shot at that swamp on the way back."

The heat rising all over the magma dome's slope quickly dried out the party's clothing, but the welcome shedding of suffocating swamp humidity turned out to be pretty much a tradeoff with the fact that the soles of their sandals and boots were being scorched by the broken ground beneath them. Dardan stumbled and fell once along the way, and even though his knees and the heels of his palms were only in contact with the ground for a second or so they still ended up blistered.

The dome had appeared as little more than a brown-gray ring around the base of the gem temple as viewed from the crater rim; here, however, its perhaps two hundred yard expanse was looking considerably more intimidating. Steam and sulfur-laden smoke oozed out of everywhere here, making the convex dome surface look like a field of tiny volcanoes. Insistent as the swamp was otherwise it was making no claim to this convex, gem-topped dome of a hill, allowing the barrenness of the dome to stand in stark defiance to its green surroundings (and thus making the dazzling crystal structure gleaming at the dome's peak stand out even more than it might have otherwise.)

Numerous as they were the steam-venting fissures weren't the only obstacles.

"Keep clear of those irregular outcroppings ahead," Sinbad called back to the rest, still leading the way beside Jason. "From the looks of them they may be unstable."

Actually they turned out to be far worse than that.

Dotted around the upper extremes of the slope were small promontory-like spots, each one sporting a cluster of sizeable rocks piled atop it. Sinbad and Jason had drawn to within about twenty feet of the lowest pair in their mutual path when those seeming piles of rock – and about half a dozen others surrounding them – rose up from their crouches. Very roughly human-shaped, though at least twice as large, the creatures righted themselves and assumed open stances as the seams between the rocks that comprised their bodies glowed with a dull orange-red fire.

"Magmatines," Orpheus said, his voice filled with awe. He'd been traveling closely behind Jason and Sinbad, who both risked a very quick glance his way. "Crafted by Hephaestus, fired by Hades...and designed to defend places like this from the likes of us."

"How do we defeat them, Orpheus?" Jason asked, his gaze quickly back on the small army of terrifying creatures that they suddenly found themselves facing.

"Unknown," Orpheus said. "Regrettably, to this point no one has."

Sinbad took his focus off the magmatines just long enough to shoot Jason a look.

Jason smiled back at him grimly. "Thanks Orpheus," he said without looking back that way. "Now get ready to be the first or die trying."

The magmatines, their seams growing brightly now, charged down the hill as one. The dome itself shook with their stampede-like barrage of footfalls, making it hard for their targets to keep their feet.

"I guess they aren't big on warnings," Sinbad said, setting his heels firmly and brandishing his scimitar. "And I've got a feeling my steel will be of minimal use against these brutes."

On the guardians came, massive and lumbering.

Chosen as much for dexterity and combat instinct as resolve by their captains, the party for the most part managed to duck and dodge the initial downhill onslaught. Belaricus took a glancing blow that set his sleeve ablaze, but other than that the magmatines' imposing charge left them both empty-handed and working to nullify their momentum so as not to end up too far downhill from their opponents.

"We *could* just outrun them up to the temple," Pollux said, blade at the ready beside Havar as the guards and the intruders assumed new standoff positions.

"Then what?" Sinbad called over to him. "I see no door to let us in and close them out."

"Perhaps we should have circled the temple and checked all its sides before heading up the hill," Jason said, the razor sharp tip of his gladius pointed at the impermeable-looking torso of the nearest magmatine. "My eagerness allowed me to lead us into this."

"So far so good," Sinbad said as he watched the magmatine nearest him sidling back up the slope his way.

Jason cocked his head. "Interesting assessment," he said as the magmatine prepared to charge him. "Care to elaborate?"

The creatures charged again.

This time not everyone got clear.

Nall was a little too frightened by the one that came at him. Backing up too quickly he stumbled and fell backwards. He didn't have long to scream about the searing hot ground before the magmatine caught up with him and stampeded over him like a fiery bulldozer, leaving in its wake charred remnants in the rough form of the mangled trespasser.

Ahmad had been backpedaling more or less parallel to Nall and, seeing him fall and be simultaneously crushed and fried in a split second, ended up catching his bad foot on a fair-sized rock and falling as well in the next moment. Rolling over, his skin sizzling in half a dozen spots, he realized that despite the pain and damage he wasn't going to be able to get up before the same magmatine that had just steamrolled Nall did the same to him.

Survival instincts nullified the searing pain long enough for him to realize his spear might well stop the magmatine's charge. As the fearsome guardian barreled in at him he sat up and drove the spear's butt end into the ground. This he did just in time, and the obviously unprepared alchemical monster could do nothing to avoid impalement as Ahmad tipped the weapon into its chest.

The long tip found a seam in the magmatine's chest and disappeared inside. The spear bowed as the creature's great momentum was deflected. The instant the magmatine's feet cleared the ground the glow in its seams died, and as it came back down to earth it shattered and cast itself out in all directions like the pile of rocks it resembled.

Ahmad popped back up on his good leg, his tunic smoldering, staring at the molten stub where its point had been. "Sinbad!" he called out.

"I saw!" Sinbad yelled back at him. "Well done."

He turned to the others, who were pretty much all busy dodging the magmatines that remained. Others had arrived to reinforce the first half dozen as well, such that even counting the one Ahmad had just eliminated it was now more or less a one-on-one battle by this point.

Casualties were currently one to one too, and neither captain was eager to see that ratio continue.

"Use Ahmad's strategy," Sinbad hollered to the others, giving perhaps a little too much credit with the word strategy. "Separate them from the ground and they die. Those of you with pole weapons move down below and be prepared to set them to catch your opponent's charge. And remember, they must be raised clear of the ground!"

Despite the simple concept the battle took at least twenty minutes and left the party weak, exhausted and a bit scorched. But victorious, and that was the most important thing. Better still they'd managed to dispatch the previously unbeatable enemies completely with only one verifiable casualty.

Still Nall was gone, Makili was despondent over his friend's death and Pentelus had completely vanished. No one had the slightest clue where Jason's first mate had gone, and not one could remember him being involved in the battle at any point. He'd disappeared early on, apparently, though no one knew where or how.

"The cracks here aren't big enough to have swallowed

him," Dardan said.

"Aye," Havar said, nodding at his side as they both looked down over the slope. "And we'd see his body as we can Nall's if he'd been ..."

He trailed off, his eyes having incidentally locked with Makili's teary ones.

"Sorry," Havar said earnestly. "I didn't mean to..."

"We all know we face death on such journeys," Sinbad said. "Let us hope Nall's death proves to be a sacrifice necessary to achieve a greater good."

"I can assure you," Jason said to them all, even though no one was specifically looking his way, "if we succeed here your friend's sacrifice will save many other lives."

Chapter Seven

Seemingly having taken out the last line of defense, the party – its numbers down to ten – indeed made it up to touch the smooth vertical sides of the great gem "temple."

"How do we know it's hollow?" Havar said. "Perhaps this is simply a great gem, one to make us rich beyond our wildest dreams."

"Certainly, Havar," Raoul said. "You carry it back to ship for us, would you?"

Had they not lost a comrade getting there the mirth that ensued would no doubt have been heartier. But the gloom still lingered, as did the sight...and smell...of Nall's charred bones.

A quick encircling of the supposed temple's base revealed neither any sort of obvious entrance nor – to the general relief of all – any more magmatines.

"No doors," Belaricus said as the party finished their circuit and came to rest back where they'd started. "You'd think if this were hollow it would have a way in."

"We haven't finished checking it yet," Sinbad said.

"What do you mean?" Belaricus said, his broad brow furrowed. "We've been around the whole thing!"

Jason caught Sinbad's drift first.

"Of course," he said, glancing up. "We haven't checked the top of it yet."

"The top!" Orpheus said, his eyes suddenly bright. "Where the gods would want to enter. Of course." He looked up that way as well. "How exactly do we check the top?"

How indeed: it loomed at least forty feet over their heads.

"Back down the slope," Sinbad said, his words evoking a few groans. "More vines. Havar and his mighty bow should be able to put an assembly of some of the lighter ones across the temple roof to the other side, and we can tie heavier vines to the end of that and pull it back across to replace the thin vine with something that will bear our weight. Then we anchor both ends of it down and up we go."

Belaricus was glaring at him. The rugged fighter grunted. "Simple as that, huh?" he said.

"Simple solutions are rarely the right ones, my friend," Sinbad shot back. "At any rate, unless someone else has a better idea it's that or we go back to the ships for more actual rope."

No one argued that a trek down to retrieve some of the ubiquitous vines and creepers found from one edge of the jungle to the other wasn't the best available option, so that's what they did. They'd apparently vanquished the magmatines for good, they quickly discovered, since nothing harassed the volunteers – Orpheus, Belaricus, Dardan and Raoul – as they descended, retrieved the natural materials they needed and returned.

Havar required a few tries to get the job done. He kept undershooting, clearing the near edge of the temple roof but not getting over the critical far edge as well, until Sinbad figured out that power wasn't the problem. He added critical dead weight to Havar's already heavy arrow, and fired with the same brute force this higher momentum object went considerably farther…and soon enough, the arrow was dangling from a short length of vine off the far edge of the roof.

Split into two parties by then, the one on the far side cheered and the one on the near side heard them and fed out more of the thinner vine, lowering the dangling arrow so that their counterparts could eventually catch hold of it and pull the vine taut. They gave a signal by jerking on that end and soon a much heavier vine was snaking up the near side of the temple, across the top of it and down the other side attached to the end of the lighter one.

Once the heavier vine was anchored at both ends several of the better-rested men set about scaling it.

The sun was at the crater's rim again by the time Makili, Jason, Dardan and Sinbad, having searched the entirety of the temple's effective "roof" and come up empty, gathered together at the center of the broad, flat expanse of crystal.

"I don't understand it," Jason said. "Surely the entrance must be here," he added, looking around. "Yet there is no sign of it anywhere."

"I guarantee you there is a way in, Jason of Thessaly," Sinbad said. "And just as assuredly I say we can find it."

"I believe you," Jason said. "And I suppose that considering this is a place safeguarded by the gods we are probably foolish to have been looking for an obvious entrance made for such as ourselves."

Sinbad craned his neck and gazed up at the thick clouds gliding by far above.

"From what you say your gods look down from the skies," he said. "If they ever return here at all they would likely enter from the top, as we have surmised. And their love of symmetry would command one seeking entrance to find the center of this surface, as we have here. By all reason – if reason applies – we should be standing at the entrance at this moment."

All four men looked around from where they stood clustered together.

"What if it's on the bottom?" Jason said.

The others turned his way bearing surprised looks.

"Good point," Sinbad said, digesting the concept quickly. "You say the gods who created those rock guardians rule over your underworld? Why would such custodians need or want to put this temple's entrance anywhere else BUT below ground?"

Jason shook his head. "Your reasoning is flawless," he said. "But to expect logic and sense from many of our deities is...well, unreasonable."

Sinbad smiled.

"Interesting system of government you have."

Jason shrugged. "We mortals were given little choice in the matter," he said. "But what of you? Do your people not worship the gods as well?"

"These gods," Sinbad said, "you have seen them?"

Jason showed a grin. "With my own eyes," he said. "I have stood atop almighty Zeus' great chessboard and chatted with him – and the other Olympians – only to learn I was merely standing in there for what they were using me for here...a pawn. Your people ...?"

"My people have many beliefs, some varying widely from others. For my part I have come to think that we look without for what is actually within, but as you say you have spoken with your gods so they must by that reasoning exist. What they in fact are, I suppose, is the question. My creators? If so then why am I just now hearing of them?"

"Why indeed," Jason said, smiling warmly. "For my part I'd say you are indeed a wise man."

"You must admit it's interesting that such powerful beings as those which preside over your lands do not do so over mine as well. Surely their control must be more limited than they would allow."

"It would appear so. You have never run afoul of such magical beings?"

"Oh, I can't say that exactly. We've encountered djinns before. They sound a bit like your gods, only more... solitary. More independent from one another, surely. And then there are the Fates, beings alleged to guide and control our affairs. I trust in them, but am not all that certain they physically exist. They seem more concepts to me."

"We also believe in the Fates," Jason said. "Though unlike my interview with the gods I have never laid eyes upon them. They are said to guide even the gods themselves."

"Hierarchies and unseen forces," Sinbad said. "I tend to believe there's much more going on in the heavens than we can know, my friend. Among these great 'gods' to which you refer tell me, can you call any of them friend?"

"Only one," Jason said, staring up at the sky. "But she has already helped me greatly…and as much as allowed."

"Can you speak with her?"

"Yes…when *she* wishes it. And it's been a long time." Jason suddenly looked wistful. "Too long, in fact. I suppose I really should have considered seeking her guidance before now …"

The others were all looking his way – and, thanks to Dardan's insider info, also exchanging wary glances. But the great screech that rent the still air in the valley in the next moment ended any speculation on Jason's mental state, at least for the time being.

***

Everyone saw it at once.

The great winged serpent rose into the sky a few hundred yards distant. To a man those atop the gem and at its base were stunned, for the creature had virtually appeared out of nowhere. A second earlier they'd been surrounded by nothing more threatening than steaming jungle-swamp, but now the terrifying beast – a thick and sinuous gray pit viper with great membranous mid-body wings – was gliding in at the temple, propelled along by huge undulations of those wings.

The horror got there in seconds. Sweeping low over the top of the temple it forced the foursome there to dive for cover. Caught in the creature's buffeting wake they all found themselves rolling along and had to flatten out to keep from going off the far edge. Sinbad caught Dardan or he would have gone, and side by side they quickly turned to watch the monster banking away.

Down below at the base Belaricus, Makili and Havar readied their bows for the monster's return. Atop the temple the others scrambled to their feet and – lacking such projectile weapons – debated their slim options. They didn't have much time to do so because despite the bird-snake's immense size (its body was longer than the Argo) it proved to have a tight turning radius in flight.

Sinbad and Dardan watched the monster swoop in on them again. Makili and Jason had ended up a little ways away from them and as the creature bore down on the upper surface of the temple it became evident that it was specifically targeting the two men who were standing near one another.

With only hand weapons Makili and Jason simply got clear of the strafing run as quickly as they could. Jason found himself out of range soon enough to turn and watch the attack. He saw a flourish of arrows spray up from beyond the nearby edge; one shot through the gigantic creature's left wing, making an insubstantially small hole, while the others hit the hard gray scale plates on the monster's underbelly only to shatter and/or glance harmlessly off.

Jason saw Dardan and Sinbad both wait boldly until the very last second before jumping to try to clear the clutching eagle-like claws that the monster had been holding in tightly against its body (and thus virtually concealing) until that moment.

Dardan got clear because the quickly adjusting bird-snake monster didn't go for him. Forced to choose it went for Sinbad, whose dive wasn't quite good enough to keep his shirt from getting snagged by a single talon hooked behind his shoulder. The fabric was tearing as the creature dragged him along, but not fast enough: Jason saw that his counterpart's scimitar wasn't going to be of much help either against such a "back attack" but he was too far away to help.

Sinbad went over the edge.

His full weight, finally clear of the surface, ripped his shirt free of the talon almost instantly. Momentum carried him, and as he went over the edge he was greatly relieved to see the taut vine. He grabbed it as it passed beneath him and did a fast full body pivot around it. He ended up dangling there near the top as the monster cut another sweeping arc.

Sinbad looked down. Ahmad, Raoul and Orpheus stared back up at him from the base of the vine, where they'd staked it to the dome rock, their faces masks of concern.

"Come down!" Ahmad yelled up at him. "Get out of the open or you'll have no chance."

Sinbad almost did just that, but then a thought hit him.

"No," he hollered down. "Take the end of the vine off that stake and pull it tight. Wait until you feel it go slack, and when you do stop pulling. Then keep your grip firm and brace yourselves."

The monster was coming back already. There was no time to chat about it anymore so – hoping the men got it – he quickly pulled himself back up onto the top of the temple. Figuring he was being targeted once more he let go of the rope the instead he was back up safely and went into a roll across the glass-smooth surface. His ploy worked. The sweeping, grabbing talons just couldn't get hold of his constantly tumbling form. Unable to hover at all the beast was forced to give up, sweep off and circle in preparation for yet another try.

Sinbad wasn't waiting for that. On his feet in a split

second, he hustled over to the middle of the temple-spanning vine.

"It's obviously targeting you," Jason yelled over at him. "Come stand with us and see how it…"

"NO!" Sinbad yelled. "Stay clear."

Taking aim he slashed the vine, his blade ringing as the temple's immaculate surface abruptly ended its arc. Under tension the near side of the severed vine instantly retracted.

Sinbad lunged for it in case the men had misunderstood him, but they hadn't: it went lax in the next moment. Sitting up he quickly made a slipknot – the monster was sweeping back in again – and, rising, worked a few feet of vine through the open-holed knot as the hideous slit-pupiled face raced toward him.

The monster's right claw came thrusting in at him, talons spread wide. He didn't flinch until the claw tips were nearly around him, and in that last possible second he made sure to get the looped rope over one of those outstretched talons, even at the price of being grabbed.

And caught he was, in a fearsomely vicious grasp that, had it lasted longer than a second or two, probably would have killed him right then and there.

But no sooner had the beast cleared the temple than it felt the full weight of not one but four men jerk it downward by the wrenching of a single digit. As that "finger" twisted and cracked the monster was forced to release Sinbad, who grabbed the rope and slid down it even as momentum carried the shocked and suddenly agonized monster in a tight arc down toward the ground.

Sinbad alit gracefully beside Orpheus and the others, whose eyes were uniformly wide as they watched the giant snake-bird slam awkwardly to the ground atop a host of the lava dome's steam vents. Springing up quickly, shrieking and hobbling, it turned and bellow-screeched at the tiny humans that had injured it and brought it down. Then, appearing to recover its strength a little, it turned back toward the swamp and – with a couple of unsteady running steps – flapped its wings and took off.

But it wasn't high enough. Its wingtips clipped a couple of tall banana palms and it went down less than a quarter mile out.

Sinbad stood watching until the beast sank below the treetops while, at his back, Orpheus, Ahmad and Raoul celebrated. Meanwhile atop the temple Jason, Dardan and Makili were able to keep the thing in sight for but a moment longer, yet in that time they managed to witness something decidedly strange that none of their comrades were in position to see.

The monster shrank out of sight.

They saw it come down, landing in a fairly open bog that featured few trees. For a couple of seconds they bore witness as it struggled and squirmed there, beating its wings against the cattails, water lilies and mucky swamp water. And then, most oddly, it simply shrank down like a deflating balloon until it finally disappeared behind the treetops lining the near edge of the bog.

"What kind of creature can do something like that?" Dardan said.

Jason shook his head. "I don't know," he said. "But it wasn't that badly injured, and whatever it just did looked quite intentional to me."

"What do you mean, Captain?" Makili said.

"I'm saying we may not have seen the last of that particular guardian."

***

Had any among the party in fact been there at the swamp where the monster splashed down, flailed and then appeared to have shrunken away they'd have certainly learned some interesting things. First off it hadn't vanished, it had merely shriveled down to its original size and form. Second, that form – face down initially in a muck of lily pads and dirty water – was of a human being. A woman, apparently in her thirties, with long, wavy hair the color of flames (albeit dirty, moss-covered flames at the moment) pushed her face up out of the muck and, dripping with it, glanced around.

Third, she had a habit of talking to herself.

"Well, THAT was embarrassing," she said, hardly even realizing what a muddy mess she was yet. She pushed herself up, disturbing a snake that launched at her and sank its teeth into her milky white calf.

"Ow!" she yelped, looking down.

The snake was already rotting to ashes from the head back like a burning fuse. She smirked.

"See what you get?" she said, but then she noticed her badly broken finger.

And – in quick succession – her scrapes and bruises, the hitch in her hip and the fact that she and her actual clothing were covered in swamp muck.

"And see what *I* get," she muttered. "I won't be underestimating dear Sinbad again."

She looked down at her bosom and saw the chain of long crystals there. Like everything else the crystals were mud-splattered too so she unclasped the chain and dipped the whole assembly into the water. Bringing the crystals out relatively clean she held them up and looked them over.

She sighed.

"I can't believe I'm down to seven," she said. "That had better be enough."

She pulled one of the clear crystals out of its base and put the necklace back on. With the crystal's six counterparts safely against her skin again she closed the one she'd taken loosely into her palm. Holding her hand out before her she closed her eyes.

"Take me to my lair," she said.

She crushed the crystal.

And vanished.

Chapter Eight

"The flames are beautiful," Medea said. "I regret only that I must witness them from so far."

"Victory over Shardesan is at hand, my lady," Baylmos said. "Despite what we've heard of their skills these eastern peasants are no more capable of defending themselves than any we've seized before." Beaming with pride, he stood at his leader's side and stared off at the city from the edge of their remote camp. A bright orange halo lit the left half of the distant city. Baylmos swept his hand from left to right before their faces. "We are irresistible. As our will rolls over this city so it will soon claim all of Aderadad."

"It is not enough to defeat them, Baylmos. You know that."

Hardened as he was even Baylmos' eyes grew wide as his commander's words sank in.

"By your word, my lady. Down to the last man, boy and male infant it shall be done."

"The women will lament, the girls will cry," Medea said. "But in the end they'll be free, and I will show them a better way."

"And I, my lady?" Baylmos said, curiosity for his future momentarily overcoming his fear.

"Obedient men are rare, Baylmos. You are one of the precious few."

ig_ er

Baylmos smiled hopefully.

"Now go," she said. "I want to watch the city burn alone."

He nodded, bowed and zipped away without question.

Medea threw her inky locks back and stared off at the star-blotting curtain of smoke and flames, lost in thought.

But she wasn't alone for long.

"You're doing quite well, my dear."

Medea didn't turn. She allowed the fiery-haired woman to move up right beside her elbow.

"Why doesn't it quench my thirst?"

"Your thirst is great, Medea," the woman said. "Each such conquest can at best fill only one portion of the hollowness within your heart, leaving much more still wanting."

The woman who had been Pentelus – and a gigantic winged serpent – waited but Medea didn't respond; she just kept staring off at Shardesan.

"I heard you give the purge order again, by the way," she finally said. "I suppose it's not that important to me either way but I still don't see the point of it."

"The point is they are cursed, Circe," Medea said. "From birth. Cursed with selfishness and arrogance and ready to sell out all they claim to stand for at a moment's notice. I am actually being merciful. I spare them. And more importantly I spare the poor women they would otherwise live to use and mistreat."

"Not to belabor a silly point," Circe said. "And I'm as against this 'men rule because their muscles are stronger' thinking as you, believe me. But either way I'm thinking if we eventually take them all out there may be some issue with no longer being able to procreate as a civilization."

Medea showed her tired eyes to Circe, her irises lit with distant flame.

"You place more value on our continuing existence than I do."

Circe just stared at her for a few seconds.

"You're a fine student," she said when Medea finally turned to stare off at Shardesan again. "I regret that I have not been able to alleviate your suffering more quickly or effectively."

Medea looked her way again, offering a pained smile.

"You've done more than I believed anyone could," she said. "Forgive my distracted state of mind, grandmother. It's good to see you again." For the first time she noticed the cocoon of clear amber gel encasing one of Circe's fingers, the only evidence of the wizard's having been snagged and slammed down bodily into a swamp mere hours earlier since her clothing was once again immaculately clean. "What happened?" Medea said. "Are you all right?"

"It's nothing," Circe said. "A spell went wrong. I'll be fine. This is just protection until it heals."

"Well, as I said I'm very glad you're back. I…I'm not in the right state of mind, I don't think…"

"Nonsense. You're in a fine state of mind. You think people do what you're doing every day? This is demanding. I couldn't do it. My social skills are deficient. I get mad at people and suddenly they're not around anymore and I need new people to get mad at. It's a vicious cycle."

Despite herself Medea almost chuckled.

"There, you see?" Circe said. "You're fine. Now quit moping. I have to go off and check on something but I'll be back soon to cheer you up some more."

She headed off, going just far enough from camp to pull a small round mirror from one of several silk pouches that hung from her waist.

She closed her eyes and incanted.

"Flesh of my flesh, spirit of my spirit," she said, "allow me to see through your eyes."

The mirror fogged and an image coalesced in the little cloud. Ten men variously stood and sat near a blue-white crystal wall, eating and talking.

Circe opened her eyes and saw the tiny live image.

"Closer my pet," she said softly. "But carefully!"

The view in the mirror jerked, rose slowly and moved forward. Approaching the originally distant encampment at a measured pace, the view soon dropped back down quite close to the dome surface and the men were momentarily lost to Circe's sight. The view was swerving between boulders, and when it finally popped up again the nearest of the men were no more than thirty feet away.

"Good," Circe said. "Well done."

The view held there. Circe frowned at the sight of Sinbad.

"I don't know why the Fates sent you," she said, staring at him. "But I won't let you stop me."

She glanced down at her throbbing fingers. When she looked back at the mirror she was a little surprised because Sinbad appeared to be squinting right at her. Then, even worse, he started walking towards the mysterious little viewpoint in the mirror.

"Go, little one," Circe said. "Don't let him catch you."

***

Sinbad couldn't see Circe's homunculus as such, as the tiny creature had the chameleon-like ability to mimic its background. What his sharp eyes and keen mind *had* picked up on, however, were the little bits of gravel that he'd happened to spy falling off a nearby rock for no particular reason. Curious, he had taken a few tentative steps toward the oddness and in doing so triggered more of it. This second gravel scattering he saw clearly, not out of the corner of his eye like the first. Something moved across the rubble-strewn slope and then deflected upward, but all Sinbad could make out as the source of the disturbance was a wavy line or two and some distortion.

And then it was gone.

For just a moment Sinbad heard an odd sound above the steam and swamp hiss: a faint flapping of small wings, as though a small bat were nearby. Then that faded away.

Sinbad scanned the shadowy landscape for a few moments. Coming up empty he finally turned and went back to the others. Orpheus was absently plucking at his lyre.

"What is it," Jason said, noticing the concern on Sinbad's face. He peered out at the slope of steaming vents and rubble and beyond, to the dark, screeching and growling swamp. "Something out there?"

Sinbad shrugged. "This place is strange," he said. "I am listening to my senses but not relying on them at this point."

"So is that a yes or no, Captain?" Havar said.

"I saw nothing I could rightly call a threat. But despite the peace we are experiencing I'd say we all need to stay on our guard, and no less than three of us should be awake at all times as the others rest."

No one disagreed or asked more about it. Instead talk quickly returned to the main topic: how to get into a temple that had no apparent doors or even windows. And of course having arrived at their objective – through no easy effort – the whole "why" of it was building up quickly now, still unspoken, beneath the more genteel question of how.

"I still think the gods would have the entrance below," Dardan said. "Hades and Hephaestus make their kingdoms here on Earth. They wouldn't put the way in on the top, they'd put it on the bottom."

"Yes," Orpheus said, stopping his idle tune-picking momentarily. "Unless Zeus commanded them to put it on top," he added, then went back to softly plucking his bronze strings.

"Even if we had shovels we wouldn't be able to dig

through this," Pollux said, stamping at the rock beneath his foot. "Shovels are for dirt. We'd need picks and axes."

"The Argo has the tools we'd need," Jason said. "IF there proves to be a need."

"You're a seasoned traveler," Sinbad said, locking gazes with Jason. "Surely you've been in at least one dilemma involving these gods before?"

Jason smiled. "More often than most would want to remember," he said, and his men chuckled knowingly.

"And you're here among us to tell of it," Sinbad said. "How did you resolve your previous impasse?"

Jason stopped sharpening his gladius, set it and the whetting stone aside and rose.

"Quite simply," he said. "I called the gods of Olympus cruel and declared that in time all would learn to live without them."

"Yes," Belaricus said. "Then he cast one of their sacred tokens into the churning waters in his rage and that deity rose and saved the Argo and its crew from a watery grave."

"With all respect to Triton or Poseidon, whoever that was," Jason said. "I have to believe he would not have been there if not for Hera."

"You speak of this friendship with a powerful being," Sinbad said. "Might she not be inclined to help you once more, if only out of friendship? After all, you are requesting only information…not help in any physical sense."

Jason looked grimly to the stars, which were just beginning to twinkle as night fell in earnest.

"Not even out of friendship now," he said wistfully. "For in my successes I have committed the same grave mistakes as her own consort, and whatever my motivations – as his – I have in the end proven just as flawed as any other. Perhaps worse than any other, for I was given the power by my own desire and in the end saw it fall to ruin."

"Forgive me," Sinbad said, bowing graciously. "I will ask no further. And I cannot speak for my men but in my case, having used the phoenix charm already, I too am out of favors owed by powerful beings." He glanced around at his men. "Anyone owed a favor by a genie or the like?" he said.

No one answered.

"So that's it then," Jason said. "We're here stuck by our mortal wits until we can figure out how to get into this place."

"Not necessarily," Ahmad said. "We can leave."

"Nall's death shall not be in vain," Sinbad said quickly. "For better or worse – and to repay our debts to Jason and his men – we will do our best to find our way into this place."

Chapter Nine

Sinbad heard the song in the middle of the night, with Ursa Major looming brightly overhead. Soft, hypnotic – the type of tune that fascinates the mind like a flitting and hovering hummingbird. Thinking Orpheus was on watch he turned that way and saw to his surprise that the bard was fast asleep, his face buried in his arm under his shaggy black hair. Looking around Sinbad spotted the three current watchmen – Raoul, Makili and Dardan – a few yards outside of camp. They were playing dice on a flat rock top and keeping their voices low.

And they did *not* appear to be noticing the almost voice-like notes he was hearing.

He sat up quietly and looked around. Havar, lying nearby, grumbled and flipped over onto his other side. Sinbad decided to rise. Moving, it seemed, as though without disturbing a single pebble he glided out of camp. Once he was well clear he cupped an ear in an attempt to discern the direction from which the music was still coming. But it didn't help. The sound was coming from everywhere.

Still unnoticed by the guarding trio he ventured even farther, moving along the side of the temple until he reached its corner.

Rounding that edge he noticed something strange right away: Beyond the base of the magma dome, kept clear by its constant steaming heat, the swamp rose dark and ominous as it did everywhere else, but here a small oasis of light presented itself, a little blotch not far beyond the rise of the first swamp palms. From his vantage point well up and away from the strange green glow Sinbad could only see it as an emanation rising from treetops.

His curiosity got the best of him. Unsheathing his scimitar he descended the slope with it at his side at the ready.

At the magma dome's base he passed cautiously into the swamp, minding his steps while keeping on track toward the emerald radiance the best he could. Down there the glow wasn't rising high enough to be seen above the palm tops so Sinbad was forced to work more or less blind and hope that he was staying on course despite the zigzag path the swamp demanded he travel.

He nearly fell into a bubbling, steaming pool that lay hidden behind a boulder. But his quick reflexes sent him leaping and tumbling over it and – though he ended up covered in swamp mud – kept him from serious injury.

He spied the light again at last. Pushing through the spiny, sweaty undergrowth he wound up breaking through into a clearing. He froze in his tracks, unable to miss the fact that the glow was coming from the decidedly non-murky pond directly ahead. Sinbad moved up to it slowly and, keeping a close eye on the nearly still waters, knelt down to touch them with his fingertips.

He tasted the water, immediately noticing the expected salt.

The music stopped. And in the very next moment Sinbad heard a giggle.

He rose brandishing his scimitar and spun about.

No one was there.

"Come in and wash off."

Sinbad studied the water again.

"I appreciate the offer," he said. "But as a gentleman of Aderadad I'm obliged to politely request a formal meeting first."

"Your mistrust is understandable."

"And your voice is familiar. You are Vrona, or someone imitating her."

"I am she. I heard your request."

"Why would someone who claims to be a guardian of this place be interested in fulfilling my request to be allowed access to it? Aren't you trying to keep me OUT of that temple?"

There was no immediate reply. But Sinbad's keen eyes noticed the moment the stars' reflections began to twist and distort atop the pond's surface.

Something rose from the water near the edge, but it was not a form as such; instead, the water itself humped up into an odd hill-like mound, which then proceeded to swell and assume a more intricate form even as Sinbad backed warily away.

The shape of a woman manifested: a statuesque hourglass figure in three dimensions, even the long locks of which were inexplicably twisting curls of clear water. Rainbow shimmers pulsed up, down and throughout the mesmerizing form as it grew detailed enough for Sinbad to make out its starlit face-like features.

"This is what you are then," Sinbad said, lowering his weapon but a little.

"Are you so much more?" the entity said, its lips moving with the words, its transparent eyes blinking. "A few specific elements, all of which simply arrange into a matrix to turn you into a rigid and easily damaged shape and imprison you there."

The form changed then, growing opaque.

Now a beautiful woman stood before Sinbad, unabashedly nude and smiling.

"Is this better?"

"Undoubtedly," Sinbad said, lowering the scimitar a little more as he fought to withhold a smile. "But not necessarily if the rest of the men happen to see you."

"Unlikely here, Captain Sinbad."

She moved up onto the relatively dry rim that separated the pool from the nearest edges of the mucky swamp, walking toward Sinbad. He reflexively brought the blade up a few inches again.

"I assure you I mean no harm," she said, stopping with her bare toes squeezing into shore mud.

"In my experiences the assurances of water nymphs, sirens and the like mean very little. We had to sail to Jakarli and take on hydra-men just to cure Rashid of an unmentionable disease he contracted in the arms of one particularly evil..."

"I am no flighty temptress of the waters," she said, looking indignant.

She glanced down at her impressively bare body, thought about it a moment and then shape-shifted again. She still looked basically the same after the quick alteration – shiny black hair, emerald eyes, aquamarine skin – but socially critical portions of her skin were now covered by stylish-yet-rugged-looking clothing.

Sinbad grinned. "I'm not judging you by your choice of looks."

"You're not judging me," the being said, its coyly, shyly apologetic advance having given way to entirely sober responses in a split-second. "I'm judging you. And the rest."

"You're judging us," Sinbad said. "So when do we hear the verdict?"

"I'm not here to stop you, Sinbad. But the games being played here are larger than you know. If I help you gain access to the temple tell me: how much of your trust will I earn?"

"Why ask me? Why not ask the man who wishes access rather than the man who is helping him in order to return favors?"

"Jason and his men did you less service than you believe. The Argo deliberately held back its advance and let you approach this island first, knowing all along that it might well still have been guarded by the sentinels of the gods."

Sinbad's brow furrowed. "Let's say I believe you," he said after a long moment's deliberation. "He didn't know us. Perhaps it was my fault for not wishing to stand off and meet the strange vessel at sea so that we could discuss the island first. My instincts typically guide me well...or at least they once did."

"There's a reason for that too," the woman-shaped being said. "And the help I can actually give you is quite limited...a single favor, in fact. And know that even in doing that I am taking a great risk."

"Prompting the simple question of why."

"I will tell you what I have told no one before," she said. "My name is Vrona, as I told you upon our first meeting. My great-grandfather is the god Triton and before you ask yes, I do have some of his abilities as an inheritance."

"So this Triton..."

"Triton has nothing to do with this place. He and his sons and daughters have no obligations to it."

"Yet you claim to serve here."

"The story is complex. Here beyond the edge of the water – where I can remain but a little longer – the realm cannot hear me tell you of these things. And as our privacy is limited by time you must choose between learning more about me and gaining insight into the nature of this temple."

"I would prefer to know more of you and your motives," Sinbad said. "But of necessity and obligation I must have the insight."

"Fair enough. Know then that access to the temple may be found atop it at its center, as you have already guessed. And beyond that ..."

She had trailed off deliberately and was looking him right in the eyes.

"Beyond that?" Sinbad said.

"Beyond that I can only say that one in in your number holds the keys to many doors, and suggest you consider that in the grand scheme of the Fates yours is at best a *minor* dilemma."

Sinbad didn't have time to ask what she meant because the instant she'd finished she grinned and her body collapsed into a puddle of water that seeped back into the pond.

"I'm sure that's useful," Sinbad muttered to himself, watching the pond return to stillness. "I'm just surprised in your faith in my ability to remember your words."

Remember them he did though, likely because he had little else to do but ponder them as he made his way back up to the camp. Rounding the corner and seeing that the three guards were still at their game he headed their way, still pondering the words.

One in your number holds the keys to many doors...

Someone was holding out? Why? Who?

He'd kind of forgotten the fact that he hadn't risked washing off in Vrona's pool. The caked-on layer of mud, dried and flaking, caught the fading campfire light quite eerily at just about the time Makili happened to glance over and see the captain shuffling somewhat absently back into camp.

"Monster!" Makili shrieked, backing away and pointing at Sinbad...and then tripping over a low rock and going head over heels backwards as the other guards spun about.

"No, just me," Sinbad said, putting a hand up and coming into brighter illumination as the rest of the party, awakened by the yell, shook the sleep out of their eyes and brought them to focus on their dirty captain. "Long story short don't sleepwalk around here."

Chapter Ten

The next morning came early for the party. Sinbad hadn't slept any more, absorbed as he remained in sorting out Vrona's vague "hint" up until the first golden beams of morning light lit up the vine-covered western crater wall and shook him from his reverie.

Orpheus' Song of Daybreak swept gently over the party, peacefully and sweetly – and inspiringly – waking the last sleepers, albeit a bit shy of their full eight hours.

"What's the rush," Belaricus said groggily, propped half-upright and rubbing an eye, "someone find a door?"

Orpheus stopped and lowered his lyre to his lap. "Belaricus," he said, "you're just grumpy because you know you're next up to make breakfast."

"By the gods you're right," Belaricus shot back. "So I say again, what's the rush?"

"We're not going to stay here forever," Jason said, rising. "One death is already too many and…"

Sinbad caught his gaze – deliberately, it appeared – and Jason cut himself off and walked over to his counterpart. A couple of the men were watching him but Belaricus' griping and requesting Dardan and Orpheus help him put together the breakfast mess had most everyone else's attention.

"I received – *something* – last night," Sinbad said quietly to Jason.

"Indeed," Jason said, softly as well. "How far across the swamp did you have to swim to get it?"

"I could have returned clean. But like you I have limited faith in so-called higher beings."

"I won't ask any more then. Well, one thing: what DID you receive?"

Sinbad recited Vrona's words. "It means nothing to me," he said. "None of my men carry keys nor would have any use for them."

Jason's eyes lit up. "One of mine does." He turned to the others. "Orpheus!" he hollered, and beckoned the legendary bard over.

Orpheus didn't rush. "Bards don't fall in line," the poet-musician-scribe had often said. "Yet we can be trusted to serve."

"How are you at climbing?" Sinbad said to him when he finally drew up.

Orpheus shrugged. "I made it down here, didn't I?" he said. "Plan to make it back out too. These hands may be fine instruments but that hardly makes them incapable of pulling their weight."

"Good," Jason said. "Your music...you often speak of keys..."

"Yes," Orpheus said, "and no matter how clearly I demonstrate them the great majority of the crew generally misses them anyway. Why?"

"'One among you holds the keys to many doors'..." Sinbad said. "Yes, if you work with keys I suppose it doesn't matter that they are intangible concepts."

"So?" Orpheus said.

"So up we go."

***

Up they went, just the three of them. True to his word Orpheus was a good climber, and soon he and Jason were following Sinbad to the center of the gem.

"Here I believe the keys are to be used," Sinbad said, stopping there. "How I don't know."

"Was there more to the 'something' you received, perhaps?" Jason said.

"Yes, something that seemed to make no sense. Let me try to recall. Something about ours being but a small dilemma in the grand scheme of the Fates."

"Sense or not," Jason said, "I can see little in the way of assistance there."

"I need to try to recall the exact words," Sinbad said. "I may be getting something wrong."

Orpheus had unslung his lyre from his back and was cradling it. He plucked a note.

The entire magma dome rattled, but nowhere was the vibration – which pumped thick jets of smoke and steam out of the normally oozing fissures all around the temple – anywhere near as powerful as it was atop the temple itself. Up there Jason, Sinbad and Orpheus all staggered, struggling to hold their feet as the note resonated the surface beneath their soles with a numbing intensity that mimicked the still-vibrating harp string.

Orpheus finally realized his contribution to the ongoing seismic jostling and damped the string. The quake stopped, but it was too late: a steam-like cloud was rising before the trio, almost as though that exact center spot had suddenly become very cold and was causing the moist air over it to spontaneously condense as fog.

Orpheus, Sinbad and Jason fell back as one, the latter pair quickly pulling out their blades. Orpheus slung his harp across his back, swapping it out at remarkable speed with his own invention: a heavy wooden ball on a very strong and light ten foot chain, tethered by a palm-crossing strap such that the ball could be launched, knock its target senseless and then be snapped right back into the tether-wrapped hand with a sharp chain jerk.

By all rights the fog should have dissipated quickly from the bright sun and steady breeze, but in fact the opposite was happening: it was becoming denser, more impermeable, with each passing moment.

A somewhat oversized male face, bearded and regal-looking, emerged from the middle of the dense, roiling white fog. Though its inscrutable gaze conveyed no direct menace as such all three men regarded it quite warily. When the rest of the being's form followed its head out of the haze Sinbad was the only one to relax.

The great creature, tawny-furred, big as a rhinoceros, settled into a lion's sitting stance. The fog billowed and bubbled at its back as it turned its dark, narrow eyes on one man after another. Those eyes settled on Sinbad last.

"A sphinx," Sinbad said, sheathing his scimitar. He urged the others to do the same. "My father told me of them. Magical. Our weapons are useless here. This being has a far sharper weapon – its wits."

"Flattery will gain you nothing, Sinbad son of Sinbad," the creature said. "You know my kind, obviously. And likely you also understand why I stand here at the entrance to this place."

"You would ask riddles of us," Sinbad said while the others – who still hadn't lowered their weapons – watched the exchange. "Should we give the answers you desire we gain access to pass."

"Not quite."

Sinbad's faint smile, born of confidence, faded.

"Oh, it's true that IS the method by which one gains entrance to this temple. But in this case I'm not here to monitor admissions to this shrine."

"Then why *are* you here?" Orpheus said.

In the next moment the answer came, most frighteningly, in the form of spontaneous manifestation of a ring of identical sphinxes that instantly surrounded the human trio.

The first sphinx glared at Jason, ignoring the appearance of its mirror image twins.

"To defend it," the creature said, and it rose off its

haunches and stepped forward.

The three men backed up. Sinbad's scimitar was back out whether it would be of use or not.

"Sinbad of Aderadad," the original sphinx said, its great voice booming across the temple's upper surface, "Jason of Thessaly, Orpheus of Thessaly: You all stand in violation of the laws of Lord Zeus. Mortals are not allowed to open the portal to this most hallowed of places. Only the blood of almighty Zeus himself permits access here. And to compound your impudence you have failed to request an audience in the proper key!"

The sphinx was still advancing, its hulking form almost seeming to grow. The men continued to back up, glancing all about themselves. The only thing preventing fight-or-flight was the fact that the other sphinxes weren't moving; however, that rigidity was quickly running the three retreating men out of elbow room.

"I suggest we…" Sinbad said, but the main sphinx cut him off.

"Run."

Run they did. For their lives. Weaving and dodging, they quickly zipped through the encircling gauntlet of apparently slow-starting sphinxes and – once clear – made beelines for the vine. The nearest of the sphinxes were virtually on the trio's heels as they sped over to the edge. There was no time to pause so Jason, the first to arrive, leapt over the edge in a desperate lunge. His gladius fell free and dropped as he caught the rope with both hands and slid down as fast as the singeing rope would allow.

Orpheus had dropped his weapon so his hands were free. Like Jason he took a leap of some faith, and because of the deflection the rope experienced under Jason's sudden added weight he alit not grabbing the rope so much as coming down on it with his waist. His tunic saved his belly skin worse than blistering as he rode that way halfway down to the ground before finally catching himself with his hands, swiveling around the rope and making his precious palms take the last bit of friction. He landed on his feet as Jason had seconds earlier and quickly jumped clear ahead of Sinbad's descent.

Sinbad had accounted for the deflection, so his jump brought him down at just about the right angle to snag the rope with both hands. He watched Orpheus land before sliding down to join him and the rest.

From below, as Orpheus ignored his burning gut skin and studied the moderate damage to his hands, the rest looked up to the top of the temple. Because of the beveled edge of the temple top they couldn't see far enough back to spy the sphinxes.

"What was the big rush?" Makili said. "You all look like you've seen ghosts."

Jason shook his head. "Worse," he said, accepting his fallen gladius back from Belaricus.

"Are you all right, Orpheus?" Sinbad asked, moving over to the bard.

"It'll be a while before I play again," Orpheus said. "But I will trade that for my life."

"You won't need to play again for a while, I dare say," Sinbad said. "We will not gain access to this place; that much is clear."

"Why not?" Dardan said. "Sounds like you made progress, anyway."

"Yes," Belaricus said. "Are we just talking about someone up there wanting to fight?"

"No," Sinbad said, "it goes well beyond that. This is the temple of one called Zeus, and only the blood of that being will permit entrance. So this place remains closed to us."

"Not necessarily," Jason said, a strange spark lighting his eyes.

"What do you mean?" Havar said.

"I mean I know where to find the blood of Zeus."

Chapter Eleven

The Argo's storm-beaten sails dripped in the bright morning sun. A rugged, dry-looking chunk of land loomed dead ahead, less hospitable in appearance even than Kryptos Island.

"That's it," Jason said.

Turning to the others at the prow, he rolled up the map.

"What's it called?" Sinbad said, staring at the fast-approaching terra firma.

"It has no name," Jason said. "At least not to us. It's where Zeus compelled Hephaestus to construct monuments to the gods of Olympus."

"And monuments have blood?" Makili said.

"No," Jason said. Then he quickly reconsidered. "Well, *sometimes*. But I think the only one with blood here is not using it anymore."

"That's right," Belaricus said. "Jason killed Talos the Great by draining its life blood."

Sinbad raised an eyebrow and turned Jason's way.

"And that's the only threat here," he said, "this giant you slayed?"

"WE slayed it," Jason said. "With advice from my Lady Hera, I might add. And all I can say is we encountered nothing besides Talos here."

"Talos was enough!" Belaricus said, and he, Jason, Pollux and several others within earshot who'd survived

86

the Fleece Voyage all laughed heartily.

"Then this should be a nice break for us," Sinbad said.

"I doubt it seriously," Rashid said. "And I've repeatedly requested you not say such things."

"You'd prefer I'd have left you behind to finish the repairs?"

"No offense captain," he said. "But if I lose one more hand there may soon arise the issue of who handles my personal hygiene."

"The island isn't too large," Jason said, too focused on the task to appreciate Rashid's dark humor. "We should be able to search it from end to end in no more than three days."

"Time well spent if the blood of Zeus is to be found here," Sinbad said, turning his way.

"I can guarantee nothing, as I've said. Hera told me Zeus had other plans for him. For all I know he may be long gone, but considering this island's proximity to Kryptos it seems almost destined we should return to make certain."

They made anchor in the same narrow-necked pocket bay where the Argo had once been mangled nearly beyond repair by a hundred foot tall titan of bronze. As they rowed to anchor all free hands and the pair of guests studied the shattered remains of the defeated titan from the port rail.

As they were mooring they got their first look at the inland side of the shattered bronze torso and couldn't help but notice the tall piles of sand behind it.

Sinbad went along as Jason and a hastily assembled party hustled down the beach to look over the odd mounds, all four of which turned out to be at least ten feet tall at their peaks. The source of all that sand, which had been sitting there as such for long enough to have sea grass growing on the sides of the conic mounds, was instantly obvious: several eight foot tall tunnel entrances potholed the area between the piles, each of them dropping down about seven feet and then curving and flattening out to become lateral tunnels. Each one of the tunnels angled immediately toward the side of the massive hollow torso.

"What could all this be?" Sinbad said, standing beside Jason.

"This is his work," Jason said. "He was looking for Hylas."

Sinbad glanced around. "Do you think he found him?"

Everyone else was scanning the area as well. Jason was the first to spy the cairn of huge boulders perched at the crest of the nearest hill. His focused study drew the others to look that way.

"I would say so," Jason said.

***

A prepared search party set out from the Argo about an hour after the impromptu party's return. Orpheus recounted the tale of the Argo's crew's experiences there from his scrolls as he, Jason, Rashid, Sinbad, Pollux, Calpius, Andoros and Farno ventured into the Valley of Monuments.

The eight strong party soon paused as one, to a man struck by the incredible sight before them: ringed by mountains, barely dwarfed by them, a forest of titanic statues towered over an eerily still valley.

All of the statues within visual range stood posed atop broad pedestals. Sinbad stared off at the nearest pedestal – the only one, it appeared from this end of the valley, not to sit beneath a titanic figure.

"I'm guessing that was Talos' spot," he said.

"Yes," Jason said. "And let's hope it proves to be the only one missing its figure."

They moved on.

Passing the pedestal of Talos they saw its door was still ajar.

"The work of the man we seek, no doubt," Pollux said, studying the shadowy gap. "Takes a god to steal from a god I suppose."

"Heracles is no god," Jason said.

Sinbad spun about and locked gazes with him. "Yet he has the blood of one?"

"Father's side only. His mother was as mortal as any of us."

Sinbad was regarding him with mild uncertainty. "Let us hope that will be enough then," he said.

"Yes," Jason said. "And let's continue to hope he's still around."

Some clues that Heracles had at least spent a bit of time there soon presented themselves.

LOTS of pedestal doors stood partially open. A couple of them had been ripped off their hinges completely, no small feat considering the size of said doors and hinges. And one door in particular turned out to have ended up a long way from wherever it belonged.

"Look at that!"

Calpius had stopped and was craning his neck back and staring up at one statue in particular. The rest paused as well and followed his gaze. Amazingly, a door had been rammed halfway into the posterior of one particularly stern-looking male figure.

"Who's that?" Sinbad said.

"Hades," Jason said. "Zeus' brother."

"Interesting," Sinbad said, staring up at the three inch thick door that protruded from a hole ripped in what appeared to be even thicker metal. "I'm guessing Heracles isn't big on his uncle."

"Are you joking?" Pollux said. "He doesn't even get along with his father!"

"Hades judges mens' worth and their behavior in life," Jason said. "He earns some enmity."

Sinbad was still studying the impact spot far above, marveling at the force involved in creating such brittle shearing in thick metal fifty feet off the ground.

"Looks like he's been judged himself," he said, provoking a few chuckles that might have been louder had most of the Argo's crew not actually dreaded Hades out of cultural reflex.

They continued on, past more ripped-open pedestals, and eventually reached the center of the huge Y-shaped valley. They stopped there and Sinbad suggested splitting into two groups to search the other arms of the valley simultaneously.

"We could finish this and be back at the Argo by nightfall," he said. "Tomorrow we can search the mountain peaks and then the shoreline from the ship itself. If he's here we'll certainly know by...LOOK OUT!"

At his warning the party looked up as one and saw the gleaming spike of gold he'd been alert enough to spy as it streaked down from the cloud-dotted sky. Everyone scattered except the person most directly in the shimmering spear's path, who boldly assessed the speed and angle and decided to stand his ground.

The golden javelin impaled the ground not two feet in front of Jason's motionless toes, coming down dead center between them.

"Missed, curse the gods!"

A huge man, hulking and broad-chested, his face nearly invisible beneath long gray-streaked hair and even grayer beard, glared at the party. At least a hundred yards distant, he made an obscene gesture with the hand that wasn't swinging the sloshing golden goblet around.

"I was aiming for your jewels, Jason!" the man hollered. "You're lucky Dionysus has such accursedly wondrous wine. Now, wait right there just a moment."

He bent over, his half-functioning reflexes struggling to allow him to set his goblet safely down on the ground. And the second the obviously drunken bear of a man dared to let go of it he feared its stability, reached out and accidentally tipped it over. He reared up angrily.

"Now you've gone and made me spill my drink!" he roared. "You truly ARE cursed."

He bent awkwardly over his broad chest and belly again, searching a pile of rocks for something.

"Heracles!" Jason yelled, his hands cupped around the sides of his mouth. "Wait! Don't…"

Heracles bolted upright again. He more or less got the resultant staggering backpedal under control just enough to cut his former captain off.

"DON'T YOU 'HERACLES' ME!" he bellowed, and his supernaturally powerful roar echoed most intensely and unnaturally off the mountainsides all around. "You abandoned me here, Jason. You left me here to rot. Left me here with Hades and Hephaestus – hey, did you know Hephaestus doesn't like my father? Also, old dad doesn't seem to care."

Jason tried to counter.

"But Hera assured me…" he said, but Heracles cut him off again.

"HERA!?!"

His thunderous voice was so intense that it loosened rocks, gravel and even some small boulders and sent the debris tumbling down the surrounding slopes.

Heracles found his focus just in time to notice Jason gesturing to the others, subtly urging them to advance slowly, and the moment Jason turned around and took his first step to lead the way the demigod froze the Argo's captain and everyone else in their tracks.

"NO!" he boomed. "I told you to wait right there."

The party obeyed, holding where they were. They watched as Heracles bent over and searched the rock pile. Reaching down at last, he came up in the next moment bearing a piece of broken marble that looked like it weighed at least a hundred pounds. Heracles tossed the yard thick chunk of rubble up and down in his huge hands a couple of times.

"Yeah, that'll do," he said to himself. He looked up from the rock to the landing party, explaining, "I needed to find one that will fly right."

He reared back and let go in a surprisingly fast motion, flinging the big rock with the same apparently nominal effort a normal person would exert tossing a fist-sized piece weighing but a couple of pounds. The rock streaked in at Jason.

This time he knew he wouldn't be able to hold his ground. But he still faced Heracles boldly, only stepping aside at the last possible second and even moving so minimally as to feel the rush of wind in the projectile's wake.

"This will resolve nothing," he hollered at Heracles.

But Zeus' drunken and quite angry son was already picking up another big rock.

"Maybe not," Heracles yelled. "But it's fun!"

He flung another boulder. Jason had to scramble to get clear this time, so hard was the rock thrown, and he ended up sprawled on the ground.

Everyone else had scattered, taking refuge quickly in small groups behind the nearest pedestals. From around the corners of these barriers they watched Jason's daring showdown.

"I don't think he's in a chatting mood," Sinbad called over at Jason from beneath the statue of Artemis. "Maybe give him some time to cool off."

"No," Jason shot back. "It's all right. I know what I'm..."

"Look out!" Orpheus yelled from over behind the other pedestal, which sat beneath a titanic Apollo.

Another potentially deadly rock came skipping like a pebble toward the Argo's captain, who actually caught a scraping blow across his right hamstring this time...and only eluded far worse damage by flattening himself down head to toe against the arid soil. Without hesitation he popped up in the wake of that still-bouncing boulder and scrambled over to where Sinbad, Rashid and Farno all stood watching.

"Perhaps you're right," he said to Sinbad. "He may need a little more time."

Another boulder shattered against the side of the pedestal in the next moments, casting a spray of high-speed fragments that the foursome saw shoot past them.

"When I tell you to go away, Jason," they all heard Heracles bellowing, "I don't mean go hide behind my auntie's statue and wait until I fall asleep to sneak up on me! I mean take your precious Argo and the wondrous Fleece you've no doubt been parading around as king and go back where you belong!"

Before Jason had a chance to respond the shriek of rushing air echoed out over the valley floor. Seventy feet or so above the foursome's heads the surprisingly well-aimed rock struck the shaft of Artemis' drawn arrow just behind the arrowhead, neatly snapping the arrowhead end off.

Only the noise saved the quartet, who looked up at the sound only to see the arrowhead coming down at them point first. All of them dove clear, to a man hitting the deck as the ponderous piece of metalwork slammed into the ground. The point sank in at least two feet, far enough to hold the rest of it upright, where it resonated like a rung tuning fork.

Heracles' great howl of laughter shook the hills.

"Pretty good shot, huh?" he yelled. "Did you all survive that?"

Gathering themselves together, working their way quickly back up on their feet, the other three saw Sinbad gesture for them not to reply.

"What, nothing to say?" Heracles yelled. "I know I didn't kill you ALL. Hello?"

Sinbad moved away from both Heracles and the protective wall, backing up until he could see Orpheus, Andoros and Calpius behind the other pedestal while still taking advantage of the shielding provided by Artemis' pedestal. Seeing Calpius glance his way he waved, saw Calpius wave back and alert the others, and then proceeded to signal them to stay quiet and remain where they were.

"HELLO?" Heracles was still taunting them. "What about it Jason, nothing more to say?"

Sinbad moved back up with the rest.

"Don't indulge him any further," he told Jason. "See what he does."

What Heracles in fact did was quickly grow bored with the effective standoff.

"Well, THIS is no fun," he finally growled. Spying his goblet he went over and snatched it up. "You have a nice time out here. Jason. All of you. For my part I'm going to see if my old friend Dionysus has anything left in that allegedly eternal barrel of his. All this sunlight is giving me a headache!"

He turned and staggered away, ambling off in no apparent hurry down the right arm of the valley. But he didn't go all that far. Casting a glance back (and not quite noticing that the landing party was peering very discreetly out at him), he angled over to a partially open door in a pedestal decorated in grape vines and clusters. Above the pedestal the vines continued to rise, swirling up the ample form of the smiling male statue whose bare feet graced the pedestal roof itself.

With one final quick look back Heracles slipped through the doorway. He pulled the huge door closed with what appeared to be relative ease.

The door closed with a resounding boom.

Sinbad and Jason locked gazes.

"Well," Sinbad said, "you've said your deities have some issues. I suppose it was unrealistic to expect anything different with the offspring of one."

Jason shook his head. "I understand his frustration," he said. "Both he and I apparently expected him to find his way off this island when his self-assigned quest here was complete."

"He asked you to leave him behind," Sinbad said. "Was any promise made of you returning to pick him up?"

"Not as such. But in his current state I don't think such details will make a lot of difference."

"So what do we do?"

"We wait for now." Jason accepted Sinbad's wineskin, slugged from it and handed it back. "Even the son of a god can only remain inebriated for so long."

"For all our sakes let us hope you're right," Rashid said, taking the wineskin from Sinbad and chugging a fair portion. "The man seems pretty tough. And I most certainly hope he is not prone to hangovers."

Chapter Twelve

The party never really got a chance to find out whether they could outlast a demigod's drunken bender. The perytons attacked first.

Monstrous eagle-like avians with the heads and horns of stags – that is, if stags typically had long curving yellow fangs and glowing blood-red eyes – the terrors didn't come in flying. Rather they had caught the scent of their intended prey while on foot and stayed that way, keeping downwind and approaching stealthily until they had drawn within visual range of their targets around one final pedestal edge. Gathered together by then beneath the towering bronze effigy of Artemis, the landing party had no clue that the clever hunters were closing in on them until it was too late.

By then the horrors were charging from both sides, some of them having broken off from the rest and circled around the pedestal. Before weapons were even in hands a pair of long, vicious jaws had clamped into Calpius' neck from behind, and in the next moment great flapping wings were hammering the early evening air and the Argo crewman's already limp body was being lifted off the ground.

Absorbed with this ghastly sight, Andoros was also caught off guard. He screamed as, turning about, he found himself staring point blank into a pair of those pupil-less red orbs. A huge pair of claws wrapped around him, clamping his arms to his sides, and the beast's powerful wings lifted it and its prey up and away.

Sinbad and Rashid went back to back, scimitars flashing. Jason nimbly dodged a set of shredding antlers and drove his gladius into their owner's neck; its agonized howl, a logical hybrid of eagle screech and deer grunt, pierced the battle scene. The shocked creature swooped away, raining blood down on the vicious melee.

Farno drove off one peryton only to look up and see another descending on him. His scream was cut off abruptly as his head disappeared inside the beast's wide open jaws, and in the next moment his kicking and flailing form was rising into the sky beneath pounding wings.

Pollux managed to nail the peryton that was struggling to make off with the squirming, heavyset Andoros with an arrow that caught it in a wing joint. With only one working wing the beast flapped back down to Earth, landing on top of Andoros. Pollux hastened that way to lend help but suddenly found himself rising, clutched by the shoulders by painfully powerful claws.

Something streaked through the gloom, something that was moving fast and straight (as opposed to the bobbing, swooping assaults of the perytons.) Whatever it was slammed into the torso of the beast that held Pollux in its clutches, and with force sufficient to drive the creature and its load at least ten feet laterally with a single jolting impact. Damaged and stunned, the peryton dropped Pollux and crashed to Earth.

Pollux crashed heavily, but despite the impact he was on his feet again in a second scanning his surroundings.

Another strange lateral-streaking something came whistling overhead. This one nailed another peryton, square in the head this time, and dropped it from the dusky shadows; it slammed limply to earth.

"Damned chickens!"

Heracles rounded the corner. He looked every bit as angry and maniacal as before. He was stomping toward the battle, a rock as big as his own demigod head clutched with near shattering pressure in one hand and his goblet in the other.

He stopped and looked the battle scene over. A peryton's slashing antlers had shredded the front of Jason's tunic and the fabric was already darkening with the captain's blood. Rashid was holding his own well against not one but two perytons that had given up hovering over him and had landed to take him on in a frontal two-on-one assault unimpeded by flapping wings instead. Behind him Sinbad was taking on only one, which was bobbing and diving at him over and over only to be thwarted again and again by Sinbad's parrying thrusts. As Heracles continued to watch, the stranger with both his hands looked his way.

Heracles saw Sinbad's wary gaze. He drew back the stone in a split second and let it fly.

The projectile nearly took off the head of the peryton hovering over Sinbad. The captain had to jump back to avoid the plummeting monster and in doing so slammed into Rashid's back and sent him staggering awkwardly toward the pair of beasts he'd been fighting.

"Hey!" Rashid cried, pushing back.

"Apologies, old friend," he heard Sinbad say from behind him.

And then he was being pulled back by strong hands.

Rashid turned and saw Sinbad had done it. And then he saw why.

Heracles came jogging in and slammed into the side of the peryton on the left. So hard did he hit the beast that it left its feet and crashed heavily into its partner, leaving them both in a flailing pile of wings, hooves and snapping, slavering jaws at the demigod's feet.

Heracles chugged the rest of his drink – there wasn't much – and hurled the goblet aside. Lunging forward he reached down, hefted the top peryton and – spinning with it like he was preparing to toss a discus – launched the monster at another that was hovering some thirty feet off the ground nearby. Caught by surprise the flying peryton and the flung one went down together in a heap that slammed to earth so hard neither of them stirred afterward.

In a mere few seconds Heracles turned the tide of battle. He took the second downed peryton and gave it the same treatment, knocking out another of its airborne brethren. These two landed separately but just as hard as the first pair and neither of them moved after impact either.

The rest appeared to take stock of their rapidly dwindling numbers. They gave up and, screeching with what sounded like serious indignation, took off in a significantly reduced pack numbering about seven.

Sinbad and Rashid stood side by side, both of them eyeing the big man. Pollux hobbled up beside them, keeping weight off his left ankle. Orpheus helped an even more disabled Andoros with an arm slung around a shoulder and together they came up to join the others.

"You're welcome," Heracles said to the small assembly. "Now get off my island."

Picking up on the slightly distracted stares of his audience, he caught the hint and spun around.

Jason stood there smiling, the front of his tunic slashed and stained from top to bottom and side to side.

"Thank you old friend," he said. "Without you we would no doubt…"

He didn't quite finish because Heracles leveled him.

***

Jason awoke hours later. For a few seconds he just stared groggily up at the crescent moon.

Then Orpheus' concerned face blocked it.

"You all right?" Orpheus said.

"I suppose," Jason said. He rubbed his sore jaw. "Mostly, anyway."

Orpheus moved back so that Jason could push himself up on one elbow. The Argo's captain rubbed his severely bruised jaw and cheek again and looked around.

"Guess I had that coming," he said in low voice.

"Quite frankly and with all respect I was going to say it if you didn't, captain. But in truth we ALL left him here. Not just you. And it wasn't really any of us at fault to begin with, rather his insistence on ignoring our pleas that stranded him here."

"Well, unlikely he was going to punch himself," Jason said with a grin. "Maybe he'll feel better now and decide to be civilized. Not that I'm going to count on it."

Jason sat up and looked around. Sinbad, Rashid, Pollux and Andoros were all seated together about forty feet away. To a man they all looked tired and ragged.

"Where did he go?" Jason said to Orpheus, sitting up.

"Same place he came from," Orpheus said. "He took out enough of those beasts to drive them off, knocked you out, mumbled what sounded like some sort of half-apology to us – I'm guessing it must have been for his odd behavior – and staggered right back to Dionysus' vault."

Jason got on his feet. He and Orpheus walked over to the rest.

"I'm glad to see those creatures didn't get you, Andoros," he said, looking at the big man.

"He was too heavy," Pollux said. "Gave me plenty of time to regroup and shoot."

"And now I owe you a life debt," Andoros told him. "From the looks of it likely to be repaid before we even leave this accursed place."

"You owe me nothing," Pollux said. "Unless the opportunity arises, I mean …"

There might have been a few chuckles were the party

not two men down.

"Well," Jason said, his jaw setting grimly. "I would say it's my job to make sure that the opportunity doesn't arise. This ends now."

He turned and took a step toward Dionysus' distant vault but Sinbad stopped him.

"He looked like he wanted to kick your unconscious body on the way out," he told Jason. "Maybe he'll be less hostile toward a respectful stranger." Sinbad smiled.

Jason thought about it a moment. "I can guarantee nothing," he said at last, conceding the task. "Go in my stead if you wish, with my thanks, and may the Fates grant neither of us regrets it. Hopefully you are right: isolation and drunkenness notwithstanding, Heracles should have no reason to show a stranger discourtesy."

"*Hopefully*," Sinbad said, removing his scimitar belt. "But if not please drag me back here and keep me company until I wake up."

Chapter Thirteen

The monsters were everywhere. Nightmarish visions clad in thick armor they hardly looked as if they needed, they lumbered here and there without apparent organization, seemingly intent only on getting their fair share (and if possible more) of the chaos and destruction all around.

Broad, flat faces with thick-ridged brows over pupilless white eyes and uneven rows of great fangs, their visages somehow combined the most terrifying and intimidating aspects of ape and reptile. They stood ten to twelve feet in height, but they weren't really standing so much as tromping around.

Flames and smoke rolled out of the second and third story windows lining the market square. Distant and not-so-distant shrieks and screams peppered the constant crackling of flames. Bodies – as many civilian as mercenary soldier, perhaps more – dotted the close-fit paving stones.

Through this gauntlet of ongoing destruction and havoc strolled Circe the Witch.

From the looks of it she was utterly unconcerned with the potential for harm to herself. The supremely powerful magician swept along in a curiously spotless sky blue robe of veils, exposing much of her strawberry pale skin if in fact most of it indirectly. Black eyes smoldering beneath flaming locks, she looked like she was out for a casual stroll in a beautiful park.

A ragged-looking woman, her hair stringy and unkempt, her eyes wild, came rushing up to Circe. The witch's abyssal orbs found her and she paused. The woman lunged forward, bending at the same time. She threw herself on the ground a few inches in front of Circe's stiletto-heeled boots.

"Please!" the woman said, groveling. "The soldiers are all gone. There is no one here who will resist you. Please...I beg you..." She raised her eyes slowly up to look into Circe's face. "Spare us...please...we only want to live..."

Circe lowered her chin and her dark gaze met the woman's.

"Stand," she said.

The woman stood, rattling like an autumn leaf in a stiff breeze.

"Calm yourself," Circe said. "What is your name?"

The woman seemed almost completely confused by the witch's behavior but did her best to comply. Still trembling, if not quite so hard after a few deep breaths, she finally answered.

"Narelda, my lady."

"Narelda, tell me of your family that I might understand your plea."

"My family?"

"Yes. Are you alone?"

"No...no, I'm...I've got a husband and two children. And my parents are alive as well. And two sisters."

"The children: male or female?"

Narelda looked even more puzzled if possible, but she was too terrified not to answer.

"One of each."

"Very well then, Narelda. I've been out here for hours now, walking around and enjoying all this, and the whole time I've been thinking 'By Hecate these people are spineless! Is there not one among them who will at least approach me to bargain?' And just when I was about to give up and go find better entertainment while my soldiers finish reducing the place to ruin here you come. I'm glad now I didn't disintegrate you as I'd contemplated on your approach. I'm relieved I didn't judge by appearances or condemn you because of how it might look if anyone of consequence happened to see us doing this."

"I...I...my lady?"

"Narelda, today is your lucky day. I'm recruiting. So here's the deal: I can either kill you now – slowly and with special care since you've already eaten up a lot of my valuable time here – or you can accept a commander's post."

Narelda fell back, completely unsure of anything at this point from the looks of it.

Circe sighed. "It's a great job. You look fit...well, relatively. And I could use a couple more gutsy women to make this all go down right."

"If I take your offer you'll spare the city?"

Circe shrugged, glancing around. "Oh, there's only so much I can do about these guys. They follow orders when they're right here around me but the ones that aren't right around here...well, monsters will be monsters, you know? But I will spare *you*. And I treat my commanders pretty well."

Narelda contemplated it just long enough to test Circe's patience.

"I don't have all day," the witch finally said. "I guess slow disintegration it is ..."

"Wait!" Narelda said, her tear-filled eyes growing wide as Circe's hands went up and crimped into aggressive-looking claws courtesy of her flawless sky blue nails. "Wait...I accept."

"That's more like it." Circe lowered her hands. "By the way I have no idea how to disintegrate someone slowly.

But a quick one is still pretty bad."

Narelda was looking around. One of the hideous beasts, its huge jaws slavering, jogged past with a screaming, flailing child under each arm. It had a nasty grin on its face and snorted at her.

Before Circe could mention the single caveat one of her granddaughter's chaos soldiers, running flat-out, nearly crashed into her. She put a single hand up and – though the beast's wildly swinging head suggested it shouldn't have even noticed such a gesture – it froze in its tracks. The thing went rigid, saluted the witch and then turned and charged off.

"See?" Circe said. "We made them big, tough and scary but we had to make a bit of concession in the mental faculties region because…well, deep thinking can get in the way of great achievement."

"Ma'am?"

"The name is Circe," the witch said. "And…Narelda, was it? Yes. Well Narelda, I'll tell you what: you do as I say, pass the test and I'll let *you* have control of this – what does Medea call them? – ah yes, this garrison. YOU can save this place." She glanced around. "Or at least what's left of it."

"Anything, my lady…I mean Circe…please…"

"Very well. There is but one test of loyalty applicable to such situations. Pass that and you may save some portion of this place. We're moving on to Aderadad anyway."

"What must I do?"

"Very simple. You mentioned sisters, a mother and a daughter?"

Narelda's eyes somehow got even wider. "My lady?"

"Yes, you did. Go and get them. My commanders' kin are welcome guests at Medea's camp, so long as they get along."

"Thank you my lady!" Narelda seemed genuinely grateful, but only for a moment before vague worry began to cloud her face. "And my father? My husband? My son?"

A creepy grin grew quickly on Circe's face.

"That's the catch, you see," she said. "Medea's got a real thing about men. You may have heard this whole scourge is about not sparing the menfolk. Not my issue but I am obliged to respect her since we work closely together." Her grin widened as she saw the horror dawning in Narelda's eyes. "These soldiers are going to kill them either way," she said. "You beat them to it and the job – and what's left of this town – is yours."

Narelda's jaw was slack and no words were coming up.

"Or you can say no and I won't even spare the girls and women. My crew would love that. They really relish the whole genocidal sweep concept. Monsters, you know."

Chapter Fourteen

This time Heracles hadn't slammed the massive vault door closed. A gap about a foot wide (by nearly twenty feet high) loomed before Sinbad, its darkness still impermeable due to the bright mid-morning sunlight. Poised noiselessly beside the gap, he had been listening to the voices within for a solid twenty minutes.

They were sporadic and sharp, those short outbursts he'd been hearing on and off the whole time. Sometimes one comment immediately followed the previous one, sometimes there were as much as half minute delay; that is, if indeed what followed was a related response, it was hard to tell. Most of it was unintelligible to Sinbad because of the chamber's echoing, but by this point he'd at least figured out that much of it sounded like emotional outbursts with a significant commiseration component.

One grumbling voice was obviously Heracles: deep, self-assured, more angry than miserable.

The other voice liked to chuckle from the sound of it: Its tone went up and down but quite often there was gentleness in it. Its owner seemed to get the most tickled when Heracles sounded the maddest.

Sinbad, on the other hand, was patiently waiting for Heracles to sound the least mad.

And at the moment he was sounding as unemotional and low-key as he had since Sinbad had quietly tiptoed up to his current position.

So Sinbad rapped three times on the vault door.

"Go away Jason!" Heracles hollered.

"Yeah," the other voice said. "We know you've been out there listening."

Sinbad went for it. He leaned forward and stuck his head into the gap.

"You are correct that I've been here," he said to the darkness, still nearly sun-blinded. "But I am not Jason, I am Sinbad."

"I don't know the name," Heracles called back. "You must be one of Jason's NEW fools."

"I'm not an Argonaut," Sinbad said. "I've got a ship of my own."

He heard a bit of communal chuckling.

"Oh, a fellow captain then! Well that's just fine... another man with a mission, no doubt?"

Sinbad laughed. "I suppose I've had a few, yes," he said. "We all have our purposes, no?"

"Not all of us!" the other voice, its bluster a fair match for Heracles, called back, amusing its owner so much he went into a prolonged giggle.

Heracles hollered over the mirth.

"Come in then," he said. "This shouting is giving me a headache."

Sinbad did just that, slipping through the doorway into the vault.

"You're no Greek or Roman," Heracles said, looking him up and down. "I'd have figured only they were foolish enough to venture here."

"I hail from a land east of those, a place whose name is likely of little concern to you."

"He's from Aderadad," said the other man, who was not quite as muscular as Heracles but similarly huge and robust. His eyes were more bloodshot than Heracles' – no mean feat – and his round face, ringed in curly black locks, featured a very broad mouth with lips stained purple with wine. Leaning over toward Heracles he said with obviously mock confidentiality, "They're very polite, his people. Sobriety is often honored in their culture. So as you might imagine I've had little to do with them!"

Hearing every word – as obviously intended – Sinbad did a gracious bow. He rose, smiling.

"Sinbad, son of Sinbad," he said. "I bring you both hale greetings on behalf of Margiana, regent of Aderadad."

"His mother," the other man told Heracles, again in that fake whisper meant to be heard.

Sinbad's eyes grew wide.

"You must be a djinn," he said. "How else could you know...?"

"A fair guess," the big man said, and he chugged more wine from his goblet, letting it splash down on a toga trimmed with grape vines whose fabric absorbed the excess but remained pristine white. "Those you call the djinn are our distant cousins, you might say. Weaker. Renegades who decided to do it their way for one reason or another."

"A thousand pardons," Sinbad said, "but I introduced myself with the implied expectation that all here would do the same."

The big guy smiled and leaned over toward Heracles again.

"See what I mean about the politeness?"

"I would prefer not to offend. Let me try again: I am Sinbad, son of Sinbad, captain of the Chimera and by the will of the Fates obligated to return a favor to Jason of Thessaly."

Heracles burst into throaty laughter. He slapped his broad, dirty knee.

"So that's it!" he said. "Of course. He roped you into this and he sent you in as an errand boy to plea to me for help on his behalf. I knew it. Did he tell you he left me here for…how long is it, Dionysus?"

"That's a rather personal question!" his drinking buddy roared.

His giggle fit was punctuated with a monstrous belch so potent that the bronze vault walls and ceiling rang like bells for seconds afterwards. He made no apologies, in fact complimenting himself instead.

Heracles looked a little pained, as though the distractive mirth was irking him.

"Seriously …" he said wearily.

The moderately rotund man's mirth continued until Heracles' rising irritation showed in his eyes and silenced his friend. The man closed his eyes, his brow wrinkled (from the smoothness of his forehead this didn't happen all that often) and he went silent for but a second, as though focusing.

"Okay…okay…ten years, four months, a week, three days, four hours, five minutes..." the man finally said, "…you want any more detail let me know and we'll count seconds."

Sinbad was marveling at him again.

"Dionysus, god of wine and reverie," Heracles said, nodding toward him. "And a good man, as you no doubt claim to be. Sit and drink with us if your people are as amicable as he says."

***

Sinbad learned a lot in a short time.

"Bottom line is Jason trusted Hera," Heracles said. "Mom's off limits thanks to Dad but I'm not. And that I accept as fair. What's NOT fair is not seeing one ship land here in – what, ten plus years – and having to deal with not just those accursed perytons over all that time but the damnable loneliness of it all to boot.

"At least those monsters are decent eating if you get the fire right. There's nothing you can do about the fact that you're alone though. And for so long." He raised his goblet, which he'd just refilled from a golden cask, and slopped wine that should've drenched Dionysus but didn't as he saluted the god. "They say my kind can't be reduced to begging, Sinbad. But I was. I'm not proud of it but I WILL face the truth. In the end it grew so maddening that I pleaded to them. Almost every last one. And only one came to help."

He caught a gentle nod from Dionysus and all drank.

Sinbad was doing well considering he was all mortal and what he was drinking was not really meant for such. Glad to be seated, he was smart enough not to trust his tongue and just went on listening.

Dionysus shrugged. "Hera and Hades – whom I believe does not appreciate this young demigod's tendencies toward justice and defending the weak, thus reducing the flow of corrupt souls to Hades' beloved Tartarus – compelled Zeus to issue an edict banning our kind from taking Heracles from this place. Poseidon has standing orders to sink any vessel approaching this island except Jason's beloved Argo, and it was starting to look like Jason wasn't ever coming back to check on his stranded crewmate."

"Dionysus took pity on me," Heracles said. "I accepted his admittedly enjoyable companionship with the stipulation that I might continue to partake heavily of his Earthly justice and rail to him of my pitiable state." His head drooped and he shook it. "And that I have done indeed ..."

"THAT he has done indeed," Dionysus echoed, shaking his head and smiling at Jason.

Heracles quit running his fingers through his tangled salt and pepper locks and looked up to the others. "And maybe that's it," he said. "Maybe the pointlessness of self-pity is the lesson I was here to learn."

"Let's hope the lesson wasn't forgiveness," Dionysus said, grinning at Sinbad.

Heracles rose...unsteadily, teetering. Then he found his center.

"No," he said. "That's it. Forgiveness isn't why I'm here. I should have seen it." He looked to Sinbad. "Do you see it Sinbad, son of Sinbad?"

"You wish me to say?"

"I do."

Sinbad felt he had to stand. He did his best to do so smoothly and held his form admirably rigid against a noticeable tendency it had at the moment to want to falter and flop back down onto the cask he'd been using as a seat. Summoning his focus he looked Heracles right in the eye. They were as close to nose to nose as Heracles' projecting chest allowed.

"I don't profess to know your ways," Sinbad said. "But if your isolation here was meant as a lesson, which you seem to believe, then I'd say the lesson is that perhaps one's concerns should not allow them to forget the needs of others. And now you attack your former captain and as I understand it one of your most trusted friends merely because he didn't come rushing back to this distant and hostile place to make sure you didn't need the help you'd already rejected?"

Heracles swelled up, making himself appear even more menacing somehow.

Sinbad didn't flinch. He did waver on his feet ever so slightly a couple of times, but that was it.

Heracles gave up his bluff at last. His glare faded as he exhaled the long-held breath heavily; reeking of dry, extremely potent wine the wind blast washed over Sinbad in a wave.

Like Dionysus, Heracles didn't appear to be a big one for manners or apologies.

"Well yes, I suppose," he said. "But when you say it like that you make me sound like I'm trying to punish Jason for my own...grave...faults." A light was glimmering in those pink orbs. "Which come to think of it is sort of why I'm here in the first place." He glanced up at the ceiling, exposing even more bloodshot eyeball surface. "Nice one Dad. Got me that time."

Heracles looked around. Sinbad stood before him, smiling but saying nothing.

"Right then," Heracles finally said. He turned and nodded to Dionysus. "It's been fun," he told the god. "I owe you one old friend."

Dionysus raised a hand and gave him a minimal salute.

"Off to kill Jason then?" the deity said.

Heracles shook his head. "No," he said, and he turned to look Sinbad in the eyes. "This odd but charming fellow has granted him a reprieve, if perhaps but temporary. Good that he doesn't remind me too much of that OTHER visiting captain." He looked back to Dionysus. "I'll hear Jason out and *then* decide whether or not to flatten him like a bug."

Chapter Fifteen

Heracles wasn't liking what he was hearing.

Particularly the part about Jason not saying what his goal was in getting inside the temple.

"I don't like the sound of it Jason," he said, nearly sober, his hand still slightly bent into the right shape to hold that goblet even though he'd left it back in Dionysus' vault. "If you can't give me a little more I may have to kill you."

Jason strode right up to him.

"Do it then," he said. "But take my word that I have a reason worthy of the effort."

"Worthy?" Heracles said, not backing down. "I'll say. Worthy of getting your crew killed. Worthy of finally checking on an old friend when his blood will serve your purpose!"

Ten yards away, on the far side of the campfire, Sinbad sat lotus style on the ground, a sort of meditative or trancelike expression on his face. He'd returned in a most curious state from his venture, one so unusual for him as to even raise Rashid's eyebrows: He and Heracles had come to the landing party weaving and wavering, the two men occasionally even propping up against one another's shoulders – apparently to keep balance – along the way. Rashid had guided his uncharacteristically drunken captain to that spot by the fire, where Sinbad's mind was currently wandering elsewhere.

Rashid sat nearby atop a chunk of marble that Heracles had tossed there, one large enough that no one else was going to be moving it. The Chimera's first mate's eyes were wide at the sight of the Argo's captain going toe-to-toe with the obviously still smarting demigod.

"All that is lost can be regained," Jason said. "I can tell you that much."

"Ah, so that would be my time here then?"

"As I said, all that is lost."

Heracles regarded him uncertainly. Jason stood firm and Heracles actually turned away first.

"I'm not sure what faith to put in what you tell me, Jason," he said, glancing around at the rest, and he turned slowly back to the Argo's captain. "I hear you achieved your goal and found the Fleece. Did it bring you what you dreamed it would?"

"I sought it to wrest Thessaly from the hands of a usurping tyrant. To that end no, it did not."

"You have it with you, then?" Heracles looked around.

Jason shook his head. "A story in itself," he said. "One I will share with you soon."

"Yes, yes, I understand. We all understand, Jason. You get into my father's earthly temple and everyone lives happily ever after. And here I thought Orpheus was the one with the entertaining campfire stories."

"I'm sorry I can't tell you more, Heracles." Jason looked around. "I apologize to you all. But Pentelus, may he rest in peace, told me that secrecy was of utmost importance. He is – he *was* – a student of the mysterious ways of the gods. He said they all watch great endeavors, and I can testify personally that this is so. They can see us all even now. And they are likely watching to make sure we follow their rules."

"Their rules?" Rashid said, and he rose from his rock seat and strode over to them, where he bowed quickly. "Don't their rules also forbid mortals from gaining entrance in the first place?"

Heracles turned to him. "Some of their rules matter more than others," he said. "It's best to know which ones those are, although I don't suggest you come to me as an expert on the topic. I seem to get that wrong quite often." He looked back to his former captain. "All right Jason," he said. "I'm willing to give you that blood, but on ONE condition."

"You have but to name it."

"Good. Then I wish to follow you right to your final destination. I'm completing this mission. I want to be there when you find this miracle, close enough to wring your neck if it's not all you promise."

They locked gazes for a few tense seconds. Rashid backed away.

Heracles thrust an arm out.

"Deal?" he said.

Jason locked forearms with him. "Deal," he said. "I wouldn't have it any other way."

Heracles stifled a grin as their grips increased. "Nice try. But I don't think we're quite back to that level of trust yet. I'll believe it when I see it."

"I will do my earthly best to make sure that happens, old friend," Jason said, doing all he could not to let Heracles see him suffering from that painfully potent grip. "Whether I have one arm left or both." Heracles let him go, almost smiling for the first time, and both turned to see Rashid looking down at his hook. "No offense," Heracles said. "Tell you what: after this is done you and I will go see my wonderful half-uncle Hephaestus and I'll beat him into making you something nice."

Jason looked surprised. "You honestly think you can beat a full-blooded god into submission?"

Heracles' grin was the epitome of self-assurance.

"There have been many days here, Jason – MANY days – where I wanted nothing more than to find out."

If Sinbad heard any of this he wasn't acknowledging it

in any way. He just continued to sit there, staring into the campfire, until an increasingly concerned Rashid finally went over to him an hour or so later and gave him a gentle push on the shoulder.

Sinbad came out of it immediately. He turned and looked up to see his first mate offering him a ragged, smoking peryton rib.

"Hungry, captain?"

"No Rashid, thank you," Sinbad said. He still looked strangely dreamy.

"Are you all right?" Rashid said. "Sinbad?"

"I'm fine. Better than that. Dionysus was right: in wine, indeed, truth can be found."

"Captain?"

Sinbad finally came the rest of the way out of his distracted state. His eyes met Rashid's and he spoke in a voice quiet enough to be hidden by the crackling campfire.

"Vigilance is demanded of us now, Rashid. There is much more here than meets the eye."

Rashid looked around.

"With due respect, Captain," he said softly. "What meets the eye here is already too much."

***

There was no dawn as such. For the first time in what Heracles said was countless months the skies were angry sheets of gray, purple and black clouds across which played nearly nonstop webs and streaks of angry lightning. Thunder echoed through the valley in rapid-fire fashion and by daylight the faint winds of the previous night had picked up noticeably and were frequently driving through the camp in fairly strong gusts.

Undaunted – in fact quite the opposite, if anything – Heracles decided to delay the trek back to the Argo to test this bold stranger who'd talked him into what in his mind had amounted to an apology.

"Just curious how well-rounded captains have to be where you're from," he told Sinbad, smiling. "I thought maybe you'd want to go tussle a few rounds or exchange blows to prove your mettle."

"I've seen your strength," Sinbad said. "I'm not sure what losing quickly and badly in a wrestling match with you would prove to either of us, or in fact anyone here."

Heracles laughed heartily and turned away, but Sinbad stopped him. "Of course ..." he said.

"Enough Heracles," Jason said. "We need to go now and don't have time for..."

"That said," Sinbad went on loudly, addressing Heracles' broad back, "if you would so much as allow me to mix dexterity in with strength in some sort of contest I think we might have a match."

Heracles turned slowly back around. "Dexterity?"

"Of course. Every bit as vital to a true and complete physical contest as strength. Remember, you can punch me all the way back to Aderadad – given you send me the right direction and allow for the wind – but ONLY if you actually land the blow."

Heracles swaggered toward Sinbad, a grin manifesting fully at last beneath all that unkempt facial hair.

"I'll give it my best," he said, drawing back a clenched fist.

Sinbad offered Heracles an unflinching smile. Heracles saw it, paused only for a second – and then threw the punch anyway.

Heracles' huge mitt came to a stop with its knuckles inches from Sinbad's motionless jaw.

"How did you know I wouldn't hit you?" the demigod said, withdrawing the hand.

"I didn't," Sinbad said. "But from all I can tell you're not the sort to enjoy a one-sided fight."

Heracles shrugged. "I don't mind joining one," he said, "on the underdog's side, of course. But you're right. I don't start them. So, what's this contest you propose?"

"A throwing competition," Sinbad said, gesturing around. "We pick a spot somewhere well away from here and see who can hit it first. We start from here and count throws."

"My count will be easy," Heracles said. "Provided someone here can count up to one." He looked around and saw a couple of faint smiles. "What do we throw? Oh wait...I've got it. Wait here."

"Heracles...please ..." Jason said.

"Now Jason, this won't take long. I waited you out for a decade. Indulge me."

He turned and hustled off as fast as anyone had seen him move to that point, headed for a nearby pedestal. Passing the door he'd ripped off its front long ago he sped inside. Seconds later he emerged from the doorway and stepped out into the shadow of the figure atop the pedestal, in this case the great sculpture being that of a slim but sinewy female titan whose raised arm held aloft a leaved wreath meant to be placed around the head (like the one Orpheus wore, except completely encircling.)

Heracles was bearing two very shiny silver discs about a foot in diameter each. He held them up. They were thin, no more than half an inch thick.

"Discus!" he yelled at the rest, who came jogging over to him.

"Actually they're Nike's victory charms, I think," Orpheus said.

Indeed the profile embossed on the surfaces of both discs – in a very coin-like centered fashion – was the same as that of the goddess from beneath whose likeness Heracles had "borrowed" her presumably treasured possessions.

Heracles looked back and forth between the disc in his hand and the huge bronze face far overhead. He shrugged.

"Somewhat appropriate then, don't you think?" he said

energetically, without a hint of concern.

"Indeed," Sinbad said, eyeing the discs. "If perhaps only for the one carried by the victor."

"Again Heracles," Jason said, eyeing the frightening skies, "perhaps we should be on our way."

"Again Jason, you owe me this at least," Heracles said. He tossed Sinbad one of the discs and showed only minimal appreciation at best when the Chimera's captain's deft hands and powerful arms absorbed the fair amount of momentum the demigod had imparted into it. "Tell you what, we can pick a target that's on the way out of this monument to collective Olympian ego; that'll save some time. And the rest of you help yourselves to anything you want in any of these vaults. There's a lot of treasure in some of them if that sort of thing thrills you. Not much magical but just grab something: you never know."

"But Heracles," Jason said, "wasn't your taking of something from here the reason we were forced to fight Talos?"

"Exactly. And now Talos is destroyed. Take what you want, my friends. The gods have no use for it and thanks to your captain they no longer have a watchdog to ensure it all stays in this forsaken place. Just don't take more than you can carry: we don't want to leave looking like looters either way."

As Sinbad and Heracles got together in preparation for their impromptu game the winds, already potent enough to topple a momentarily unbalanced individual, picked up considerably. Not only were the gusts becoming more frequent with each passing minute, they were growing in strength as well. Some were virtually gale force, and these were lasting four or more seconds more often than not.

Orpheus had to hold his holly head wreath by hand. Jason, meanwhile, quietly slipped about telling his men – and Sinbad's as well – that it might not be such a good idea indeed to take anything from the valley of monuments. He got few arguments. Only Heracles was willing to defy the gods to such a degree, but as the Argo's contingent all agreed – confiding to each other as the impromptu two-man competition began – that was no big surprise considering for him it was a "family thing."

Heracles and Sinbad settled on Talos' pedestal as the goal.

"Might take two," Heracles said, his grip on Sinbad's forearm much lighter than the one he'd had on Jason's. "But only because the door we need to throw these through is on the far side from here."

"Two?" Pollux said, staring down the long valley. "That must be well over a mile away!"

"That plays to my 'skills', I'd say," Heracles said, casting a smirking glance at Sinbad. "I suppose I have to thank you for that."

Sinbad smiled right back at him. "Only if you win," he said, and gestured for Heracles to go first.

Heracles' brow furrowed as he considered the increasingly unpredictable and more potent wind gusts and – far more daunting by far – the forest of statues and pedestals that more or less guaranteed that no throw aimed to pass through them all was destined to make it without striking a great bronze arm, leg, torso, weapon or shield.

"A fair challenge, Captain," he said at last. "An awful lot of things up there to stop a good throw well short of its goal." He looked to Sinbad, who was not far beyond arm's reach at his side, and saw the captain give an appreciative nod. "A test of wits as much as anything," he said, turning and studying the great monuments again. "I could try to throw it over everything, but at this angle I'll hardly be covering much ground." He kept looking…and getting more frustrated. "Yes, a good test indeed. I suppose accuracy is called for. Find the best possible gap and give it a solid fling."

He finally decided on a spot.

"Don't try this yourself, lads," he said to the rest, and went into a throwing stance.

Heracles let it fly: hard, because he seriously wanted to be able to brag about that hole in two.

But he sacrificed just a little too much accuracy for force. And it was very funny.

His throw glanced off Aphrodite's wrist (the one not holding the mirror) and, deflecting sharply upwards with a resounding clang, shot right up into her brother Ares' nose. So fast was it still traveling that when it impacted the inside of the statue's head the force was sufficient to lift the head nearly a foot. The head came back down loudly and awkwardly, the great weld beads that had held it in place on the bronze neck for countless years shattered, and then it toppled in almost comical fashion down the front of the statue's torso and shattered thunderously into several huge pieces on the valley floor.

Everyone was staring at Heracles, who looked much less angry than might have been expected.

"Don't worry about it," he told the rest. "That's Ares. He's a jerk anyway." He gave it a moment's thought and then added, "Maybe don't take anything from HIS vault; no need to push it." He looked over at Sinbad. "Don't say it," he said. "I know. It'll take one fine shot to make it in two now."

Sinbad merely smiled.

"Your turn," Heracles said. "May it be half as entertaining as mine."

Sinbad bowed sharply and turned to consider the challenge.

Aiming carefully, he wound up and took his best shot.

But he hadn't thrown the discus.

He'd rolled it. Underhanded.

Hard as he could.

The sharp-edged disc had as much momentum on it as the mortal had been able to muster; it skipped along, streaking between the two nearest pedestals and continuing on. Some of the party decided to chase after it but Sinbad, Rashid, Jason, Orpheus and Heracles all took their time and walked. In the end it rolled far past where Ares' facsimile noggin lay in fragments. Heracles found his disc and pried it out of the inside of the top of the head with modest effort despite the fact that the tempered steel disc had embedded several inches into the forged bronze.

"I throw from here now?" he said, looking over at Sinbad.

"Aye," Sinbad said. "Or the nearest spot you can find that has ample room for your throw."

Heracles decided he had enough clearance there once he'd cast the large chunk of Ares' statue's head aside. He took careful aim and let fly again.

This time he made it through all the gaps.

And beyond. WAY beyond.

All applauded, but the applause faded quickly when the disc continued to shrink in the sky.

"Hope we can find it again," Heracles said, striding up to the rest and moving through their midst. "Sometimes I overdo it a little."

No one dared to mention he wasn't going to make his goal in two throws. They marched on, the roiling skies continuing to threaten but not yet unleashing the fury they appeared to be holding. As it turned out Sinbad's "roll" had deposited his discus almost three times as far from its point of origin as had Heracles' first toss. Picking up the discus, Sinbad took aim once again.

"Please," Heracles said. "Feel free to roll it again if you wish. I just wish I'd have known my opponent only *looked* like a man."

But Sinbad didn't take the bait. True, he didn't roll it this time; but in fact he wasn't about to anyway. He'd planned a different tack on this shot.

He threw it with a great deal of force, keeping the shot

low. And he aimed it right at the side of the pedestal directly ahead and to the group's right. The discus clanged off the pedestal wall about ten feet off the ground and, still climbing, angled off the other way and almost immediately glanced off another pedestal. Now heading back to the right again it continued over to the sloping wall of the valley and impacted there, where it happened to come down and continue on rolling along its edge once again.

No one knew what to make of this odd shot except Sinbad, who stifled a little smile.

They moved on.

"Looks like yours is up again," Heracles said as they spied Sinbad's disc.

"Go on," Sinbad told the group. "I will wait until you're in position to judge this last throw."

Heracles contemplated that for but a moment before erupting in belly laughter. Some of the others laughed as well, if not quite so thunderously, and even Jason, Orpheus and Rashid were giving Sinbad curious looks.

He merely shrugged and gestured again for Heracles to go and find his disc.

"Please," he said. "I need to consider this shot a moment anyway."

The rest finally moved on, leaving him behind to fetch his disc. Sinbad did indeed consider his next throw closely for the next few minutes, right up until the party – gathered well ahead at the side of the statue-less Talos pedestal save for Heracles – were hollering back his way.

He sized up his challenge one more time and let fly.

This time he went high instead of low. VERY high. Instead of aiming through the remaining handful of statues and pedestals he had targeted the steep hillside beside him. He threw the disc such that it was standing on edge, and it came down high on the arid hill that way as well.

And it began to roll.

Descending only a little as it went it zipped along the just less than vertical slope, kicking up dust and rubble in its wake. But after about a hundred yards or so, and to Sinbad's obvious disappointment, it clipped a rock, jumped up, came back down...and slowed. His spirits obviously fell as his discus finally slipped over onto its side and came to a grinding, sliding halt still high up that wall.

He heard Heracles' distant laughter. Make that his VERY distant laughter.

The demigod had indeed seriously overthrown. But he was in the clear now, and strong enough to make up for the overshot with ease.

"It has to go in the door, right?" the demigod hollered at the party, who'd turned to look his way. "Well, get a good eyeful of THIS!"

His discus came streaking in at Talos' pedestal so fast it was virtually impossible to see. But again he'd put a little too much on the throw, and despite its impressive accuracy the shot didn't go in the shadowy doorway; it did go into the pedestal wall, however, sinking at least half of its breadth deep a foot or so from the door.

His curses rang out across the valley. Particularly loud thunder answered him, causing the knees of a few in the party to buckle a little. Heracles headed toward them, ignoring the fierce weather above.

"Sure," Pollux said to Andoros as both studied the demigod's relatively unhurried pace. "He's not worried. His father won't thunderbolt *him.*"

"He'll put his next shot in," Rashid said, watching Heracles' swaggering approach. "He can't miss once he pries it loose. That will be four shots. Captain Sinbad can only hope to tie at best, and even then I don't see how he can reach his disc to try. It's over. Let's get out of here before your gods decide to strike us down in our tracks!"

"I agree, Rashid," Jason said. "We've indulged this foolishness and pointlessly risked our lives out here too long. At least back in the Argo this lightning can't reach us."

Rashid nodded. "IF we get there."

They and the others watched as Heracles passed by them and up to Talos' pedestal. Without hesitation he pulled his disc out of the shrine, glanced over at the landing party and then tossed the discus in through the pedestal's half-open door.

"Four," he hollered over at them. "Not pretty but I don't think our captain from exotic lands will be able to get all the way up there to take his last shot. Not even Zeus could…"

An intense bolt of lightning struck only yards from the demigod, the concussion knocking him flat as nearly deafening thunder filled the valley. The ground was actually shaking.

Sinbad's discus was shaken loose.

No one even noticed the latter because they were too worried about those skies. Though it should have been noon it looked almost like midnight, dark and dense as the storm had become. And that single downward-cast bolt had changed everyone's priorities anyway.

Heracles got back on his feet, staring up at the sky.

"Are you all right?" Jason hollered over at him.

"I'm fine," Heracles said without looking his way. "Father never cared for my arrogance. Of course he's got a lot of things he does and doesn't like, don't you?"

"Heracles!" Jason yelled. "STOP TAUNTING HIM!"

Heracles turned and threw his erstwhile captain an angry glance.

"Get to your ship, Jason. This is between him and me, and I don't want anyone else to get in the way of what he thinks I have…"

He stopped because he'd spied something small and shiny – and moving – out of the corner of his eye. Sinbad's shaken-loose disc was coming his way. Having resumed its long journey it had skipped along, descending more steeply, picking up plenty of momentum and finally rolling onto and off of a short projecting ledge with enough accumulated speed to hurtle through the dark air. Coming down still on edge on the valley floor it had actually passed by its intended destination, gone into a wide spiral and by the time Heracles spotted it the disc was curving in toward Talos' pedestal.

Heracles watched slack-jawed as the discus went right past his sandal tips and rolled in through the door.

Sinbad had just caught up with the others. They all turned to him as the disc finished its roll.

"I suppose I should have worked out more of the rules of this game," he said. "But to me that's still my third throw."

Chapter Sixteen

They hustled back to the Argo as fast as they could go, hurrying Heracles along the best they could and doing everything possible to keep him from launching any more skyward-aimed curses and taunting. As a somewhat stretched-out pack they passed under the great stone arch through which the giant Talos had once tried to grab fleeing Argo crewmen.

The Argo was in sight.

And of course the sails were all furled.

"That's not good," Sinbad said as he and Jason ran along on either side of Heracles (nobody else would get anywhere near the unpredictable demigod.) "I hope your men are practiced at setting sail."

"We haven't had to worry about it in a while," Jason shot back. "I share your hopes."

Because the pair were corralling the still-angry Heracles they too were lagging behind as he was. Others well ahead of them, drawing to within hearing range of the ship, were already yelling "Drop sails!" and "Weigh anchor!"

"Are we sure we should be using sails in such unpredictable wind?" Sinbad said. "The only outlet to this bay is narrow."

"You wouldn't risk sailing out of it?"

Sinbad grinned. "That's not what I said ..."

The landing party's lead members reached the ship's mooring point and waded out into the breakers, headed for the rope ladders.

The sky rumbled, ear-splitting baritone thundering that shook rubble down every slope on the island. Lightning streaked madly across the sky, jumping around the underbelly of the storm in blinding arcs.

The two captains and the demigod splashed out into the surf and waded to the rope ladders. As they hauled themselves up separately, Heracles tearing one side of his ladder and ended up scaling awkwardly the rest of the way using two of them, they could hear Pollux shouting commands. By the time Heracles finally hauled himself up over the rail and set foot on the deck most of the Argonauts were at their rowing stations.

To a man they were all rowing hard, but they weren't going anywhere.

"Heracles!"

Sinbad was calling to him from the prow, where even the captain's just-added strength was not proving a sufficient addition to allow the two other Argonauts at the anchor station to crank the anchor free of its mooring.

Heracles strode forward. Sinbad told the Argonauts to stand clear, an order they perceived as odd only until they turned and saw the broad-chested "wild man" coming their way. At that point they were happy to comply, letting go of the anchor spool's handles and backing away.

Heracles bypassed the spool and, kneeling down, grabbed the heavy chain at the grommet where it passed through the hull. He pushed himself down into a crouch, still grasping the links nearest the inner hull wall, and then came up abruptly while simultaneously jerking back hard on the chain.

The anchor came flying up out of the water at frightening speed. Heracles let go at just the right moment such that the hissing, smoking chain went limp and the fast-rising anchor had slack again: the potentially deadly projectile hurtled up over the rail.

Heracles caught it with one hand, stopping it with a thick metal barb just inches from his nose.

He turned to Sinbad as he set the man-sized forging down with a heavy thud.

"What was that you were saying back there about dexterity?" he said.

Sinbad grinned.

Freed in that single moment, the Argo was instantly retreating from the shore under full oar. The storm still threatened away above, but save for that one bolt that had nearly blasted Heracles all the fireworks were still well overhead. At the helm Jason shouted commands, slowing the ship as they reached deep water and ordering its prow turned toward the outlet to the sea.

Sinbad and Heracles stood side by side at the prow looking down at the intently working Argonauts manning the oars.

"I'd think you'd want to join them," Sinbad said. "We could be at sea in a minute or two."

"Looks to me like they have it," Heracles said. "Besides, Jason says it takes too long to figure out how to balance me out when I…"

The deck lurched sharply upward and tilted in one single huge motion.

When it came crashing back down seconds later an immense crustacean claw thrust up past the starboard rail. The great claw snapped at the air, its pincers sounding like a great metal gong as their serrated business edges slammed together.

"That's no ORDINARY giant crab!" Heracles roared upon hearing that decidedly inorganic clang, bracing himself on the port rail and watching the claw swinging and clutching.

"There are *ordinary giant crabs?*" Rashid, who'd crawled up beside Sinbad and the demigod, said.

"It's mechanical," Sinbad said, keeping low and up against the rail. "Even this ship's deck weapons might not stop it."

The Argo lurched sharply again, to the same side – port – tilting so acutely that way as to nearly dip that side's rail and all those clinging to it, including Heracles, into the bay. Heracles found himself looking nearly straight up at Sinbad and Rashid, their sandal-clad feet dangling free as they clung to the starboard rail that had tipped over so far that it was more or less directly over the demigod's head. The Argo's weight ultimately (if only barely) overcame the crab's uplifting force after a few long, terrifying seconds and the ship flopped back onto its keel, revealing to the crew and their guests that a second massive claw and a titanic but decidedly mechanical-looking crab face had joined the first claw to form a terrifying visage hovering high over the deck.

Snip! Crack! A claw cut effortlessly through the middle of the forward mast, bringing the upper half of the thick wooden beam toppling down right atop the massive crab's back and making its obviously metallic orange-tinged shell ring like a huge bell. The behemoth didn't even seem to notice.

Crunch! The other claw sheared off a big chunk of the aft rail, to which the unfortunate Peronicus had been clinging. He shrieked as his grip failed and he went into the churning waters between the ship and the monster.

"Enough of this," Heracles said, rising. "Hephaestus hasn't made a toy yet that I can't whip."

He timed his move like the demigod he in fact was, planting a heel against the base of the port deck rail and waiting until the bobbing far rail was approaching the best possible angle with respect to his target. When it looked right he took off, and he landed only two strides on the prow deck before leaping. Using the starboard railing as both stepping stone and launching point he crushed a bit below one sandal as he pushed off it.

131

One thing few had ever seen Heracles demonstrate was the strength of his legs.

He flew across the thirty plus foot gap between the starboard hull and the monstrous metal crab so quickly and easily that had he not managed to snag hold of the front edge of its shell he might have skipped right down its back and ended up in the water behind it.

Clutching the thick shell Heracles flopped about on the tilting, shifting orange surface, unable at first to even get in a punch because he was being forced to concentrate on just keeping his grip.

The left claw smashed down amidships, crushing barrels and crates and sending the crew scattering. Many were already jumping over the port side and swimming for safety – even though they were having to paddle AWAY from shore to do it.

Heracles felt himself sliding forward and went with it, seeing the destruction that was being wrought on the Argo. Flying bodily over the edge, still clutching it tightly, he let himself pivot until he felt his momentum moving in the right direction.

Then he let go.

He shot past the first eyestalk and nearly missed the second as well. But his aim had been good enough, and the inhuman strength in his outstretched fingers was ample to allow him to snag the side of the second stalk. Cupping his hand instead of grasping, he spun his formidable bulk around the stalk; and as he came over the top of it he was able to thrust out his free hand and get hold of the first as well.

He ended up hanging from them both, a sight that might have been comical had the situation been much less dire. Heracles' bulk had bent both stalks downward such that their tips were both aimed down at the water. Behind him great mechanical jaws opened and closed.

The monster reared back, drawing away from the ship.

Jason had been watching the whole thing. "Drop

sails!" he ordered from the rail.

"What?" Malayus, the drum master, said, his eyes huge.

"We'll have no control," Pollux said. "The foresail is gone!"

Only one face staring back at Jason didn't look at least as stunned as those of the Argonauts.

"He's right," Sinbad said. "We need to get clear fast."

"But Heracles…?" Rashid said.

"Don't worry," Jason said. "We won't leave here without him...again."

A gap of perhaps thirty yards had opened up between the titanic metal crab and the ship since Heracles had made his move. That span nearly doubled again in seconds once the mainsails were lowered (and even before their whipping lower edges could be secured.) Other sails were being set as well, with each Argonaut, Rashid and Sinbad rushing here and there across the debris-strewn deck, slip-sliding on wine and cashews as they worked to secure every untethered rope. Jason steered, glancing over at the handful of men who'd jumped ship every few seconds to make sure his barely controlled Argo didn't accidentally mow them down.

Meanwhile Heracles was in sort of a bind. Still dangling from the eyestalks, he was having little trouble overcoming their hydraulics to keep them bent down the wrong way. But the crab's pincers had entered the fray and he was having to twist, bend and pull his torso around to avoid their potentially bisecting grips.

As the clank-snapping pincer swipes grew ever closer and more rapid fire he realized they would eventually get hold of him. So he decided to beat the claws to the punch.

He timed an incoming assault, drew himself up above the great swipe and let go of the antennae. He dropped onto the claw – it was the larger one – deliberately coming down between its fixed and moving fingers. His big hands caught the edges of both and held them from coming together just above his waist. The paralyzed claw drew up high, doing its best to overcome the great resistance.

The sky was riddled with streaks and webs of lightning as Heracles pitted every ounce of his power against the automaton's chariot-sized claw.

Having forgotten about the Argo, which was circling – sort of – as freed-up crew members sought to bring its deck guns to bear, the monster threw its lesser claw into the fray. With repeated hard kicks Heracles was keeping it at bay, but his divided attention was weakening his critical battle with the right claw.

"We've got to help him!" Orpheus shouted, watching helplessly from the rail.

"We will," Jason said, steady as humanly possible at the wheel. "As soon as he's clear of our shot!"

He had a point: the titanic machine was fighting its battle with the enemy more or less at eye level now, having brought its claws down, so in effect it was holding Heracles as a flesh and blood shield against any potential Argo retaliation.

The alternately telescoping and retracting eyestalks were trained rigidly on the stubborn demigod. The pesky left pincer kept at it, causing Heracles to lose his beloved Nemean Lion-skin cloak to the bay's churning waters. And the fierce right claw was doing its best to end the long life of a legend.

"Someone has to do something!" Andoros hollered.

Chapter Seventeen

Someone in fact was already doing something. Sinbad had rushed over to the deck gun where Pollux and Dimitrius, the Argo's best big gun shot, were struggling to find a clear trajectory to the monster.

"Let me try," he urged the pair.

Dimitrius turned to Pollux.

"Worth a shot," Pollux said with a shrug. "He beat Heracles in a test of physical skill."

Dimitrius turned, saw Sinbad's earnest stare and backed off the handles of the gun. Sinbad nodded sharply and stepped into his spot. Bending a little he looked through the crosshair glass even as he got used to the feel of the heavy pedestal's swivel.

"Keep it steady Jason," he called out.

Before Jason could answer a sharp splintering sound from above signaled the final collapse of the uppermost portion of the main mast, which the mechanical crab had clipped several times. Both the top trim sail and the eight foot long section of mast that had supported it fell free and sent Argonauts scrambling as it crashed to the deck.

Jason said nothing, being far too focused on compensating for the sudden thrust shift...in addition, of course, to dealing with the ongoing siege of erratic wind blasts.

Sinbad ceased aiming and fell still, but for just a

second.

He pulled the trigger.

The ponderous javelin exploded from the deck gun and streaked out across the frothy waters.

The projectile speared into the central joint of the crab's front left foreleg, slipping into the narrow gap between the upper surface of the huge ball hinge and the upper leg section and prying that gap wide open.

"You missed!" Dimitrius yelled.

"No he didn't," Jason hollered back.

The impact had driven the crab back; not much, but enough for that leg to have to retreat a step and thus display the restricted movement the firmly wedged javelin was inducing. The disability was just enough to compel the crab to favor that side and cease its secondary claw attack to use that limb for balance.

Much like a real crab might, it was now rotating awkwardly around its center, shaking its impeded limb with each backpedal as that side's claw struggled against its own design in an all-out effort to grab the hilt of the javelin.

And that was all the break that Heracles needed.

"If I ever *am* to be beaten," he grunted, summoning his supernatural strength, "it won't be by one of Hephaestus' accursed MACHINES!"

Heaving with all his remaining energy he forced the pincers open.

Harder, harder he pushed, straining the lengths of his muscles and tendons in a desperate attempt to force the mechanism beyond its limits before surpassing his own.

CLANG!

The flexible pincer broke free, the exposed joint spouting gears, nuts, bolts and springs. But that shower wasn't in itself dangerous; what was – and what Heracles nearly caught a spray of – was the same lava "blood" that Jason had managed to drain from the great Talos' body years earlier.

As the useless claw reeled back, flinging the hissing liquid all around, Heracles saw the blistering arcs of titan blood descending toward him as a shower and dropped clear just ahead of it.

He splashed in about twenty feet or so directly beneath the monster's jaws and popped up in the hard-to-tread water staring up at its underside. Heracles saw the javelin fall back out and watched as the titan ceased its stumbling.

He watched it step back, which it did much more ably with the impediment removed, and realized instantly that it was doing so in order to try to find him again. The body stayed more or less level but the eyestalks telescoped out fully while simultaneously tilting down to focus on him. The great and complex jaws clinked as they gnashed, as though this particular automation could actually get angry.

Sinbad's second shot caught the thing right between those snaking eyes.

Caught by surprise the stalks recoiled and turned in on the still-vibrating javelin, giving the huge mechanical construction the momentary look of having its eyes crossed.

The left claw came up and the eyestalks parted to allow it to grab the javelin, which it did without error. While it was working to pull the weapon out Heracles was checking out its legs, looking for a way back up on it, but to his dismay he saw that the choppy waters and randomly stepping limbs promised to make the task extremely challenging.

He gave it his best shot anyway, even as the titan was succeeding in pulling out the deeply lodged javelin at last. And Heracles was still going for it when, mere seconds later, Sinbad's accurate eye fired another one clear down the aquatic automaton's throat.

Even this didn't stop it though. Seeming to realize Heracles was still below it somewhere, the giant backpedaled again.

But one incredibly powerful thunderbolt ended its reign of terror in the next moment.

***

As their eyes slowly readjusted in the wake of the blinding white lightning strike all beheld the smoldering titan's abrupt immobility. Smoke billowed from here and there beneath the ship-sized carapace's edges. The crab's great legs, their joints fused solid by the forge-like heat, were boiling the stormed-churned waters around them. The eyestalks were lifeless now, hanging down in limp arcs in front of a gigantic maw forever stilled.

And in the frothing bay beneath that huge mechanical mouth the body of Heracles floated limply.

"Get to him!" Jason shouted, fighting the sluggish helm.

But Sinbad was already boldly diving into the rough waters to retrieve the bobbing demigod.

Belaricus and Aesthenes joined him, and just as well: it took all three to haul him to the ladders, battling the waves all the way. Luckily Jason ordered a sail-furling maneuver that swung the arcing Argo tightly in and brought it up right alongside the four men.

Those who'd jumped overboard, meanwhile, were nearly exhausted from dogpaddling. Jason sent several men over the port side and had others man the rail there with ropes to aid in that rescue effort while others helped Sinbad and the others haul Heracles up on deck.

Jason passed the helm to Dardan and rushed over to his fallen friend.

Orpheus was checking the demigod's pulse on his thick neck. Before Jason had even arrived Heracles had recovered enough to realize there were fingers on the underside of his chin.

"I'd move those," Heracles said without even opening

his eyes, "if you want to keep them."

Orpheus snatched his fingers back.

"I'd say he's alive," the bard said, glancing up and seeing Jason's concerned face.

Heracles sat up.

"I'm all right," he said. "Could use a little breathing room."

To no one's surprise, not even Sinbad's or Rashid's, he gruffly shooed off potential helping hands and eventually struggled to his feet on his own. Like many on board not otherwise engaged he was noticing that the strange storm was suddenly breaking up.

"Heracles …?" Jason said.

"I'm all right Jason," Heracles said. He turned and looked beyond the rail to the smoking, steaming metal crab. His gaze tilted downward a little from the ever-frozen metal maw and there beneath it he saw his Nemean Lion cloak bobbing in the water. "I'll have to go get that back though."

"What happened?" Pollux asked him. "The lightning… Zeus…?"

"Aw, that's just the old man for you," Heracles said, and he looked up at the dispersing clouds again. "He's always been like this. If a fight loses steam he loses interest and ends it himself."

Chapter Eighteen

Repairs required only two days thanks to the presence of the quick-recovering son of Zeus, who made five-man jobs into one-man jobs and could do just about anything with his bare hands except smoothly cutting wood planks and rails. In all the Argo had been away from Kryptos Island and the Chimera a week already, and both Rashid and Sinbad were rightly quite eager to get back and see how the repairs on their own far more extensively damaged ship were going. With luck they'd already be done, at least by Sinbad's generally accurate calculations.

They were on the open sea again, just shy of halfway back, and they'd been making good speed. As they cut along beneath the stars under full sail just around midnight Sinbad – who'd volunteered for night watch – found himself running into a sleepless Jason amidships.

"How's Heracles?" Sinbad said.

"Physically fine despite that shock. None but a god, they say. And of course still grumbling. Says Zeus didn't trust him to win that battle and stepped in. It's been an issue for him before."

"Well, for my part I'm glad his father *did* step in. I still wasn't liking our odds." Sinbad paused a moment, his brow furrowing. "What was that thing?"

"Apparently when Talos was destroyed Hephaestus was tasked to make a replacement. At least that's my best guess. Its blood was like the giant's."

"And that was meant to keep us on the island, just as Talos was, because we'd taken things from the vaults?"

Jason nodded. "I allowed the same mistake twice, this time with full forethought," he said. "Surely we should learn from our mistakes."

Sinbad smiled. "I have found that an old mistake may on occasion wear a clever new disguise."

***

Well over the conversation the chameleonic homunculus wafted, its diminutive wings flapping fast and hard but making nowhere near enough noise to be heard on the deck. Through its eyes Circe watched the two captains speaking.

But she couldn't hear them, and she dared not take her precious spy any closer.

"There's nothing to be done where you are, my pet," she said aloud, her voice echoing around the spacious cavern that had been her lair for centuries. "Fly ahead of them. To Kryptos. Find the other vessel. I sensed something there ..."

Her brow knitted.

Ceasing her remote viewing she walked over to one of several bookcases, the sum total of which held shelved a virtual library of mystic knowledge.

"Very primitive...primal..." she said, scanning the spines of the ancient tomes, "...something born to dominate...to control..."

She closed her eyes and swept one arm gently back and forth in front of her.

A single ponderous tome with a dirty, beaten maroon cover that looked like leather lacquered in thick, clear blood pulled free of those on either side of it and wafted over to Circe's hands. Strength belying the looks of her pale, slender arms took hold of the ages-old volume and bore the instantly returned full weight of the age-old relic without any sign of strain.

She opened her eyes and stared at the embossed glyphs on the cover.

"'Before the Titans'," she said to herself. "Well, that's a start anyway …"

She carried it over to the book podium, set it there and waved a hand through the air a few inches over it. The book's cover pivoted open and one at a time the pages turned. Circe scanned each quickly, constantly adjusting the rate of page flipping with faint finger gestures.

Images flashed past: horrifying, hellish artistic renderings of great monsters dominating and devouring hapless primitive humans wearing animal skins rather than clothing. Some of these nightmares were almost humanoid in appearance, albeit in general much larger than actual humans; others were just the opposite, favoring distinctly non-human aspects like tentacles, antennae, manifold eyes and mouths, mouths and eyes on the ends of tentacles and – incredibly – even more bizarre things.

"Liking *this* already," Circe said.

She halted the page advancement near the middle of the book and scrutinized one page in more detail. The page featured two columns. The left column was made up of rows of the same symbols that were obviously lettering while the right featured hand-drawn sketches of objects.

Each object corresponded to one of the symbol rows.

Circe's wicked smile broadened.

"Holy symbols of their high priests," she said. "And knowing the way Kronos works, ideal prisons for the deities themselves." She looked up from the book and stared absently across the obsidian-tiled floor of her lair's central chamber, looking through rather than at the many wondrous objects she'd acquired over an already unnaturally long life. "*This* is what I felt," she said. "I'm certain of it now. Must be down below."

She directed her gaze back down to the ancient book and its summary symbol table.

"That's a lot to remember," she said, scanning up and down the list of dozens of supernatural entities and their holy symbols. "So much for traveling light."

With a single incantation – and with her fingertips on the book – she shrunk the tome to the size of a pocket mirror. Then she snatched it up, closed it manually and slipped it into her stylish waist pouch. With that done she took hold of her necklace.

Only four crystals remained.

Circe frowned. "There had better be enough," she said. "Not like I can go back for more."

She glanced around her abode.

"Wards!" she called out loudly to the room.

Two enormous phantom hellhounds, hulking translucent blue specters around ten feet tall at the muscular shoulders, materialized (or rather semi-materialized) instantaneously and immediately went on patrol, weaving through Circe's accumulated wonders. One of the pale beasts passed right through Circe.

She looked momentarily ecstatic.

"Ah," she said dreamily. "Can't beat that chill."

Her eyes focused on one of the larger of her prized possessions – her most recent acquisition, in fact: the skull, hide and fleece of the rarest of rams. The strangely beautiful golden relic lay draped across the lifeless lower limbs of an odd tree that appeared most ancient. The tree featured few leaves yet nearly twice as many flowers, all of which were scattered sparsely across the ends of the handful of upper limbs. The flowers looked like pink dogwood blossoms.

But Circe wasn't looking at the tree.

"I'd certainly like to take you along," she said to the fleece. "But you don't seem to work as a cloak."

Circe removed one of the crystals and steadied herself.

"Take me to…" she said, ramping up pressure on the

somewhat fragile crystal.

But just as the crystal was about to crack she caught herself.

She took a deep breath and closed her eyes. She concentrated.

And her body changed shape. Clothing, waist pouch, necklace…everything melted and re-formed in an instant into the form and apparel of Jason's missing first mate.

Circe-Pentelus exhaled heavily and then went on to carefully look her/himself over.

"Focus Circe," he-she said. "Wouldn't do to forget the touches of realism."

She closed her eyes and concentrated once more and in the next moment Pentelus' garments went from loom-perfect to appropriate for one who has been wandering aimlessly lost in the jungle on Kryptos: rips and ravels appeared here and there in the fabrics of his garments, spots went threadbare, a sandal strap frayed and tore.

"That's better," the disguised witch said when Pentelus looked sufficiently damaged. "Should sell the story, anyway."

The Argo's first mate set himself. "He" adjusted his grip on the crystal.

"Take me back to where I left Kryptos Island," he said, and he crushed it in his palm.

He faded out, leaving the terrifying guards to their chamber-pacing.

***

Pentelus reappeared right where Circe had left Kryptos: thigh-deep in mucky swamp.

"The things I do for absolute power," he said, shaking his head.

Getting the most unpleasant task out of the way immediately, he took a deep breath and dove headfirst into the warm, algae-saturated pond. Popping up almost immediately, spitting out mud and strands of swamp grass, he glanced around. Finding his view of the temple blocked by the treetops and seeing no witnesses he closed his eyes and concentrated.

Pentelus rose up out of the bog.

Completely out, that is.

His sandals dripping muck he floated over the twenty or thirty feet of intervening swamp to the muddy bank of the pond; once there, though his eyes were still closed, he came down gently on supportive soil as though he knew exactly where he was anyway.

Pentelus opened his eyes.

He shuddered, already miserable with the steam, the flying pests and his mucky coating.

"It's true what they say," he growled, swiping at mosquitoes. "The path to the mountaintop runs through the swamp."

He made his way back toward the magma dome through the intervening jungle quickly. Seeing the steam columns growing considerably more frequent ahead even as the trees and undergrowth grew sparse, he slowed his advance to keep an eye out for a clear view to the temple.

He finally got it.

A small encampment was still up there. He could see Havar and Raoul among the half dozen milling about up at the base of the temple.

Pentelus did a last second once-over to make sure his reappearance would look as realistic as possible. He had a story to sell, and the first part of the sale was purely visual. Once he was satisfied that he looked ragged enough to have spent nearly a week lost and disoriented in the marshy swamp, he took up a vigil focused on the remaining landing party and waited until one of them happened to look in his general direction.

Turned out that person was Ahmed, who went off in the right direction to answer nature's call about ten minutes later. His snakebite-induced limp nearly gone, he happened to glance up just in time to see Pentelus stagger out into the open.

Keeping the act going, Pentelus didn't look up – not even at the sounds of Ahmed's distant shouting. Instead he took the cries of alarm and calls for help as cues that he'd been spotted and feigned a collapse, cleverly falling and splaying his body across a waist-high boulder in the middle of a barely steaming puddle so as to minimize contact with too-hot surfaces. The stone was hot beneath his chest and burned his cheek a bit anyway, but knowing everything else nearby was probably much worse he resigned himself to what he hoped would be a short stint on a relatively mild barbeque grill.

Pentelus heard the shouts of Ahmed and a couple of others drawing nearer and he lay virtually still there, flopped across the side and top of the rock, waiting for them to come to him.

"I don't believe it!"

Pentelus heard Raoul's incredulity.

He smiled.

Chapter Nineteen

To Sinbad and Rashid's mutual dismay the Chimera appeared far from seaworthy.

In fact, as the Argo approached to within a mile or so, all aboard could readily see that beyond those mountainous rotting decacheire carcasses, through the clouds of scavenging gulls surrounding them, the Chimera didn't look like it had been repaired much at all.

"I think we've got a problem," Rashid said.

Beside him at the rail, Sinbad said nothing.

But Jason, next to both of them, did.

"I see no movement," he said, staring off at the battered vessel. "Where is everyone?"

"I have no desire to guess," Sinbad said, likewise scrutinizing the Chimera, "nor to risk this ship and its crew bringing it any closer to such an inexplicable sight. It's possible we haven't been noticed yet; if we veer starboard we can hide the Argo behind the decacheires and set deep anchor there. Then Rashid and I will make use of your landing craft to investigate."

Jason turned to him. "A sound plan," he said. "Except for the part about it just being the two of you."

Heracles strode up before Sinbad could protest. He'd obviously overheard Jason.

"That's right," he said, striding up to the three, his ponderous steps creaking the Argo's floorboards. He saw the trio turn from the rail to meet his gaze and he locked his with Sinbad's. "You came to my island, pulled me away from a perfectly enjoyable multi-year drunken binge with one of the few Olympians I actually like and I wound up having my father embarrass me in front of the entire Argo crew. Which was only the latest addition to a long list of annoyances the old man has tagged me with, but that's beside the point...the point being that you two may be fine fighters and wise men, but from the looks of it you might benefit from a little extra muscle here. That is," he added, his eyes rolling skyward, "if a certain great pain in my tail keeps his big nose out of it this time!"

Sinbad was far too wise a man to turn down such an offer.

Accompanied by Belaricus and Pollux as well, Sinbad, Rashid and Heracles took one of the Argo's pair of eight-man rowboats in to shore, keeping to the right of the rightmost monster carcass and finally drawing up about a quarter mile down the beach from where the Chimera sat anchored. Once they'd grounded the boat the five gathered themselves up and headed off down the beach.

As they drew ever nearer the Chimera something strange could be seen: Not only had no repairs been effected, it appeared even more damage had actually been done. The deck cabin's door, the door of the captain's cabin in fact, along with its frame and several adjoining feet of both wall and roof were missing; in place of it all loomed a gaping hole, its edges frilled with the chamber's bent, splintered and broken wall boards.

Rashid, in the lead, turned and pointed at the shadowy hole but Sinbad met his gaze and nodded to signal that he'd already seen it. Rashid fell back to his captain's side.

"What do you think?" he said. "Looks like they were attacked. Something smashed in the deck cabin."

"If anything the cabin was ripped open rather than smashed in," Sinbad said, shaking his head. "Those broken planks at the edges are bent outwards, not inwards."

Rashid squinted. "You're right," he said at last. "Looks like something burst it from the inside."

Heracles, trailing the pack, saw the pair talking but couldn't hear them.

"What are you two on about?" he said with more volume than discretion. "Please do share."

Whether his virtual shout triggered what happened next or not was debatable. The timing was suggestive of such nevertheless.

"Look!" Pollux said, spotting the motion on the distant deck first.

At least some of the Chimera's crew had survived the destruction that had left the deck cabin blow out. More and more it seemed, for now they were popping up one after another and filing over to the pair of rope ladders that hung from the starboard rail.

Sinbad had the landing party hold up.

"Something is strange about this," Sinbad told them. "Look at the way they're moving."

One by one, with only a few rungs separating each from the previous and next, the crew were descending the ladders. Each crewman to reach the bottom let go, stepped clear and watched and waited as more descended beside them.

"Doesn't seem so strange," Belaricus said. "They look like a well-organized team to me."

"Exactly," Sinbad said. "That's NOT the crew we left behind."

Rashid was counting.

"Fifteen…sixteen…seventeen…"

He turned to Sinbad, looking decidedly puzzled.

"Captain, unless I miscount that's everyone," he said of the Chimera's crew as the last couple descended into the midst of the rest. "Everyone but those we left at the temple - Havar, Makili, Ahmad and Raoul…and you and I!"

To a man the landing party was entirely focused on the Chimera's crew, all of whom were now coming toward them in a broad cluster. They seemed purposeful but in no great haste, and Rashid was the one to voice what everyone was thinking.

"Look," he said. "They're all moving in step!"

The Chimera crew's right knees were all bending at the same time. The lefts likewise matched.

Everyone but Heracles reluctantly drew and readied their weapons. Heracles just stood there, clenching and unclenching his fists at his sides.

"These are my crewmen," Sinbad said, ignoring Rashid. He shifted his gaze quickly from Pollux to Belaricus before letting it settle with hard focus on Heracles. "They are my friends," he went on, glancing at the other two again. "We talk first and defend ourselves only as necessary. Fight to disarm and disable, and ONLY if we have no other choice."

Belaricus, Heracles and Pollux all nodded, albeit with varying levels of obvious uncertainty.

"I'll do my best, Sinbad," Heracles said. "But sometimes there's a thin line between a knockout punch and a death blow."

"Then I'll do my best to make sure you don't have to tread that line," Sinbad said. He looked over at Rashid. "Stay back," he said. He looked around at the others. "All of you. If I run into problems I want you all to have enough time to ready yourselves."

He didn't wait for a response. Turning back around to face the approaching crowd he caught his first good look at the faces of his crew.

Their eyes gave them away as the living zombies they were: vacant, dull, pupils too large for the ample light, staring not at Jason but through and well past him as he came their way. They were all bearing arms, but even those with bows and arrows were just holding them, not aiming them at him or any member of the party as such.

They were simply striding relentlessly forward.

As Sinbad continued toward them he sheathed his scimitar and held his hands out at his sides, palms open, fingers wide.

His four comrades watched as Sinbad met his crew and they folded in around him. He vanished in their midst.

"Your captain is a bold man," Pollux said to Rashid.

"Captain Sinbad has boldness to spare," Rashid said, his gaze fixed on the confrontation. "It is his wisdom that we must earnestly hope has not run into short supply."

***

Sinbad's head, rising slightly above the rest because he was in fact taller than most of them, bobbed in the midst of the others for a very tense minute or so as his allies watched. And then, most unexpectedly, the Chimera's crew parted as one to reveal their captain still standing, apparently untouched. He gestured to the others, beckoning them to approach.

They did so, albeit cautiously, with Rashid and Heracles leading the way.

"What's happening?" Rashid said as he and the others pulled up into the midst of the quite zombie-like Chimera crew.

"Well Rashid," Sinbad said, "it appears their god requests an audience with us."

"Their...*god*...?" Rashid looked absolutely confused but so did the others.

"Yes," Sinbad said, sounding quite matter-of-fact about it, as though this sort of thing happened all the time. "I volunteered to speak to him myself but they say no, we all have to come up and meet him personally. Jason and the rest of the Argo's crew too eventually, they're telling me."

Most of the zombie-like crew nodded slowly.

"And you said yes?" Rashid looked more than a little

pale. "More gods. ALL we need."

"I could hardly say no now, could I?" Sinbad said. "After all, I'd be disappointing so many of his loyal followers…right out here in the open…"

Rashid looked around, taking note of the plethora of bows and arrows.

"Lead on Sinbad," Heracles said. "You've gotten me anxious to meet this fellow. What's his name anyway?"

He got almost twenty responses, all identical and eerily synchronized into a chorus.

"Molo," the Chimera's crew said as one. Then again… and again…and again, as a chant.

"Molo…Molo…Molo…"

"I'm guessing his name is Molo," Sinbad said, and his dry quip seemed to make the chant pick up pace.

"Molo. Molo. Molo."

"What do you figure he wants?" Heracles said over the repetition, looking to Sinbad.

"Good question," the Chimera's captain said. "I suppose my first guess would be more recruits."

"Molo! Molo! MOLO!"

Unable to miss the growing hostility and impatience of the crew Sinbad suggested his party comply and get moving right away. He turned to face the ship again.

"Per your request," Sinbad told the handful of semi-blank faces directly in front of him. "Here we are, at your service. Take us to your leader."

The Chimera's crew opened a passage through their ranks, and once Sinbad and the others were through it and on their way to the ship the crew spread itself into a horseshoe shape to pen in and guide those they were escorting from the sides and behind.

Heracles cast angry glances here and there as the procession neared the ship, but those with whom he locked gazes didn't exactly react as he'd hoped. They sort of stared right through his focused glare, further frustrating him. His fists were clenched so hard that by the time they reached the rope ladders his huge knuckles were white as bone.

Sinbad went up first, followed by Rashid, Pollux and Belaricus. Heracles came up last, slowly and while casting glares that fell on annoyingly unresponsive faces. Stepping over the rail and onto the deck he saw that the others had already been guided over to a spot in the middle of the deck…right across from the big hole in the cabin.

Heracles moved up behind the others.

"That's his lair?" he said. "An outhouse with the front door torn off?"

"Molo…Molo…Molo…" the crew chanted, surrounding their "guests" on the Chimera's littered deck. "Molo…Molo…Molo…"

That pretty much did it for Heracles' last nerve.

"All right," he growled. "Enough of this."

Pushing through his friends he strode up to the decimated cabin front. There he stopped, set himself and addressed the shadows beyond the gaping hole.

"Let's get this done, shall we?" he thundered. "I don't have all day to mince and curtsy for some pipsqueak little wannabe …"

The shadows themselves seemed to be moving. Unfolding. Pressing one another for space.

The immense being broke more fragments of the cabin wall and roof as it pushed through the tight-fit hole it had made. Reddish brown skin extruded out into the daylight.

Molo rose fully to his nearly twelve foot height and spread his muscular arms – thick as tree trunks and not dissimilar to them either in their mottled shades – wide. He appeared to be stretching.

He stretched again and even yawned, all the while ignoring the uncharacteristically large (but relatively tiny) human standing before him as well as everyone else on deck.

Finished at last, he brought his gaze down to meet that

of Heracles.

"Well, well," he said, scrunching up the minimal features on his wide demonic-looking face. "You're a very large one, aren't you? Probably think you have great strength."

Heracles shrugged. "I can generally take care of myself," he said. "How about you?"

Molo leaned back and his great laughter generated so much wind force that it caused the tattered lower mainsail to billow. He looked back down at Heracles. Reaching up, he idly tweaked at the tip of one of his pair of huge curving ebony horns (he had another two sets of shorter pairs framing his face as well, these like armor studs.)

"I am Molo," he said. "I have killed and eaten thousands of your kind. I have crushed their armies and relished the sweetness of their infants as they slid whole down my throat. I was a scourge, a plague upon these feeble lands, for countless centuries. Back before your kind built your hovels, when they hid in caves and risked their lives tiptoeing out of them to steal the scraps of nature they so craved to ensure the continuation of their miserable existences."

Heracles folded his arms over his chest, his unflinching gaze locked on those huge blank eyes.

"Sounds a little before my time," he said calmly. "Guess I'll have to take your word for it."

"Not necessarily," Molo said. "In fact allow me the honor of a brief reprise ..."

Heracles lowered his arms. He moved to his left, sizing up his huge potential opponent, who quickly realized his intention and did the same. They were slowly circling one another, and even Molo's newly devout followers joined Sinbad, Rashid, Pollux and Belaricus in backing up.

"I'm quite willing to accommodate you," Heracles said. "While you're still able, would you mind answering one question?"

"While I'm...?" Molo roared again, his great belly

laugh shaking the Chimera's boards. "Wit AND brawn? You must have been quite popular while you were still alive!" After a few more monstrous chuckles – and a bit more circling, during which Heracles glanced briefly up into the air over Molo's great shoulder – the beast-man relented. "Very well," he said. "I'll indulge you. What is it you want to know?"

"I will admit I have no idea what kind of creature you are," Heracles said, continuing to circle and then glancing up oddly again as he returned to about the same spot where he'd done it the first time. "And I see you have no wings. Now, I'm not going to be so rude as to ask where in my grandfather's realm you came from but I'm really curious as to whether you can somehow fly even without wings?"

Molo considered the question for a long moment, still sidestepping to match Heracles.

"My powers are such that I have no need for flight. A trivial talent at best."

"I see," Heracles said.

He came to a halt and did something odd: after glancing warily around at the circle of friends and possessed foes he looked back up at Molo and, raising a single finger up in front of his own face, beckoned the great entity to lean down as though he we wanted to share a whispered secret with the brute.

Molo drew back a little, his leathery brow furrowing. Heracles kept flexing his finger.

Apparently curiosity overcame suspicion because the mind-controlling giant finally caved; bending, he brought his huge and intimidating visage rushing down toward his opponent.

Heracles saved his move for the last possible second, bending slowly at the knees as Molo leaned in to look him eye to eye.

He came up with the force of the demigod he was, landing an uppercut on Molo's left jaw so potent that the huge being actually rocketed up into the air.

"Thanks," Heracles said as he watched the stunned entity streak skyward.

Utterly shocked and more than a little dazed, Molo's eyes didn't even register awareness until his exaggerated arc was nearing its peak. And he had no idea that Heracles had aimed so well that he was about to come down very, very hard on the jagged upper end of the broken-off mainmast.

Deity or not, the ancient entity's short revival came to an abrupt end as the ragged mast rammed through his torso dead center. Initial momentum sent four or five feet of the mast through him right away and his wriggling, flailing bulk slipped slowly down it that far again or more in the next moments, with Molo's dark heart's blood slicking the mast down all the way.

Heracles himself barely remembered to get out of the way before a disgusting scattering of pushed-out organs and a broad spray of sticky black ichor came raining down on the deck.

To the extreme relief of the landing party – Sinbad and Rashid in particular, of course – the Chimera's crew all came out of their semi-trancelike states at the same moment. To a man they all looked around, obviously unaware of what was going on or why they were there.

Heracles still stood alone, but not for long. Seeing that they were no longer surrounded by hostile zombies, just dazed fellow adventurers, Sinbad, Rashid, Pollux and Belaricus rushed over to congratulate him. But Heracles ignored the praise and friendly slaps on the arms and shoulders.

He was still staring up at Molo, who had grown nearly motionless save for a little reflexive twitching in his extremities.

"Nice to get to finish one on my own," the demigod said. He tilted his head a little to stare up at unimpeded sky. "Thanks Dad."

Chapter Twenty

A search of the room in which the treasure had been locked aboard the Chimera revealed not one but several telltale signs of the unexpected rise of Molo. First and foremost of these was a quite ornate staff, gold and ebony and encrusted with uncut and unpolished emeralds and rubies, which they found in halves on the floor. Additionally it was obvious from the disheveled overall appearance of the room that someone had gone through a lot of it in some kind of search. Yet if any specific treasure item was missing neither Sinbad nor Rashid, the pair who'd brought it back from the lair of the vile Caliph of Sherazahn in the first place, was able to name it. What's more – and perhaps strangest – a tiny book seemed to have actually been *added* to the treasure.

"The words are too small to read," Rashid said. "Of what use could it possibly be? No wonder whoever broke in here left that behind; it's not good for anything."

Sinbad pulled it gently from between his first mate's fingertips and looked at its cover. "The title is large enough," he said, "but I am unfamiliar with the lettering."

"I've said it before, Captain," Rashid said. "Cast it over the side. Now. For all we know we are indeed intended to learn its secrets, such that by doing so we will invoke its dark magic upon ourselves."

"And as I've replied before, Rashid, I think I'll keep

it." Sinbad smiled. "Besides, what are the odds we'll pick up a new curse the day after ridding ourselves of one?"

"We can do it," Rashid shot back. "We're achievers."

***

Hundreds of miles away at the same moment Medea's army of monsters had just run into their first significant obstacle.

The great towers, spires and minarets of Aderadad loomed tantalizingly in the distance, rising before a ridge of rugged mountains. But there, just a mile or so shy of its outskirts, Medea's creatures had slammed snout-first into something that looked to be an actual impediment (at least more so than the feeble armies and weaponry her siege had faced so far, anyway.)

The sorceress herself approached the great barrier, having been summoned by her field marshals. Jet hair flying she strode forward through the loitering ranks of snorting, growling monsters without hesitation: despite their vicious ferocity every single creature made sure to be well out of Medea's path, pulling back (and in a few cases even scrambling) out of her way.

She stepped right up to the barrier, stopping inches shy of it as though she could see the invisible energy. She raised a pale, ring-laden hand and placed a couple of fingertips against the energy. Then she spread her palm wide and pressed it against the unseen surface.

She increased the force for a moment and then finally gave up and lowered her arm.

Medea looked up to the heavens.

"There's likely an upper limit to it," she said to no one in particular. "Not that we can reach it." She brought her gaze back down. Elinnia, one of her best marshals, met it. "I wanted them to have wings," Medea told her aide. "But Circe said they'd be too damageable."

"My lady?" Elinnia said.

158

"Nothing Elinnia," Medea said. "Don't worry about it. Just coordinate with the other marshals. I suppose this verifies those rumors of the leader of Aderadad having some magical skills. I will bring this wall down soon enough, and when we march into her palace I will show her some beyond her wildest dreams."

***

Margiana stared off at the milling horde of monsters from the edge of the palace's upper balcony. Many in Medea's army carried torches – they made fires easier to set – so the distant panorama of hundreds of temporarily-at-bay soldier-beasts glittered with dozens and dozens of twinkling lights.

Seeing her intent focus Haroun, her longtime advisor, hesitated a moment before finally moving up to speak to her.

"Your barrier is working, my lady," he said. "Aderadad is safe."

Margiana didn't budge. "For the moment, Haroun," she said. "But it is hardly invulnerable."

"But my lady? Surely your magic is powerful enough to withstand any amount of physical assault."

"Perhaps," Margiana said, and she turned to him bearing a pained half-smile on her aging but still stunning face. "Unless stronger magic undoes what I have done."

"Stronger magic?"

"Look out there," she said, and they both turned to study the distant army. "Our scouts say the creatures seem without control, chaotic independents. Yet I look out there and I see...organization."

Haroun glanced over at her.

"Organization?"

"A true horde would be fighting that barrier with everything they had," Margiana said, her gaze still fixed on Medea's army. "Or they'd give up, disband and go away."

Haroun turned back to the distant sight.

"Tell me, what do they appear to be doing?" Margiana said.

"They're...just...standing around."

Haroun turned to her again, his bushy salt-and-pepper eyebrows knitted.

"Exactly," Margiana said, looking his way. "As though they're waiting for someone to remove the barricade so they can continue into the city."

"You...you think they have...mages?"

"There are many students of the mystical arts, Haroun. It's a fair assumption."

Haroun considered this, slowly shaking his head.

"It's bad enough that we no longer have the great Sinbad to protect us," he said. "With his son also gone we are at our weakest."

Margiana's obvious distress at hearing this prompted a quick apology.

"It's all right," Margiana said, giving Haroun a fairly reassuring smile. "We've done well these past five years without my husband." Her smile faded. "And our son's absence is also disheartening, but his mission is absolutely vital and you know as well as I that I couldn't have given it to anyone else."

Haroun didn't look all that placated; still, he acknowledged the validity of that last part.

"Like you my faith in Sinbad's son is nearly as strong as in Sinbad himself. But he has been gone a long time now as well."

They both went momentarily silent and fell to staring at the distant army again.

Margiana finally spoke up.

"Sinbad and I always resisted the idea of a militia," she said. "Violence breeds violence. And it worked for a long time: Aderadad and its neighbors have enjoyed a greatly productive peace for decades. Most of us have put war and armies behind."

"Yes," Haroun said. "Yet out there stands a terrifying one, and without a militia only your barrier stands between them and the devastation of our great city."

"You heard the scouts, Haroun," Margiana said, looking his way. "Other militias have stood up to them on this campaign...only to be quickly decimated."

Haroun looked puzzled again. "Then Sinbad, son of Sinbad's task is a pointless one."

Most surprisingly, this observation actually seemed to encourage Margiana rather than challenge her judgement. She smiled, her beautiful eyes twinkling, and looked up at the stars.

"So it may seem," she said. "As it often did for his father."

Chapter Twenty-One

The relentless rain that had kicked in shortly before dawn was making the return slog through the swampy valley to the crystal temple a miserable crawl.

"At least it's cooled things down a little," Sinbad said, flashing a wry smile at Jason and a couple of the others who were leading the way alongside and directly behind him.

A few yards back of him Rashid saw Heracles turn and give him a quizzical look.

The Chimera's first mate shrugged and offered the demigod a private observation. "My captain is afflicted with chronic optimism," he said. "Strand him in a blistering desert and he'll go on and on about its beautiful skies."

"I'll take him down to the Underworld sometime," Heracles said, smiling grimly. "Let's see him put a nice spin on Tartarus and Hades."

Had even one of the ten men in the vine-slashing parade chanced to look directly up overhead – into the often driving downpour – they *might* have been able to see the oddity that was traveling right along with them.

Outlined in streaks of rain the homunculus flapped easily along, its eyes feeding a constant report back to its coma-feigning owner. The little creature's chameleonic talents were limited to hiding only its own form, so the rain splashes were an odd little "flying 3d pattern" that was exactly matching the party's grueling return to the temple.

But a small anomaly it was indeed, and what's more the homunculus was shrewd enough to be staying fairly well above the swamp-slogging travelers – about sixty feet or so over their heads at its lowest. At Pentelus' psychic command the creature tilted its gaze upward until it was focused on the no longer distant temple, which glowed with an eerie yet majestic beauty even beneath the squalling skies. Below the temple the lava dome was ringed in thick steam/fog that reached almost all the way up to the base of the gem-shaped edifice.

***

Pentelus risked opening a deliberately closed eye. As he'd hoped (and guessed by the lack of nearby voices or sounds) the others were all well away from him. He tilted his head just a little and spotted them all together at least ten yards distant. Lying atop a rain-soaked blanket on the oddly unheated band of ancient lava surrounding the temple he finished contemplating his quite uncomfortable circumstances and the virtual inevitability of the approaching party's imminent return and, preparing himself and taking in a deep breath, let out the loudest moan he could manage.

Ahmad, Raoul and Makili heard him, dropped what they were doing and rushed over his way.

Pentelus put on a convincing job of acting as though he'd just awakened. Feigning confusion and weakness he squinted at the concerned faces as they rushed up, encircled and loomed over him.

"Can you hear me?" Ahmad said. "Pentelus?"

"Y-yes," Pentelus said, brilliantly feigning fogginess, his eyes rolling around. "Sinbad?"

"No, it's Ahmad. Raoul and Makili are here as well.

Do you understand me?"

Pentelus' eyes slowed their fluttering but it didn't cease completely because his eyelashes were still batting away raindrops.

"Help me...sit up..." he said.

"Are you sure you're ready?" Makili said. "You've been out for..."

"Yes...yes...I'm fine. The rain...hurting my eyes... can't see..."

The hard, oddly chilling raindrops were sharp indeed, giving Pentelus' excuse some validity.

Ahmad stood back as the others knelt down and assisted the seemingly still half-feeble first mate in sitting up. Raoul and Makili stayed crouched there at his sides until Pentelus finally convinced them he could stay half-upright on his own.

"What happened to you?" Raoul said a few minutes later, as Pentelus feigned sating ravenous hunger with a formerly dry and crusty half-loaf of bread.

Pentelus shook his head, sending chunks and crumbs of bread flying freely from his fast-moving mouth.

"Wine," he managed to say through a big mouthful, and when he saw that Ahmad wasn't in any hurry to get it to him he stopped eating just long enough to gesture sharply at it.

Ahmad passed it over. Pentelus took a good long pull on the wine and then went back to eating.

Ahmad asked again and once more got blown off. Raoul soon reached his fill of watching the least trusted man on the Argo refuse to respond to his curiosity.

"Easy enough to guess what happened," Raoul said, sneering at Pentelus. "When those beasts rose up and attacked he turned tail and fled back down into the swamp, leaving us behind to deal with them without him. He hid out there for a while and then dirtied himself up and returned to us, and when he finally DOES talk – and he will have to, sooner or later – he'll tell us he barely got away from them and was so terrified that he had no idea where to go when his senses finally came back to him."

The other two were looking uncertainly at Raoul.

"He's right."

Ahmad and Maliki turned to Pentelus, both men looking quite stunned. The first mate had ceased his gorging. He looked up at the trio.

"I lost my nerve," Pentelus said, casting the soggy butt end of the loaf down angrily. "I admit it. I'm no fighter, I'm a thinker. When those things attacked I saw no chance to defeat them. I ran. I wanted to live. How you DID defeat them I don't know, but when I eventually recovered from my panic I was so far into those wastes down there that I couldn't tell which way was which. And when I finally did manage to find my way back out and saw you up here I realized that I had to come up here and confess my shame if I ever hoped to get back out of here alive."

Raoul drew his scimitar.

"Put it away," Ahmad said. "We do not kill for such things."

Raoul didn't relent, at least not right away.

"He can't be trusted," he said, glaring at Pentelus. "What's to stop him from running again the next time he gives up on us?"

"Nothing," Maliki said, shaking his head.

"Right," Ahmad said. "So now that we know that we know what to expect. He's only here because he gave Jason that map as I understand it. So we know why, as well as why he ran...and so we'll watch him for now. And then Sinbad and Jason will decide his fate."

Pentelus hid a brief smile by momentarily bowing his head. He brought his face back up.

"I will plead my case before my captain and yours," he said. "And I will beg their mercy."

***

What the Argo's first mate deliberately held back from the three Chimera sailors was that he had an out, a very solid one that in the end got his "cowardice" off the hook. He claimed he'd figured out the secret to gaining access to the temple from the words Orpheus had left behind on a scroll…the words that Sinbad had told the bard he'd received as a message from a mysterious oracle.

"If not for what you may perceive as my lack of battle valor," Pentelus told Jason, Sinbad and Rashid (with Heracles well out of earshot and busy testing the temple's wall for the first time), "I might not have survived to figure out what you had done wrong."

His captain made the final call.

"You were not brought along on this mission as a fighter," he said. "And without your guidance we would not be here at all. You are forgiven."

Pentelus relaxed visibly. He smiled. But before he could thank Jason the captain spoke again.

"And by the same token you will not be needed at my side when we open the temple. Only the most agile and able will be able to survive the sphinxes should anything go wrong."

"Captain?" Pentelus said uncertainly.

"Tell us what you learned. What mistake have we made?"

Pentelus did something that none in his audience appeared to expect: he went mum.

"You beg for my mercy and then refuse to offer help?"

"I will tell you, Captain," he said, "as I stand at your side."

"But the sphinxes…"

"I will risk it," Pentelus said. "Like you I have come too far to be denied the sights that lay within those walls. Sphinxes can be reasoned with, those fire guardians could not. I trust my wits if not my nerve."

Gazes locked, jaws set, the two said nothing for a long

moment. Sinbad and Rashid likewise remained silent, keeping clear of a decision that was obviously Jason's to make. At last Jason spoke.

"You will be at my side then," he said. "Know that I will also watch your every move."

"I would expect no less," Pentelus said. "And considering my current condition I imagine that should take very little effort on your part."

Chapter Twenty-Two

Sinbad heard the music again that night.

The rain had slowed but was still coming down enough to keep that ring of dense fog in place around the temple. Sinbad opened his eyes. Their lashes batted away raindrops as he scanned the camp. A distinctively dank and sweet fragrance filled the air, overriding the otherwise warm and damp earthiness spiced with traces of sulfur.

Blonde hash.

Sure enough, it appeared Rashid was turning Orpheus and Dardan onto his favorite addiction. They were passing his pipe, doing little to guard because not much was happening besides their deeply contemplative chat.

"Live long enough," Rashid was saying, "and you become fairly certain you know nothing at all."

"I disagree," Orpheus said. "True that all this is subjective, brought to whatever our minds actually are by whatever our senses are. But there *are* truths to be had, I believe, intangible as they in fact all might be. This, for example: this is a truth…that there may truths, but none you can lay your hands on." Seeing Rashid's look – and the glint of his hook – the bard quickly added, "Figuratively speaking, of course."

All three men chuckled.

The song was so strong that even such an inherently

interesting conversation quickly lost Sinbad's divided focus. Making sure the three watchmen weren't paying attention he rose slowly, grabbed his scimitar and quietly headed off around the temple corner. Out of sight of the rest there he drew his scimitar from its sheath and headed down the volcanic dome slope into the fog.

He knew where he was going. And he did his best to aim there as he traversed the listless milky mist. The fog extended well out into the swamp by this point, so he wound up having to negotiate that almost more treacherous campaign as well; that is, once he'd gotten through the fogbound maze of hissing and flaming vents.

Yet he was rewarded for his dogged persistence in the end, as the fog abruptly yielded and he stepped into cool white moonlight.

Two strides brought him to the very edge of Vrona's clear saltwater pool.

The music was penetrating, affecting. Sinbad had to fight its allure, as well as an odd urge to walk out and immerse himself in the pond, a baseless-seeming whim that he figured may or may not have owed something to the tune.

"Is this your way of summoning me?" he said, his words echoing across the nearly still water.

The reply wasn't quite immediate. A few seconds passed, and Sinbad was just about to ask again when the answer came.

"Yes."

But that was all, it seemed, he was going to get.

"Well then," he said, relaxing but not quite lowering his scimitar. "I suppose you have a reason?"

"The Fates have decreed this must happen," the sultry disembodied voice said. "Even the gods obey them, and so they have declared I shall not prevent you from gaining entry should you try."

Sinbad sheathed his weapon and did a short bow. "This is not my quest," he said. "Perhaps you should be

169

speaking to Jason rather than me."

"My words would fall on Jason's pain-deafened ears. If you truly are a Sinbad – a master sage – it is your ears that must listen…and your heart that must hear."

"Then tell me what I must hear."

"I fear I cannot," the voice said. "I am forbidden from influencing the affairs of mortals, even when what happens here may well affect every single being on this world. And yet …"

Sinbad waited only a second or two before echoing her last two words. "And yet?"

"It is not safe."

Sinbad's brow furrowed. That announcement had a decidedly different tone to it, a hint of alarm atop the obvious wariness. He glanced around.

"Beneath," the voice said. "You must go beneath."

"Beneath?" Sinbad said, studying the shadowy, noisy, vine-meshed jungle surrounding the pool. "You mean beneath the water? Join you and drown happily, something like that? No thank you."

"Beneath," the voice insisted. "You'll see."

"I'm sure I will."

The voice didn't seem inclined to offer anything else without prompting. Growing annoyed by the vagueness it kept displaying, albeit in quite the alluring tones, and seeing nothing of note to be alarmed about Sinbad turned his gaze down upon the still-rippling pool surface. He knelt slowly and, leaning over, dipped a couple of fingertips into the water. Bringing them up right beneath his nose he sniffed them, smelled the salt and nothing else and thus risked tasting the water.

"You'll see," the voice said.

The music had stopped several minutes earlier but the voice was so intriguingly melodic that Sinbad hadn't even noticed until then.

Even Sinbad wasn't sure why he took the leap of faith, but that's exactly what happened. He rose, disarmed, disrobed and dove out into the odd marine pond. The water was cool and refreshing, more like night surf than any water in a swamp had any right to be, and as the Chimera's captain popped up out of the water he noticed something else: the mosquitoes and gnats that were so relentless everywhere else across the valley-spanning swamp were finally cutting him a break. Blinking water out of his eyes was all he had to do – for a change nothing small and buzzing was trying to fly into those orbs. Once that was done he had a constant and unimpeded view of his surroundings.

"I'm in," he said, dogpaddling in the pleasant waters some fifteen feet out. "Show me."

"Beneath," the voice said. "You'll see."

"I'm charmed," Sinbad said. "I must be. I'm about to drown myself for some siren temptress."

"*Beneath ...*"

"May the Fates be merciful," he said to the starry heavens, and he pushed himself under.

***

Pentelus wasn't sleeping either. He'd seen Sinbad rise and slink away, so he'd sent his little spy after him to see where he was off to on his own in the middle of the night. He'd been keeping the homunculus up fairly high, about a hundred feet or so out of respect for both the clear night over the pond and Sinbad's extremely sharp senses. So Pentelus vis-a-vis his eye in the sky proxy had been too far away to hear Sinbad doing what appeared to be talking to the pond itself; that is, until Sinbad had gone even more bizarre and decided to take a swim, at which point Pentelus' fascination with his surprising behavior had compelled him to send his living remote viewer down for a closer look.

The pond was deep in the middle, perhaps thirty feet beneath where Sinbad had submerged, and as Sinbad

171

sank slowly toward its bottom he eventually gave up trying to take in his hazy surroundings in favor of the comparative clarity to be found directly overhead.

That was when he saw it.

The homunculus wasn't invisible to him anymore. Here, through a couple of feet of water that seemed to override the creature's blending nature, its form and gray-brown color were as obvious as the stars it was blocking out as it bobbed some thirty feet or so over the pond. He studied it, watching it staring down at him, for a few seconds before Pentelus realized Sinbad was *staring right up at his spy.* At that moment, and well before Sinbad could take action, Pentelus willed the creature to fly off and hide out in the swamp until needed again.

Sinbad watched it flap away.

About then he realized he'd been underwater for what had to have been at least three minutes or so...on but a single breath. Yet his lungs weren't aching, he didn't yearn for air. He tried to exhale but found he couldn't; floating in the oddly comforting liquid ether he felt as though he were drifting off to sleep.

Maybe I'm drowning, he was thinking.

"Water is time," the feminine voice said.

And then the beautiful Vrona materialized before him. Or had she been there already? Stunningly bare as she was, hovering inches away and apparently quite tangible, Sinbad couldn't tell if she'd just manifested or if she'd been there the whole time and he'd been so distracted by the hovering homunculus that he hadn't even bothered to look around himself again until that moment.

"All things obey the commands of time," Vrona said, displaying a faint but pleasant smile that even the wise Sinbad only half-noticed at first. "Kronos may be chained below but all are bound to his system...save water. Water changes shape constantly, but water itself never changes. Even if frozen or rendered steam it is still at its core unchanged. Thus water is a shield against time."

Sinbad nodded, still wondering why he wasn't needing to breathe but taking it for granted in order to make sure he focused and got what he could from the enigmatic dazzler.

"Time," the Chimera's captain said. "This is about time?"

"It is about many things."

"The temple," Sinbad said. "What's inside it?"

"Wonders. Wonders so terrible they tempt the gods themselves and have to be locked away far from the reach of Olympus."

"Why does Jason want in?"

Vrona shook her head, looking solemn. "I cannot say," she said. "Only that you must be there if and when he attains his goal."

"Why? Am I supposed to stop him?"

"You must do as you do," Vrona said. "And I must trust that your wisdom will prevail."

"Tell me what he's doing," Sinbad said. "Perhaps I can convince Heracles and we will stop him together."

"You must find your way to the truth. Jason's singlemindedness is not the only test that stands before you." She was starting to fade out, to become less material-looking and more translucent. "Know that this pool and the other on this island are Eyes of the Sea, sanctuary to all who sail and respect her waters, and that here you are welcome."

"Thank you," Sinbad said.

Then, seeing her fadeout quickly becoming more complete, he begged her to wait.

"Stop!" he said. "Please tell me…I need to know why you are doing this?"

But it was too late. She was gone.

Chapter Twenty-Three

The rain ceased shortly before dawn.

As the angled cascade of early morning sun tilted ever downward, turning more and more of the western valley rim from dull brown to radiant gold, six figures climbed the ropes they'd brought to replace the vines to the top of the temple. When all were finally atop the sparkling edifice they turned as one and headed over to the exact center of the temple's upper surface.

They came to a mutual stop there.

"This is it?" Heracles said, looking around. "It's a little less infested with sphinxes than you described it, Jason."

"They didn't come until I played," Orpheus said.

"Yes," Pentelus said. "And the reason they came and were hostile was because you played the wrong tone." Seeing all five of the others – Rashid, Jason, Orpheus, Sinbad and Heracles – looking quizzically at him, he displayed a self-satisfied smile. "That's right," he said, and he turned his gaze on Sinbad. "You said all but the first of the sphinxes that appeared attacked you. You also said they had no wings. Those are lower sphinxes...very smart and tough guard dogs, as it were. But that's all. They appear when someone tries to break in, no doubt.

Orpheus played the wrong tone and summoned them. Had he played the right one they probably wouldn't have appeared; more likely, if anything this place would have opened its doors for you."

For a moment he watched as the others pondered this.

"So you know how to get in?" Jason finally said.

"Absolutely," Pentelus said, nodding sharply. "Play the RIGHT tone."

Several pairs of shoulders sagged noticeably and a shorter and tenser moment of silence passed before Pentelus spoke up again.

"It's not that big a deal," he said. "Orpheus, how many tones are there?"

"Dozens," he said. "Unless you want to reduce it all to the chromatic keys."

"And there are how many then?"

"A dozen. One dozen." Orpheus' brow was one of only several knitted ones around Pentelus. "Twelve," he said finally, looking quite thoughtful. "Yes, it surely must be one of them. And I guess we know A is not the right one," Orpheus said.

They all stood there pondering it for a moment.

Sinbad heard something in his head, clearly and seemingly out of the blue.

"In the grand scheme of the Fates yours is at best a minor dilemma."

"What?" Orpheus said, hearing the Chimera's captain softly mutter what he'd heard in his head. "That's what you were told?"

"Yes," Sinbad said. "Why does that...?"

"'A minor' is a tone," Orpheus said. "Or more accurately a combination of several chromatic ones, forming what we call a chord."

They debated it for a short time among them, but not surprisingly under such odd circumstances no one had a better idea than dissecting the mysterious words Sinbad claimed to have received on his previous visit to this place. After all, Orpheus had to play *something* – that was a given. Nothing played, nothing summoned (or better yet just politely opened.)

So they all set themselves, and as the sun's rays inched across the gleaming blue-white gem surface toward their collective sandals Orpheus plucked a resounding A minor chord.

The mood-laden sound resonated across the temple's upper surface.

Pale fog steamed up before them, quickly billowing higher and wider than before. Out of the fog stepped a huge phoenix, its shoulders nearly twelve feet over its massive paws; fluttering its expansive white-feathered wings the being paused before the six petitioners and then settled into a crouch like the immense lion its body more or less resembled. The decidedly human-looking head at the front of the true chimera tilted down to regard its audience.

"Entrance is permitted only with the blood of Zeus," it said in a calm yet thundering voice. "Bring it forth that you may receive the question."

"The question?" Rashid said under his breath, glancing around uncertainly at the others.

But Heracles didn't worry about the details. He strode forward, stopping only when his sizable nose had drawn to within a few feet of the sphinx's tawny chest, and forced it to crane its thick neck sharply and even pull back a little to look into his fiery eyes.

He smiled up at. "Got all you want right here," he said. "It's a bit diluted with human blood – and Dionysus' fine works – but the old man's no doubt in there somewhere. Now how do we…AHH!"

Quicker than lightning the sphinx had lashed out and poked a razor sharp claw an inch or so into the demigod's upper arm. Just as rapidly the massive arm withdrew, and from the tip of the claw a single drop of blood fell on the temple.

"Answer you this and enter then," the sphinx said as Heracles stared at him, brow furrowed, palm squeezing the wound spot. "What is it that you may give to another in its entirety and yet still stand to lose?"

Heracles went silent, considering the question. He went over it, mouthing thoughts unspoken and obviously giving the question his mental all. But he really didn't think about it all *that* long.

"Well, if it's all the same to you," he said to the sphinx, "I think I'd like to ask a friend."

The sphinx seemed to consider it. Scanning the faces of the rest one at a time, he eventually came back around to Heracles. And nodded.

"I see no reason why not," it said. "Who will be your proxy?"

Heracles didn't hesitate.

"Jason is my captain, a genius and a trusted friend," he said. "Yet strangely I feel compelled now not to defer to him but to another captain, a man I am already honored to call friend." He turned to Sinbad. "Would you mind?" he said. Sinbad smiled and shook his head, prompting Heracles to look back up at the sphinx again. "I name Sinbad, Captain of the Chimera, as my proxy. May the Fates grant he might answer your question; I cannot."

Heracles withdrew. Sinbad stepped forward and after a short pause for a brief bow of respect he took the demigod's place, although he played it a bit more politely by not trying to go quite toe to toe with his interrogator as Heracles had. The sphinx looked down at him.

"You heard the question," the bearded male countenance said, and Sinbad nodded. "Tell me then, Sinbad, son of Sinbad: What is it that you may give another in its entirety and yet still stand to lose?"

Sinbad smiled up at the sphinx.

"Trust," he said.

"Correct!" the sphinx thundered. "Enter and be welcome."

The great creature rose and retreated into the fog bank. The fog dissipated in seconds.

For a moment or two the party stood alone again, bathed in mid-morning sunlight.

"'Enter and be welcome,'" Rashid said, looking around after a couple of seconds. "It would have been nice to have been shown how exactly we're supposed..."

He didn't quite get to finish because the temple itself had just become insubstantial and he and everyone else was plunging down into it.

Chapter Twenty- Four

The six men fell as one into an impermeable darkness that instantly wrapped itself around them.

But neither the sense of falling nor the sheer lightlessness lasted even long enough for anyone to call out to the others.

The party felt solidity beneath the soles of their sandals.

But they barely noticed. All around them, staggering beyond description, were stars, nebulas, novae and even a couple of quasars.

"By the Fates," Rashid said as soon as his voice came to him. "We are in the heavens themselves!"

"Not quite," Sinbad said. "Or perhaps we misperceive them considerably from below, for if these are indeed the heavens they are oddly starless and solid beneath our feet."

Everyone else finally turned their gazes down that way as he had done almost immediately. Sinbad dropped to a knee and laid a palm on the surface that supported them, which was so non-reflective as to be virtually invisible. In fact he'd located the surface by feel, not sight.

"We're not in the heavens," he said, and he rose slowly

and looked around. "We're inside the temple."

"Impossible!" Heracles said. "All this couldn't possibly fit in there."

"I don't think that's how it works," Sinbad said.

For a few seconds they all took in their strange new surroundings.

"Well then, we're here," Heracles finally said. "What now, Jason?"

"Good question," Rashid said. "There's nothing here... I mean, other than all those stars."

"I'd say there's *something* here," Sinbad said. "But it's not meant to be easy to find."

"What do you mean?" Heracles said. "This isn't going to be another one of those tag-out riddles, is it? So far I've only been good for a drop of blood. I could use a good tussle at this point."

"Defeating a pagan deity with a single punch wasn't enough for you?" Rashid said, smiling.

"That's hardly a good back and forth now is it?" Heracles shot back. "I mean give me a legitimate challenge if that's how you find what you're looking for in this place."

"Heracles, with all due respect," Orpheus said, "I seriously doubt that's how..."

He cut himself off because a beast of a man, easily as oversized and musclebound as Heracles, had just materialized before them all. His visage was pronounced and angular, his dark eyes and aquiline nose hovering over the faintest of smirks. Clad in a gold-trimmed white tunic and golden sandals, his only other apparel was a pair of golden gauntlets so finely crafted that they looked like golden sheaths over his trunk-like forearms, his wrists and his hands.

He was looking Heracles right in the eyes.

"I am Atlas," he said. "What is it you seek here, son of Zeus?"

Jason stepped forward. "It is I who seek what is

contained within this temple. With good intent."

Atlas' gaze remained fixed on Heracles.

"You seek access to what is here on behalf of this mortal thief?" he said, the smirk becoming a noticeable sneer. "You truly are the son of one of the usurpers. For what reason?"

Heracles looked angry. He stepped forward, shoving Jason aside.

"For whatever reason he damn well pleases," he said. "He says it's a good one and that's all I need. He's my friend and he's never lied to me. Abandoned me for years yes, but he hasn't once lied. And his thieving, as you call it, was meant to liberate a populace from tyranny."

"Are you certain of that, son of Zeus?" Atlas said. "Liberation can be a treacherous term."

"Here's the deal, titan," Heracles said. "Jason wants something in this wondrous temple of yours. I'm good with that. Now do we keep gabbing about it, play chess, answer riddles or what? Because to me all of that seems like kind of a waste of our particular skill..."

The titan had lunged with amazing speed. Slamming into Heracles with fierce momentum he took the demigod down hard onto the light-absorbing floor.

That same floor shuddered beneath them as the rest, even Sinbad and Jason, jumped clear of the ensuing fracas. The five mortals struggled to keep their feet as the quake-like shaking went on.

"Should we help him?" Rashid said, his hand on his scimitar hilt.

"Don't even think about it!" Heracles bellowed from where he struggled beneath Atlas, who was trying to get a forearm out of Heracles' grasp to administer some head-pummeling discouragement.

"Right then," Rashid said, letting go of his weapon. "Spectator it is."

He and the rest stayed clear of the ensuing battle as Heracles commanded...even to the point where it looked like Atlas finally had him on the brink of defeat.

The shaking was considerably milder whenever the combatants weren't wrestling together on the strange "ground." With both of them momentarily upright and relatively still – Atlas had both hands wrapped around the battered Heracles' throat and the titan actually had Heracles' feet up a few inches off the invisible surface – Sinbad moved close to Orpheus.

"What do the bards say of Atlas?" he asked.

"He supports all the world," Orpheus said. "Why?"

"Heracles is mighty, but he couldn't do that," Sinbad said. "I'm thinking it's those gauntlets."

A spark shone in Orpheus' eyes. "Of course!" he said. "I heard something about that once. They are powerfully enchanted. The reason Zeus allows Hecate on Olympus, I believe; Atlas' sister made them amplifiers of one's own strength, and with Atlas already the mightiest Titan that allowed him to restore the balance that the War of Gods and Titans had disrupted. In fact it's…"

"Many thanks," Sinbad said, cutting him off. "Finish the story later."

His gaze was on Heracles' straining beet-purple face.

"Heracles!" Sinbad called out. "His gauntlets are giving him the edge."

"You're…you're cheating?" Heracles managed to gasp, squinting eyes locked with Atlas'.

Atlas shrugged. "Didn't say I wouldn't," he said, smiling. "Titan is a race, not a code of honor."

"No…problem…" Heracles squeezed out painfully with what was left of his breath "…just didn't want…to do it *first*."

He kicked the titan right in the groin.

Gasping, Atlas let go and collapsed to his knees. Doubled over in pain, he looked up just in time to see Heracles' knockout punch.

All the mortals could do as the kayoed titan flew limply through the air and skidded across the odd floor was stare, and as Atlas' body slid to a halt they hastened over to the severely beaten demigod to congratulate him.

"Well then," Hercules said, eyes glazed, swaying on his feet. "THAT was more like it!"

And then he passed out, slumping to the floor with his hairy face split by a satisfied smile.

Chapter Twenty-Five

The five mortals were too absorbed in Heracles' collapse to notice that six objects were now surrounding them in a perfect circle about eighty feet across. Noticing while the rest were bent over the fallen demigod, Pentelus showed remarkably little surprise and said nothing...but his pale eyes were certainly lit with inner fire. He spun around quickly while the others were still preoccupied, taking in the seemingly unrelated items one after another. His eyes locked onto the final object and held there even as the others were rising from the unconscious Heracles' sides and seeing the unique constructions for the first time.

Nothing supported the objects: From the palm-sized crystal phial to the silver calliope, each and every one of them appeared to be hovering in midair. Sinbad, Rashid, Jason and Orpheus were all studying these as well as the full-sized mirror with the jet frame, the golden torch with the apparently ever-burning red flame dancing atop it and – most intimidating by far – what obviously had to be the head of Medusa, snake hair free and undulating over and around a face-covering mask.

But Pentelus' gaze was unwavering. And when Jason saw the focus of his first mate's attention his instantly became fixed on it as well.

"Is this it?" Rashid said. "Are these things what we're

here for?"

"Orpheus?" Sinbad said.

"Surely that's Medusa's severed head," Pentelus said, looking over at it. "Remove that mask and we're a garden set. That gaze turns flesh to stone."

"Gaze?" Rashid turned to him, slack-jawed. "A severed head has a gaze?"

Pentelus nodded at it. "Snakes are still moving, aren't they?"

Orpheus spoke again.

"The Ancient Wonders of the World. The rest are sketchy at best in common lore," he said. "The Fire of Higher Knowledge, brought to Earth against the will of the Olympians by Prometheus. Hecate's Mirror, an instant gateway to any place the mind can envision. And if I'm not mistaken that's Mnemosyne's Phial, in which the eternal essence of any single individual may be captured and held in suspension."

"For how long?" Sinbad said, staring off at the phial.

"For as long as the phial's holder desires," Orpheus said. "The captured spirit is not affected by the passage of time, as I recall, but is quite well aware of it."

"A prison," Rashid said under his breath.

Orpheus gently shook his head. "Mnemosyne is the goddess of memory. In that small bottle a mortal may live as long as a deity, thus allowing a mortal to provide eternal companionship – of a sort – to, say, an immortal who's becoming emotionally attached to him or her...in one way or another."

Rashid shrugged. "Like I said ..."

"What else are we looking at, Orpheus?" Sinbad said. "That device with the pipes...what's that?"

"Pan's Calliope," Orpheus said, his voice more filled with awe than ever. "Played by a practiced hand that instrument places any and all those that hear it completely under the command of the musician...or rather the emotions he projects through it. Pan used it for orgies, allegedly. But its potential uses are unlimited." His brow furrowed as he looked over the final item, an hourglass filled with golden sand and capped at top and bottom by a pair of marquee-cut diamonds larger than Heracles' fists. "That's Kronos' Hourglass," he said. "And that's only six. There should be seven."

"Are you certain?" Rashid said.

"Pretty sure," Orpheus said, taking in each of the six in turn in a slow pivot. "Seven Wonders of the Ancient World." His wandering gaze eventually fell upon the motionless body of Atlas. "Wait," he said, stopping and focusing there. "Of course. Those gauntlets. Wearing them a deity could even wipe out his or her peers."

Sinbad was staring at the hourglass.

"What great power does that have?" he said.

"The one I need," Jason said determinedly.

"Perhaps, Jason," Pentelus said. His form was already morphing. "But not as badly as I do."

Pentelus morphed not back into Circe but a hawk, which rushed forth and snatched up the hourglass while the rest were still reeling at the sight of the bizarre (and quite fast) transformation. Sweeping out and around the mortal quartet and the dozing demigod the hawk and its large burden were hard to pick out against the dazzling dome of stars.

Jason was first to react, withdrawing his gladius and drawing back as his sharp eyes tracked the circling bird.

"No!" Sinbad said, seeing him do so.

"He's right Jason!" Orpheus said. "That hourglass controls time on Earth. If it should fall and not end up upright anything could happen …"

Jason fought hard to hold back his throw. All four men watched as the hawk swooped down at the mirror.

There was nothing any of them could do to stop Circe. Despite tucking her wings in at the last second she still clipped tip feathers off both of them as the rest of her passed into the mirror's surface, which had only a second or so before gone from dark reflection to displaying the interior of a torch-lit chamber.

The instant she was through the mirror the image faded and the glass was once again merely reflecting its surroundings. The feathers, which had been floating to the floor, dropped like rocks.

Sinbad had taken only three or four steps when he realized he was the only one rushing over to the mirror. Pausing, he spun around.

Rashid, Jason and Orpheus stood absolutely motionless. Even their eyes were frozen in place.

Sinbad's eyes darted over to Medusa instinctively. She was still masked. But her serpent "locks" weren't moving either. Neither was Prometheus' Fire: the red flames were rigid as sculptures.

"So why can I move?" he muttered.

For a few moments he merely looked around, contemplating his strange predicament and trying to come to terms with why he seemed to have been exempted from an otherwise all-encompassing freezing of time that had occurred the moment the hourglass was taken from the temple.

Then it hit him.

"Vrona?" he said, addressing the canopy of brilliant stars. "If you're behind my mobility, I thank you. But I'm not sure that alone will allow me to overcome what has been done."

He heard her answer in his mind, not with his ears.

"I have done what I can, Sinbad. The waters of my pool have temporarily spared you from the suspension of time, but they cannot save you, your friends or your people from what may in fact come to pass. Use your wits, trust your roots to guide you and work quickly, before your momentary protections fade. And you must succeed and return with the hourglass before this island's defenses, which have been triggered by the removal of one of the relics they protect, destroy your ships and men."

"My wits and my roots?" Sinbad replied, instinctively saying it aloud. "Surely you know I grew up on the streets, a petty thief scrapping to survive. And my wits? I need more than that. I need information: I don't even know where the hourglass has been taken."

"As I said I can help you no more," Vrona said. "You've been tested before, I know. But never like this. May the Fates smile upon you, Sinbad Son of Sinbad."

***

And that was pretty much all that he was indeed going to get out of her, he soon realized. Whether he called out for her aloud or merely thought it at the same "mind's volume" she no longer replied.

He looked around. Heracles appeared to be dead, but Sinbad quickly realized after a start that the demigod's barrel chest was only motionless because he too was frozen in time.

"I don't see where I have any choice," he said, his gaze fixed on Jason's frozen face. "I'm sure I'm not even supposed to touch any of these things," he said, and he glanced around at the Wonders before coming back to face the Argo's captain again. "Much less attempt to use them for my own ends, I'm guessing. But that's exactly what I'm going to do."

He walked over to the phial, the smallest item by far. He set himself, took a settling breath, exhaled it and then reached out and snatched the beautiful little relic out of midair.

He braced himself and looked around expectantly, but nothing happened.

Sinbad shrugged. "Better than I'd hoped," he said softly, and he turned and jogged over to the torch and did the same. Admiring the oddly frozen flame spikes for just a second he then spun about and hastened over to

Hecate's Mirror bearing both relics. Stopping in front of it, he stared at his own reflection. "My mind's eye?" he said. "Perhaps if I envision not a place but a person …"

His reflection faded away as he concentrated, but the image that replaced it was not that of Pentelus. Nor was it that of the hawk he'd mysteriously become.

In fact it was that of a seductively dressed woman of notable pale beauty and flaming red hair…and a complete stranger to Sinbad, whose brow furrowed at the sight of her.

As with Sinbad time wasn't stopped for her either; but then again, she was holding the hourglass. Sinbad tensed as the woman turned her icy eyes toward the mirror.

But she couldn't see him.

Relaxing just a bit, he watched her lift the dazzlingly beautiful diamond, gold dust and crystal hourglass up before her face and hold it there, studying it. Behind her Sinbad could see an array of objects – from artworks to jewelry to weapons – each of which had been set atop its own pedestal in what looked to be another place not all that unlike this one, although the floor of that broad chamber was easily visible as a grid of polished obsidian slabs.

Seeing the woman's gaze fix solidly upon the hourglass, Sinbad watched as she spoke to it.

In seconds he realized that the syllables he was reading from those alluring lips were not adding up to words he recognized, so he went into action.

Drawing his blade he rushed through the mirror, intent on sprinting the couple of yards that separated his point of view from that hourglass and ripping it right out of the woman's obviously delicate grasp. And indeed he went through, and raced at the surprised woman. But he'd only gotten halfway to her when something vaguely electric blue and mostly translucent blindsided him.

Chapter Twenty-Six

Circe's hound stayed on the aggressive, pouncing quickly on its fallen prey and snapping its ghostly jaws at Sinbad's throat. Fending off the first few thrusts with parries using the flat of his scimitar blade, Sinbad finally managed to push the superior steel far enough back into the semi-phantom's jaws to wedge it behind the creature's jagged back teeth. The powerful entity wrenched the weapon free of Sinbad's hands with a single mighty jaw twist...only to find it was still stuck with and hampered by the blade that a grateful djinn had once enchanted to deal with the spirit world as well as the material.

The chamber guardian staggered back, its thick neck swinging its brutish head around violently.

Sinbad pushed himself up to his feet in an instant and looked around.

Prometheus' Fire was hovering in midair about four feet off the ground, more or less right where it had been when Sinbad lost his grip on it. Sinbad scrambled to his feet and rushed toward it.

"Halt!" Circe cried.

Sinbad didn't freeze in place, but his feet did. They were glued to the floor, and from the feel of it the adhesion went right through the sandals and was affecting his feet themselves.

Circe smiled. She lowered the hourglass. Her second

guardian had moved up beside her, and as Sinbad watched – the torch mere inches beyond his grasp – the first guardian finally pried his scimitar out of its mouth with one clawed foot and sent the weapon clanging across the chamber tiles.

Flanked by her huge guardians Circe strode casually toward Sinbad. She told her summoned beings to stay back and they complied, halting and leaving Circe to move up quite close to her captive.

"I have dealt with your kind before," she told Sinbad, staying just clear of his reach. "Questing heroes. One bested me and commanded my servitude. Then another seduced and betrayed my beloved niece. Tell me, Sinbad – before I decide what to do with you – how you differ from such men?"

"I have never commanded a woman's servitude nor betrayed a trust," Sinbad said.

Circe grinned. "Well then," she said, "there may be some hope for you yet."

***

Once she was certain her audience was truly captive Circe dismissed her phantom hounds, which faded away like vapor.

"Jason wouldn't tell me why he wanted in the temple," Sinbad said. "I'm thinking you know."

"Of course I know," Circe said. "He wanted this."

She held up the hourglass.

"Obviously he wasn't the only one who wanted it," Sinbad said.

The sorceress' twisted little grin suggested as much, yet her response didn't quite match.

"This?" she said, rather callously shaking the hourglass. She shrugged. "Not really. Control the passage of time? Erase the past, perhaps? Why would I want to do that? This timeline is working just fine for me."

"That's what it does?"

Circe nodded.

"The so-called hero who jilted you?" Sinbad said. "Some might want to go back and change such a thing."

"Some, perhaps," Circe said, her eyes momentarily losing focus…though it came back quickly. "But it wasn't all that bad an experience, all things told. And I learned what so-called heroes are made of, which most interestingly turned out to be pretty much the same things as so-called cowards. The difference lies only in desperation, and how one reacts to it."

"So you took that," Sinbad said, nodding toward the hourglass, "even though you didn't want it?"

"I took it," Circe said, "to prevent Jason from using it. I don't want the past reset."

"You're Pentelus…or at least you *were*…why did you send Jason to the temple if you didn't want him to get his hands on what he was seeking?"

"I knew Jason could get in. I knew he'd do anything it took, right up to and including getting hold of the blood of Zeus…although I admit now I didn't know that was part of the admission process at the outset. But once he did get in I had to make sure he didn't get his hands on this."

"You say you don't want to reset it," Sinbad said. "So why were you mouthing incantations over it just before I stepped through the mirror?"

"Simple," Circe said. "Once I moved it the hourglass froze. World time stopped. It's still stopped. I was about to reactivate it so that the world can go on. I've got just the place for it right here in my little collection until this is all sorted out. So, with your kind permission…?"

Sinbad bowed. "As you will," he said, rising. "Not like I can stop you either way, nor would I without deeper understanding of all that seems to be happening."

Circe nodded sharply, then turned and walked over to the only unoccupied pedestal in sight, a carved work of black marble and gold which looked just about the right size to hold the hourglass. Sinbad waited until she'd turned completely away from him and was carefully setting the relic atop the pedestal, at which point he slipped his hand down into his pocket and brought out the phial.

She was incanting at the hourglass as he brought the phial up and scrutinized it in detail. The stopper appeared to be the same rainbow-glinting cut crystal as the body.

He hid the body of the phial by wrapping his fingers and palm around it, leaving his thumb poised with the nail just under the flared-out top of the stopper and the tip of his forefinger over the stopper top to catch the stopper in case he ended up having to pry it off. For all he knew he might accidentally suck himself into the device instead of her, so he lowered his arm to his side and waited to see if such a risk might eventually look to be necessary.

As Circe finished golden dust trickled through the hourglass neck again. She turned and came back over to Sinbad and once again stopped just out of his reach. From there she looked him up and down, an overtly sexual leer twisting the corners of her lips.

"I'm a little curious," she said. "How exactly was the stoppage of time not affecting you?"

Sinbad just smiled.

"Fair enough," Circe said at last. "I had hoped for an honest exchange, but …"

"Admittedly I am your captive," Sinbad said. "You're entitled to interrogate me, but don't tease me with phrases like honest exchange while you hold such advantage."

She was still assessing his admirable physique, and not being very subtle about it at all.

"If I were to free you," she said, "the first thing you'd do would probably involve a lot more slashing than talking."

Sinbad shook his head. "I helped Jason out of indebtedness," he said. "Until I understand all that is going on I don't plan on killing anyone. Hopefully it won't be necessary even then."

Circe laughed. "I love your optimism," she said. "The truth is it's *always* necessary."

"Let's try that honest exchange you suggested," Sinbad said. "You led Jason to that temple and then took what he wanted there before he could get his hands on it. Why?"

Circe showed a mischievous grin.

"Why indeed?"

"Because you wanted in there too. You wanted something there."

"Why didn't I take it?"

"You didn't have time. And somehow you know how to get back there to do it now."

Circe's grin widened.

"Do I?" she said. Seeing Sinbad's faint smile as his only reply she said, "What exactly did I want there then, Sinbad...and why?"

Sinbad shook his head. "I'm afraid I don't know enough to guess. Perhaps everything else. I don't know your plans, and I doubt you'll tell them to me."

Circe shrugged. "Maybe later," she said. "I *will* say your guess about my wanting something else there and having a way back was a good one. And as soon as I take care of that and a few other details I should be in a position to come back and let you in on the fun."

She reached up to her necklace, took hold of one of its three crystals and jerked it free of its connecting base.

"Mind you," she said as she held it up for Sinbad to see, "there's no guarantee this will work. I know this will take me anywhere else on Earth, but this might be a special case. Promise not to laugh if I disappear for a split second only to come bouncing back here on the rebound off a teleportation barrier."

"That would be a shame," Sinbad said.

"It certainly would. I'd probably fly into one of my rages and end up flinging your insides all across these quite hard to clean relics." Her smirk became a leer, her eyes fluttering. "And that's not really where I hoped our new relationship would go...at least not right away."

"I quite agree."

Circe's eyes widened. Her brow furrowed. "You do?"

"You're an amazing beauty. Flame for hair, skin like moonlight, eyes the color of the cloudless skies of the Great Northern Lands. A man would be a fool to throw away such an opportunity for...*friendship*."

For a moment Circe just stared at him, looking slightly stunned and a bit as though she was having to search for an adequate response.

Then she laughed, a coughed-out chortle that even seemed to surprise her.

"You're..." she said "...you're not the normal heroic captain of an adventuring ship, are you ..."

"I am Sinbad," he said, and he gave a short bow. Rising, he showed her an inscrutable half-smile. "And I am at your service...as well, it seems, as your mercy."

She was scrutinizing him now as never before; deeply, studying his eyes and facial movements, his gestures, looking for any giveaway.

And apparently finding none.

"Your wife," she said. "For surely you have one. You would leave her side to ally with me?"

"Unnecessary," Sinbad said. "I am wed to the sea herself. Call it an open relationship."

"And you would serve me above all others?"

"I go where Destiny herself directs me," he said. "For was it not her divine wind that drove my ship beyond our maps...and guided me in the end to you?"

"I don't know," Circe said with a smirk. "I wasn't there until that last part. And that's not really an answer either, is it?"

"I'm on the edge, I confess," Sinbad said. "Between my responsibilities and my interest in you and your desires and goals."

"Indeed," Circe said. She was very slowly circling him now, and with his feet stuck to the floor courtesy of her magical energies he wasn't quite able to continue hiding the phial without looking rather twisted. "What's that in your hand," she said. "Surely it's not something from the temple?"

On the spot more with each passing second, Sinbad made his move.

He popped the stopper out of the phial.

And it sucked him into it.

The phial hovered in midair, the stopper likewise floating mere inches away.

Circe's hilarity rang and echoed around her hall of magical treasure.

She strode up to the phial. "Perfect," she said, and she reached out and took hold of it with one hand and the stopper with the other. "Have to love the self-detaining intruder." She plugged the stopper back into place and held the phial up. Sinbad – miniaturized, his image crystal-distorted – was staring back out at her. "Well, you can only be SO smart, I suppose," she said, grinning wickedly at him. "And you almost had me with the sweet talk. But using a relic without knowing how? No, you're not quite up to being my consort. Sorry, Captain Sinbad. Too bad, really. As a physical specimen you're every bit Odysseus' match, and far taller. But I think you're a bit too treacherous to have at my side, skills notwithstanding."

She looked down at the nearly empty necklace, more specifically focusing on the lowest crystal-holding socket – the one that had until moments earlier held the crystal in her hand.

"Hmm," she said, looking up from that socket to the phial. "Not quite right, but I think I might be able to make it work anyway."

She moved the phial up to the empty socket, which was considerably smaller and didn't really match; that is, until a couple of words and her momentarily glowing stare brought the pewter to life and guided it to shroud itself out over both the stopper and the upper portion of the phial. When she was done the phial lay against the bare skin of her ample cleavage with its base over her solar plexus.

"No peeking," she said. "Like I said, you're not worthy of trust. But I think I can find a suitable use for you. Now sit back and watch, because – well, because that's really your only choice. And enjoy the ride, because you're about to witness not a rewriting of the past but the writing of the future."

She smiled. The crystal had grown warm in her tight grip. She held it out before her and closed her eyes.

"Take me back inside Zeus' forbidden temple," she said, and crushed it.

She vanished.

Chapter Twenty-Seven

She materialized inside the temple. But her relief at arriving where she'd intended was short-lived.

"There!" Orpheus said, spotting her first.

Thinking ahead, he'd disassembled his special weapon to make sure he could throw its heavy "knockout ball" beyond its normal tethered range. He let fly with it and it streaked quite accurately toward Circe's head. He'd thrown it just hard enough to force Circe to actually dodge it rather than stop it short via incantation. Unused to such tests of reflexes, she actually staggered back a little as the ball whizzed by her and slammed into the mirror. Amazingly, the ball merely clanged off the obviously anything-but-glass surface and bounced off into the darkness beyond the ring of relics.

Heracles was still out cold, but Rashid and Jason were on the charge as Circe sought to recover her footing. Seeing the two men racing in at her too fast to counter she turned to the undamaged mirror and envisioned not her lair but Medea, and as her niece's image appeared – somewhere amidst the ranks of her army, near the invisible barrier – Circe darted through the portal.

She spun about the instant she was through, ignoring

the surprised grunts from those of Medea's hellish soldiers who had seen her materialization, and gestured and incanted at the space through which she'd appeared.

"I can't believe they were that ready for me," she muttered. "But then I suppose not understanding the mirror they had no way out – and nothing better to do. I'll have to rethink this."

Jason and Rashid had rushed after her, side by side, blades at the ready. Rashid had dropped back at the last second – they couldn't have passed through the mirror side by side – so only Jason got a glimpse of Circe's destination before the witch spun around and magically closed the portal.

That glimpse was enough. Rashid hastened up to his side, only to find Jason apparently lost in thought...his gaze far through the mirror.

"What is it," Rashid said to him as Orpheus drew up behind them. "What did you see?"

Jason shook his head slowly. "She's with an army now," he said, his absent look gradually fading. "The most deadly army this world has ever known. We'd have no chance."

"You know this army?"

"I do," Jason said, and he turned to face Orpheus and Rashid. "And we must stop it, by whatever means avail us." He glanced around at the relics that remained. "Perhaps we have exactly what we need here."

Orpheus' eyes grew wide. "The gods hid these things from themselves because even they didn't dare risk their use," he said. "Even if we *could* somehow figure out how to use any of them, what right do we have to potentially endanger the world with their might?"

Jason turned and stared deep into the bard's eyes. "It's not the gods' world," he said. "It's not Olympus that army is trampling flat," he said. "It's *our world*." He looked to Rashid. "This is not your fight nor your captain's," he said, "wherever indeed he seems to have gone. I can ask no more of you."

Rashid shook his head. "I'll ask it of you then," he said. "Help me get my captain – and my friend – back and we'll both add our blades to your effort. I can guarantee it."

They shook forearms.

"I'll do all I can," Jason said.

And then, for a long moment, the trio fell silent as they took in the still-motionless bulk of Heracles and the array of forbidden objects.

"Two have been taken," Rashid said. "What was removed besides the hourglass?"

"That crystal bottle," Jason said, staring at the space it no longer occupied.

"Mnemosyne's Phial," Orpheus said. "She took it to capture someone."

"Let's assume she has both," Jason said. "Why then did she return?"

Both of his companions appeared to realize the answer at about the same time.

"She wants something else here," Rashid said, and Orpheus nodded. "But what?"

Jason thought about it for a moment only.

"Doesn't matter," he said at last, a twinkle in his eye. "She still wants it."

"So?" Orpheus said.

"So, old friend," Jason said as a determined smile set his jaw. "We'll take it all with us and make her come and get it…through us."

Orpheus' jaw dropped. Rashid just looked stunned. Jason's smile became a grin.

"We're not transgressing against Zeus," he said. "We're just going to get his things back for him."

He stretched his arms wide and gave both his comrades reassuring slaps on their upper arms.

"Let's go now," he said. "We've got a world to save."

Turning on his heels, he strode off toward the head of

Medusa.

"I'll get this one," he called back over his shoulder. "Orpheus, you grab Prometheus' Flame. That's probably what she really wants...the ultimate weapon. Rashid, grab those gauntlets. We'll meet at the calliope and see if we can work everything over together to that mirror. Oh, and don't put both those gauntlets..." Remembering, he spun around. His gaze focused on Rashid's hook. "Sorry. Just bring them over so we can use them to haul Heracles out of here."

Neither of the men were moving.

"Time really *is* wasting, men," Jason said. "And if we hope to have any chance at all to stop that army we'll need these relics."

He turned back around and continued toward the masked, serpent-haired severed head.

Rashid looked searchingly to Orpheus.

"I guess we ought to do it," Orpheus said. "He's played games with the gods before and he lives to tell of it."

"I'm starting to think your gods are much like our djinn," Rashid said. "For all their powers and fickleness my captain doesn't show them much respect either."

"Good luck," Orpheus said.

"You too."

They headed off to complete their assignments.

In seconds they had the head, the flame (now a mere unlit torch, as the wondrous fire had extinguished itself the moment Rashid had taken hold of the device's base) and the gauntlets gathered together in front of the mirror.

"Here," Jason said, gesturing to Rashid. "Give me one of those. You put the other on and we'll be able to carry both Heracles and that calliope through with us as well."

The debate over who would get which glove was quick.

"Are you actually left-handed by any chance?" Jason said.

"Only of late," Rashid said, showing a pained smile. "I

201

suppose I'd better take it…"

"Wait!" Orpheus said. "Try the right one on instead."

Rashid held up his hook. "Not sure it'll go on over this," he said. "Might be loose everywhere else as well."

"No…go ahead. Take that off and put the gauntlet on."

Rashid looked to Jason, who shrugged.

"The worst that can happen is that it won't work," Orpheus said. "It's worth a try."

Rashid shook his head, yet went ahead and handed both gauntlets over to Jason to hold. Then he worked his hook free, exposing the nearly straight-edged wrist stump, and stuck the hook in his belt. Jason handed him the right gauntlet.

"You said there was no time to waste," Rashid said as he slipped it on. "Yet here we are …"

The gauntlet's cuff wrapped itself tightly against his upper forearm. The smooth silver assemblage wasn't limp and empty; incredibly, it appear to be filled with not just forearm and full wrist but hands and fingers too.

"Yes!" Orpheus declared. "The lore is right. I mean you're stuck with it forever now, or at least until Atlas finds you and takes it back. But in the meantime you have two functioning hands…and one of them has the strength of ten men."

Rashid was flexing his new "hand," admiring its perfect performance.

"Would that happen if I wear this one as well?" Jason said.

Orpheus shook his head. "Lore states the gloves have but one owner," he said. "It would be useless on you. And if Rashid should put the other on as well he'll have much larger problems than the inevitable vengeance of a titan."

Rashid was nearly in a trance, still working his fingers and marveling at them.

"Very well then," Jason said. "If it's of no use to us we'll leave it, as we will likely have to do with the mirror itself since we have no way of knowing how to take it."

"What if the gauntlets are what she wanted?" Orpheus said. "Perhaps those and the mirror?"

"We can only hope they aren't," Jason said. "Either way we can't stay here forever. Come Rashid...you should be able to pick up Heracles alone from the sound of it. Go get him and bring him over to the mirror and I'll help Orpheus with the calliope."

Orpheus and Jason headed off toward the magnificent instrument. Their joint departure shook Rashid out of his daydreaming. "Wait," he said, looking confused and a little worried. "Did I hear something about titans seeking vengeance?"

Chapter Twenty-Eight

At the sight of Orpheus and Jason jointly appearing out of thin air at the front and back of a stunning silver calliope Havar dropped his lunch on his lap, yelped as it burned him and fell backwards off the rock upon which he'd been seated. The others either saw it as it happened or turned at Havar's surprised cry to see their comrades were back. So pretty much everyone was watching as Rashid appeared behind the mini-caravan, though in fairness he was barely discernible at first behind the much larger bulk of the demigod he was shoving through the portal ahead of him.

The entire camp rushed up to welcome the arrivals.

"What of Sinbad?" Makili said to Jason.

"And Pentelus?" Dardan said.

"No time for explanations," Jason said. "We must all be on our guard. A powerful being seeks these great objects and we must keep her from them."

Before he had a chance to order a retreat one was forced upon them all.

The ground shook.

HARD.

Rashid kept his balance admirably – almost effortlessly

– and, showing no strain, was the only one able to survey what was happening all around them. And Jason and Orpheus had the calliope, which they'd set down, to brace themselves against as they clung tightly to Prometheus' Flame and the head of Medusa with their free hands. Most of the others were falling all over the place.

The quake went on and on. Thirty seconds. Forty.

Rashid's voice rang out the moment the thunderous roar finally faded enough for it to be heard.

"Look!" he cried, pointing at the distant crater wall. "The sea is coming in," he said, and his finger's target changed…and quickly changed again. *"Everywhere …"*

Indeed, all around the ancient crater rim great cascades of water were dwarfing the handful of waterfalls that had been there all along. Either sea level had inexplicably just risen several hundred feet or…

"The island is sinking!" Orpheus yelled.

Wide-eyed alarm was the general rule as the party's members pivoted about, surveying their impending doom. And with only one captain present all those fearful eyes soon turned his way.

"What do we do, captain?" Havar said.

Jason eyed the ropes leading up to the temple roof. "Up there," he said. "Everyone. Once the valley has filled the water should be less turbulent."

"So?" Raoul said.

"So the undercurrents may be reduced or even gone by the time we're forced to swim."

Jason saw some of the men exchanging dubious looks.

Makili voiced the question on everyone's mind. "Then what?" he said. "Dogpaddle home?"

Jason looked him right in the eyes. "I'm open to suggestions," he said.

"Couldn't we take refuge in the temple," Makili said, "as you now know how to enter it?"

"Possibly," Jason said, "although in trying we may test

the patience of its immortal and extremely dangerous guardians."

"True enough," Orpheus said, nodding. "They didn't look too pleased at having to admit us in the first place. They let us use that mirror once…but only, you'll notice, to escape."

"We'll make such a return a last resort then," Jason said. "Anyone else have something better?"

Judging by the shrugs, head shakes and general lack of response no one did.

"Fair enough," Rashid said. "But I think we may have to tie this fellow onto me if I'm going to lug him up there. I'm still getting used to this."

He set Heracles down on the still faintly shaking ground beside him.

The demigod groaned.

The big man's eyelids fluttered as Rashid stared down at his bruised and cut face. Jason, Orpheus and the handful of others who weren't still staring at the brand new ring of gigantic waterfalls hastened over to the scene at Rashid's call.

Heracles' eyes batted open. Staring down at him he saw a ring of deeply concerned faces.

"Good scrap," he mumbled. "Did I win?"

***

Heracles got to his feet, albeit shakily since he refused any helping hands.

"I'm fine," he said, teetering, and after a couple of missed swipes he managed to push his blood-caked curls out from in front of his eyes. "What's going on, Jason?" he said. He turned and, seeing the temple wall nearby, said, "What, did we get kicked out or something?"

He saw Jason turn away and survey the crater rim again, at which point Heracles followed his captain's gaze all the way across the crater valley to the great deluges coming into the crater valley all around.

"I guess you might say so, old friend," Jason said grimly, turning back to him. "Things got a bit complicated."

For the first time Heracles looked around and noticed the calliope, the head of Medusa, Prometheus' Flame and Rashid's single gauntlet. Taking all this in, he looked to Jason and smiled thinly.

"Captain is your avocation, Jason," he said. "It's obvious by now that thief is your calling."

Organizing quickly as the ocean continued to surge into the valley, the party headed up to the temple roof. Last to ascend, Jason cut one of the two ropes at its base, asked for and got some slack and re-tied the vine end around the calliope before climbing the other vine to join the rest. Heracles and Rashid had the calliope – hardly weightless outside the temple – squeaking its way up onto the roof in short order.

They all looked out at the waterfalls. From this higher vantage point they could see that the swampy extremes of the crater were all but inundated already, rough water frothing about the tops of palm trees there.

Orpheus moved up beside Jason.

"How long do you think we have, Captain?"

Jason didn't look his way. "Hours at best," he said. "Powerful as it undoubtedly is, I'd trade that calliope for a decent raft right now."

Chapter Twenty-Nine

"A mirror?"

"Yes, our lady's own," Circe said. "And with it we can travel anywhere we want."

She and Medea stood together admiring the beautifully intricate wrought silver frame.

"And return?"

"Yes, if you know how." Circe moved up to the glass and admired herself. "As I do and as you soon shall. A simple matter, really...just an incantation to re-open the portal it creates from the other side." She looked down at the single crystal remaining on her special necklace, beside which hung the phial in which Sinbad was still trapped, reduced to a mere spectator. "I took it just in time," she said. "Down to my last teleport gem, and it's not like you can find one of those just anywhere."

"What about the barrier?" Medea said. "The army remains stalled and is getting restless; they're killing their own now because there's no one else at hand."

Circe grinned. "Good," she said, "we'll want them irritated and hostile when they hit Aderadad."

"But how? The barrier..."

"With a magical corridor such as the one this device

makes," Circe said, her attention still on the mirror, "no walls are impermeable."

Medea was looking around, this being her first actual visit to Circe's vast lair. Taking in her grandmother's dazzling collection, or rather the small portion of it she could readily see, her eyes locked momentarily on the museum's newest addition.

"That hourglass," she said. "What does it do?"

Circe's answer seemed a toss-off. "It affects time," she said. "I don't know the details yet."

"Time?"

Circe turned from the mirror and caught Medea's attention.

"Yes, time," she said. "Which we're wasting at the moment. Nothing here can augment our efforts right now, and if indeed something IS needed later we now have the means to return whenever we want and get it. The sooner we get this mirror to the front lines the better...and that much closer to victory. Once there it will be your task to protect it, and mine to direct our forces once they're through to the other side of the barrier."

"I suppose ..."

"You *suppose*? My dearest granddaughter, I would expect you to be a little more enthusiastic. Soon we shall have conquered all of the known world – well, all of it that matters, anyway – and we'll be free to rebuild it to suit our wills. And Hecate's of course: as it was in the Golden Age, once again she shall hold sway over all magic...and magic shall rule the world. WE shall rule the world."

Medea's failure to respond with anything, much less the hoped-for enthusiasm, provoked Circe even more. Medea wasn't even making eye contact because her gaze had slipped down a little ways and come to focus on the tiny man trapped in the phial.

"You worry me, Medea," Circe said, taking note of but not acknowledging the shifted gaze. "It's disheartening to see your resolve so weakened."

Medea looked up to her mentor again.

"Perhaps I'm confused," she said. "You told me once you wanted the land scoured of the infection known as man. Yet not only are you sparing many of them, you're carrying one around with you as well."

"Not exactly by choice; as I explained, he trapped himself there. Since then it's been a matter of finding the right time to dispose of him and make this device useful once again." Circe smiled and fondled the lower end of the phial, jostling Sinbad within its confines. "And at the moment I really don't have anyone better to trap in it, so I still see no hurry. This stranger has forced his way into our game, so let's let him watch for a while. He might learn a few things...before he dies."

***

"The protections won't last forever," Haroun said.

"No," Margiana said. "They won't."

"Perhaps the time has come to set aside our peaceful ways, then ...at least long enough to make an appeal to our neighbors to the north, south and east. They have the mercenaries..."

"Even if we did, and even if they agreed and sent them they'd be sending mere humans," Margiana said, cutting him off. "No match for those creatures, no matter how well armed and armored they may be. Just more pointless sacrifices."

For a moment Margiana's well-warded consultation chamber fell utterly silent.

"Then what?" Haroun finally said.

"Evacuation," Margiana said. "We may not be able to spare our beloved city, but we can save most if not all of its people."

"Evacuation? To where, my lady?"

"Away from that army...with all they can carry. Our

210

public transport can move many of them faster than that horde travels. The rest – well, we'll be there ourselves to defend the stragglers."

"Yes, you and I and Murif and Salia and a few other mages. That should be...well, quick if nothing else."

Margiana's eyes locked with those of her chief advisor. Her beautiful face was a mask of deep concern.

"This is why we are here, Haroun. The city looks to us to protect them. And we've seldom had to do our jobs, all things considered. To fail to do them now – or at least try with all we have – is to betray the trust given to us by the citizens of Aderadad."

"Apologies my lady," Haroun said, and did a respectful bow.

Margiana's gaze softened. She showed Haroun a sympathetic little smile.

"I must remain here and defend the city to my last, as Sinbad would. But I cannot command you or any of the others to do the same. You may in fact serve me best by organizing and leading the exodus."

Haroun shook his head. "You would face them alone?" he said. "Then I will stay and fight at your side. Salia can organize the flight from the city as ably as I ever could. We shall fight the invaders together, me with my blade and you with your magic. Who knows? We might even prevail."

He regarded Margiana's pained but honest smile.

"I mean," he said, "not that I'd bet that way."

"Yes," Margiana said, "but as you and I learned well long ago it can be the mere acts of mortals that end up tipping the cosmic scales."

Chapter Thirty

The swamp was inundated, its tallest trees rendered odd, wiggling-edged little green balls floating atop a new inland sea that was still rising as the great oceanic cascades continued. In the center of the ring of deluges, at that point an island within an island, the lava dome's lower edges were reacting to the lapping seawater with a thick ring of hissing steam.

Atop the temple roof the landing party studied the ever-rising waters.

"Not to be negative," Orpheus said. "But I'm not too happy about the way this is shaping up."

"Anybody owed a favor by Poseidon?" Belaricus said. He looked around but didn't see any nods or smiles. "Worth asking, anyway."

"He has a point," Rashid said. "Any of my shipmates have a djinn in their debt?"

More shaking heads.

"We don't need favors," Jason said. "We need to use our wits. There will be floating debris out there in the water. The trunks of fallen trees will bob to the surface eventually and we can cling to them until…"

"Until when, Jason?" Raoul said. "For all we know our ships have been destroyed as well. We can't bob out in the middle of nowhere forever."

Jason shook his head. "The Argo would have

withdrawn at the first sign of trouble," he said. "They had orders."

"As did the Chimera," Rashid said. "Providing they had it seaworthy by then, that is."

"Yes," Raoul said, looking back and forth between the two men. "AND assuming that they had time and weren't simply sucked under when the island began sinking."

Neither Jason nor Rashid managed much of a comeback.

***

Circe smiled. Her homunculus was relaying a most entertaining event to her mind's eye.

The tiny imp was blending well with the partially cloudy skies over the nearly twenty men who stood atop the temple watching the bank of dense fog creep up toward them. Beyond it a new (and from the looks of the still-cascading rim falls quite temporary) inland sea churned as it continued to deepen. Even the tallest trees were gone now, and though – as Jason had predicted – the frothy waves were littered with debris, some of it big enough to be used for flotation, the challenge of negotiating that up-and-down water any distance to reach, say, a decent-sized floating log was looking pretty daunting at the moment.

"Steady my pet," Circe told her familiar psychically. "I want a clear view of the end of Jason."

The scene in her mind stabilized a bit, but even sixty feet or so was proving too great a distance to make out the facial expressions on any of the hapless men.

The sorceress urged her pet softly.

"Closer," she said. "I want to see his face as he watches his men die one by one."

She opened her actual eyes. For just a moment her pupils stretched vertically and narrowed horizontally until they were the slits of a venomous snake's orbs.

She said something under her breath, a soft incantation ending in a long hiss.

And every deadly snake floating atop the foamy waters in that distant crater, every one infiltrating that potentially life-saving debris, turned its attention to the temple top, whose edges the ever-rising floodwaters were even then lapping.

Circe closed her eyes again.

"Ah, that's much better," she said, able to see Jason's face much more clearly as her homunculus hovered no more than thirty feet over his head. "Now, Jason…I have given you and your men and alternative to drowning. Never let it be said I cannot be merciful."

***

Unnaturally recovered already, most of his cuts healing and his bruises either faded or gone, Heracles had taken to strolling around the perimeter of the temple roof. Looking this way and that, up and down, he eventually wandered over quite casually to Orpheus.

"Your pipes," he said. "I don't suppose they're of any possible use to us in this situation?"

Orpheus shook his head slowly. "I tried petitioning Poseidon, Triton…even Oceanus," he said. "If help is coming it's taking its time."

"Might I take a look at them?" Heracles said.

Orpheus brow furrowed but he was not the man to deny a benevolent (and now quite sober) demigod such a request.

Heracles took the pipes and looked them over.

"They're beautiful," he said. "A gift from a lady admirer, I assume. Wealthy one from the looks of it."

Orpheus shrugged. He showed his old friend a mischievous smile.

"And there's nothing more they can do to avail us here," Heracles said. "You're certain?"

Orpheus shook his head again. "Would that they could, but I don't know how."

The master bard saw Heracles' gaze deflect ever so momentarily up to the sky.

"I think I may have an idea," the demigod said.

Heracles fell back and let the pipes fly skyward.

"Hey!" Orpheus cried, watching them streak up.

Their rapid rise ended abruptly about thirty feet overhead as they slammed into Circe's homunculus, whose death squeal shut Orpheus up instantly. Like the rest the bard saw the tiny monster's camouflaging – a consciousness-based ability – fail and watched as the mean-faced critter caromed away, shooting off sideways under momentum imparted to it by the pipes that had also broken its neck and a few other bones. Circe's ruined servant plummeted into the fog ring and vanished.

"What was that?" Makili said, still staring at the spot where it had gone in.

"A spy, no doubt," Jason said. "Servant of a sorceress. At least now she can't watch us anymore."

***

Indeed she couldn't. The empathic link had stunned her at the moment of her homunculus' demise, causing Circe to stagger back and eventually collapse. Temporarily dazed, she lay on the cold tiles in her museum. Atop her solar plexus the phial rolled a little to one side, then another, as its miniaturized and trapped occupant tumbled with it. Once it stopped – more or less – Sinbad was able to regain his senses and assess his situation. He craned his neck to look up to the stopper; to his dismay he saw that it was still firmly in place. But the lower end of the stopper was no longer hovering out of reach overhead.

He inched up toward it as quickly as he could as Circe lay nearly unconscious, murmuring softly. The phial's inner side slowly rose and fell rhythmically beneath

Sinbad in time with the sorceress' breathing. At last his outstretched fingertips found the stopper's base.

But that's all he could get on the door to his magical prison – the ends of his fingers – because of the taper of the phial's long neck. Sinbad pushed the best he could on the stopper's lower surface, but with little resistance from the glass beneath him he mostly just drove himself backwards with his efforts. The stopper didn't appear to budge in the slightest. Still he kept at it, stopping only when Circe finally recovered and sat up and he dropped nearly his own height back down to the bottle's "floor."

"You will pay for that, Son of Zeus," Circe said, her voice uncharacteristically shaky. "You might be able to walk into and out of Tartarus on a whim but my mistress has much stronger prisons."

Chapter Thirty-One

The sorceress didn't need her homunculus to watch the siege of Aderadad.

Passing through the mirror, she uttered the proper incantation and the mirror switched locales.

"Organize those brutes the best you can," she told Medea. "And keep them back until I signal."

As Medea nodded and went about doing as commanded Circe moved up to the mirror. An image of the ground just on the other side of the barrier materialized and she stepped through and reappeared immediately there, a sight that agitated the milling monsters (though it did not appear to frighten any of them.) Circe turned on her heels and, catching Medea's attention, beckoned for her to start sending the creatures through.

Despite their chaotic combat techniques the army filed through the mirror with little hesitation and relative organization. Huge as they were every single one of them had to squeeze themselves through rather awkwardly – each passage a sort of miniature birth, as it were. But despite that, once they were through the odd portal they appeared to shake off their magical teleportation experiences quickly and in general broke into vigorous jogging toward their still distant target.

"Nice to see the enthusiasm," Circe said, admiring

them as they passed by. "You don't get that all the time with manufactured monsters."

Within minutes a long, rough column of hulking killing machines was streaming across the open land toward the buildings lining Aderadad's western edge.

Her job done on the other side, Medea filed through between her minions and moved up beside her mentor-matriarch. Together they watched the soldier chain as it continued to elongate.

"Soon," Circe said absently, staring off toward the front of the contingent. "Very soon, my dear, Aderadad shall fall, its lesser neighbors on all sides will collapse with it and the known world will be ours." She turned to Medea. "Ours to enjoy, yours to command. The men and boys I've allowed to live will soon be yours to do with as you please, and should you decide to complete their extermination you certainly won't find me standing in your way."

"What of the one you carry?" Medea said, staring down at Sinbad through the phial wall.

Circe merely glanced down at the phial before looking back up to Medea and offering a little shrug. "Thanks for reminding me," she said, failing to notice that Sinbad was showing Medea a strip of turban that he'd torn off and written on with his own blood. "I suppose I could dump him out here and let your army have him, but I kind of want to do something special with him. He's been a thorn in my side and I owe him."

Medea didn't reply, she just kept staring at the words.

I CAN HELP YOU

She made sure to look back up to her mentor before Circe's attention was drawn down to the bottle, Sinbad and his message.

"Who is he?"

"The captain of a ship from this very city nation,"

Circe said. "He calls himself Sinbad – their word for 'great wise man', HAH! – and from the tales his men tell he appears to be the beneficiary of a long streak of remarkable good fortune."

"If so, how did he end up in there?"

Circe smiled wickedly. "No streak lasts forever."

Medea's next words surprised her viciously beautiful grandmother.

"Aren't you worried that you might get jarred and free him accidentally if the stopper pulls from the phial?"

"Actually, I hadn't considered it," Circe said, regaining her poise quickly. "But even if it came apart he wouldn't be released. He has to be shaken out of the opened phial."

"Oh, good. I just wouldn't have wanted him to appear from nothing so close to you."

"Thank you my dear, but rest assured I leave no such details to chance. Hecate's *faithful* servant I have always been ..."

There was no mistaking the emphasis, even as softly and with as much subtlety as Circe delivered it. Medea's chin dropped. Then it slowly came back up.

"I fell from her grace," she said. "But am I not redeeming myself?"

Circe didn't hesitate. "Of course, my dear. You are doing wonderfully. Perhaps you have not redeemed your betrayal completely, but I have faith you will. Our lady believes so as well, I believe. The Titans may be all but gone, but the greatest shall see her domain restored... through our work."

Circe turned to stare off at Medea's monstrous army. Even the trailing ranks were at least a quarter mile distant by that point, yet their bellows and eager war cries could still be heard quite clearly by the sorceress pair.

Had she spun back about she would no doubt have been dismayed at the torn look on her protégé's face. But she didn't.

"They will be there in an hour or so," Circe said. "I

think I'll get there ahead of them and watch the exodus. Have a little fun ..."

"But my lady, that's unsafe," Medea said. "Without their protection..."

Circe spun about, eyes blazing. "As if I need *them*? Those lumbering brutes do a fine mindless assault, admittedly. But protection?"

She swung back around to face the army's rear ranks again. Summoning her raw magical energies, she unleashed a dense wave of power that caused the air itself to distort as it sliced across the barren, flat land and quickly traversed the gap between its source and its targets – the lagging beasts.

The rearmost six monsters took the brunt of the force: they sprayed out like shrapnel in various directions, some in pieces, as the wave of sheer mystical energy wore itself out destroying them.

For the most part the "new" rear ranks didn't even turn around to see what had happened right behind them. The mighty concussion, which they were at least crudely intelligent enough to recognize as an "incentive" to get them to hustle rather than an actual attack, were too busy picking up their pace to avoid the same fate.

Circe turned back around to Medea, her self-satisfaction obvious.

"You were saying?" she said.

"I would never doubt your power, my lady. But even you cannot see in all directions at once."

Circe's smirk bent into a frown.

"It won't be a problem," she said, her jaw setting. "Trust me on this, granddaughter."

Medea merely bowed, displaying obvious respect.

Circe's grimace faded. Her too-red lips bent slightly up at their corners as she stared down at the top of Medea's head. "I can't take the mirror there because I haven't seen Aderadad," she said, and she watched Medea rise. "I must use another method, one that will...OH!"

She had been idly fondling the base of the phial, but at that moment Circe realized the potentially disastrous mistake she'd just come far too close to making.

"I need to shape change," she said. "Something with wings, eyes in the back of its head as well as the front for your sake...I'm sure I can come up with the right shape." She looked down, muttered to her necklace and it released the phial into her hands. "Were I to do so with this pest aboard I can't be sure he wouldn't have a say in the end product, and we can't have that."

She moved up and handed the phial to Medea.

"I'm entrusting you with both the mirror and this," she said. "Try to avoid looking into the phial and having to fight the urge to destroy yet another man of adventure. I'd really like to toy with him after all this is done. He's a bigger liar, cheat and thief than Jason."

Hearing the name of Medea's former love visibly pained her. Circe apologized.

"I'm sorry. I should have avoided mentioning him."

Medea took the phial...and her grandmother's advice, wrapping her hands about the relic's body so as to completely obscure Sinbad from her own eyes.

"Take the mirror back to my lair," Circe said. "We have no need for it. Take that as well and place it upon the pedestal that's been prepared for it. Call for it and light will guide you to the right spot."

"What about you," Medea said. "How will you return to your lair?"

Circe shifted the necklace so that the single remaining teleport crystal hung at the bottom.

"I'm covered," she said. "Go, my dear. And await my summoning when victory is at hand."

Again Medea bobbed her head, bowing quickly. "I will," she said. "Be safe."

Circe grinned oddly. "Always," she said, and she let go of the teleport crystal and retreated.

Backpedaling quickly, she opened a gap of about forty

feet between them.

Medea set herself and looked up to the fast-rolling clouds.

"Hecate, Queen of Darkness, hear my plea," she said. "Transform me that I might ensure your victory this day. Of the many creatures of Hades and Tartarus and the other wastelands below, grant me the form of the one I desire...for I know it must exist, as I can see it in my mind."

The transformation's speed only intensified its inherent drama. In seconds the crimson-tinged wizard grew into a nightmarish form: great membranous wings, like those of a monstrous bat, sprung from her erstwhile bipedal mammalian back and spread like volcanic ash jets to shroud the much larger demonic torso that was replacing Circe's pale hourglass figure. Muscles puffed out and re-solidified at many times original size. Sinews thickened. The sharp features of the sorceress bent and twisted and became even sharper and more cruel-looking until her countenance had become a true reflection of her inner diabolical essence. Her white skin darkened to heart's blood red, so dark as to almost seem to have a base of black under it...not unlike the dense, leathery skin of the deceased Molo. And like that pagan god her skin thickened, becoming like heavy but smooth leather.

The most hideous transformation by far, however, only affected the top half of her head.

Two eyes had become a ring of five.

Her great head, hovering fully fifteen feet over Medea's now, tilted such that her original pair of eyes – or rather, the fiery glowing almond-shaped orbs they'd become – were looking down upon her granddaughter.

"How's this?" she said, and as Medea continued staring up in amazement the Circe-demon tipped her head first to one side and then the other, showing her audience of two – Medea had absently lowered a hand and Sinbad was studying Circe intently – the eye on either side of her head. Gradually she turned to reveal the fifth orb, positioned in the center of the back of her head. "I thank you again for your foresight, granddaughter," she said, "and our great goddess for this wondrous new hindsight!"

She roared demonically. Half a mile away now, the trailing ranks of Medea's army didn't glance back: hearing the fearsome bellow at their backs they just picked up speed again, shoving each other aside in their uniformly independent efforts to keep clear of any more long-distance wrath from Circe.

Circe laughed.

"I hope I don't scare them all off," she said of the scrambling army. "I don't plan on doing all this by myself."

"I could command them to hold up and let you establish your presence in their midst first," Medea said.

"No," Circe said. Having un-twisted her great red-black neck she was staring off at them with her front eyes at that point. "Don't slow them. They'll adjust. Once they see I'm sparing them – well, most of them, as long as they stay out of my way – they will get used to me."

"Be careful," Medea said.

Circe just laughed.

She was still laughing as her broad wings lifted her heavy, yet sleek, powerful and eminently terrifying new body and her devil's head with five eyes into the sky. And she was giggling with glee as she flew along high over Medea's monsters and studied the rapidly nearing spires of Aderadad.

Chapter Thirty-Two

"LOOK!" Havar shouted, and his bear-bellow was more than strong enough for all atop the temple to hear clearly. "The crater wall is collapsing!"

All heads turned to him except those already staring at the same thing as he. A moment later everyone's attention was firmly fixed on the section of crater wall – hundreds of yard wide, at least a hundred high at its crumbling center – that was in the process of falling into the churning sea-within-a-sea. The constant influx had finally eroded the edges of the wide expanse sufficiently to allow the surging water to break it into great pieces which were tumbling – with eerie slowness, as viewed from the distant temple top – into the foaming torrent.

Behind this initial collapse the ocean seemed to have been gathering its wrath, saving it for the breakout moment, for the brittle lava barrier was falling only to reveal a miniature tidal wave rushing in through the breached crater rim.

Alarmed cries rang out all over the temple top. The frothing inland sea was already licking that last dry surface in the canyon, splashes surging in many yards due to the precision flatness of the structure only to sit there in thin, slippery layers owing to the very same incredibly level nature of this gods' construct.

Heracles moved up beside Jason. His captain turned

and saw him shaking his head.

"Sorry Jason," Heracles said. "Afraid I can't whip a tidal wave for you."

Jason smiled grimly. "I owe you. This one's on me."

"You have a plan?"

"No. Just saying it's on me to come up with one."

"Well," Heracles said, eyes fixed on the crest of the rapidly nearing swell, "might want to hurry."

Jason nodded. He turned from the sight of the rapidly approaching band of furious froth and looked behind their collective backs. His eyes immediately fixed on the single still-taut rope that remained after the calliope haul had claimed the other rope's anchoring.

"Everyone!" he shouted, looking around. "To the taut rope. Grab it, hold on tightly with both hands and lie flat...and if you pray, might want to do that while you're at it!"

Bearing vines, palm fronds, tree trunks, uprooted shrubs and massive water snakes that Jason and Sinbad and their crews had thus far managed to avoid, the latter potentially deadly creatures that were now caught in – and invisible within – a confusing and angering torrent, the tidal wave rippled out across the inland sea, almost doubling the sea's depth as it rolled along.

Per Jason's call everyone, even Heracles, hustled back to that remaining tight-pulled rope.

"The stakes will pull out of the ground," Makili said, looking around from his knees at all those to either side of him as they prostrated themselves, hands gripping thick vines. "We'll be swept off like leaves!"

"Just hold onto the rope," Jason, one of the few others not yet completely prone, hollered over at him from his spot. "No matter what happens. All of you. The rope is our link to each other. Hang onto that if nothing else."

Makili didn't look the least bit reassured, but he still ended up dropping flat onto his belly and locking a death grip onto his portion of the vine as the debris-laden tidal wave surged in on them all.

***

Medea stood staring at Sinbad through the glass phial's wall. He'd blood-written her another note.

IF ADERADAD FALLS THE WORLD WILL BE
CONSUMED BY PLAGUE

The sorceress just stared at him as he held the stained cloth out for her to see, ruing her fall from the priesthood. A wizard she was, a great one – but her deity's words were for her ear only no longer. Circe retained the rank of priestess. Hecate spoke to her. But Medea no longer merited equal privilege, meaning she had no higher power to beseech directly. Nor could she contact Circe, at least not while she was rampaging as Medea figured she no doubt was by now.

Among the highest of all rituals, she knew well, was the Rapture of Destruction. Circe had reached such levels, and this most sacred rite in which she was likely now participating – with relish, Medea figured, knowing her grandmother as well as she did – was not to be interrupted.

She pondered the scrawled words. Was he speaking of some sort of "failsafe" protection, some sort of caged devastation that might be unleashed by Medea's own minions and end up destroying everything? Or was it just a bluff, a ploy by this trapped "troublemaker" intended to prematurely spring him from his prison?

The phial allowed sight contact only. Sinbad was a miniature figure, fully animated, that about half-filled the lower end of the elongated bottle.

"You're lying," Medea said. "You're trying to trick me into releasing you. It won't work."

Sinbad shrugged. He drew his scimitar, lightly cut his

226

forearm, dabbed the blood and wrote more on the strip of cloth.

NONE ARE IMMUNE

Medea stared at him. Sinbad stared at her.

Medea decided to remove the stopper.

"What do you mean?" she said.

Sinbad appeared to hear her, and he was mouthing a response, but his voice was not carrying out of the device. Medea moved the open end in close to her left ear and listened, but heard no sound.

She drew it back out to arm's length again and stared at Sinbad.

"You hear me?" she said. "Nod if so."

Sinbad nodded.

"I can't hear you. But since you can at least hear my words, know that my mistress – my grandmother – claims you to be a liar, a cheat and a thief. You must then understand my skepticism when you make such a threat. In fact I'm still strongly inclined to believe you're bluffing."

Sinbad offered another noncommittal shrug.

"Your first note," Medea said. "You say you can help me?"

Sinbad nodded sharply.

"We're on the verge of world domination," the sorceress said. "What makes you think I could possibly need your help?"

Sinbad made yet another cut across his left forearm. With no space left on the cloth he wrote his response across his shirt instead, making sure to reverse the lettering so Medea could read it.

THE PAIN I SEE IN YOUR EYES

***

Haroun looked odd in armor. Had not the circumstances been so dire Margiana might have giggled at the sight of him. Once he'd been a prime sea hand, but his hedonistic tendencies hadn't exactly gone completely dormant after Sinbad's father had rescued him from a hazy half a life spent floating away in opium dens. Haroun had enjoyed quite the life, in fact, so much so that he was currently still retaining respectable status in the ranks of desirable Aderadad bachelors (he appeared to be a confirmed one.) But social form and state defender form were not the same thing, and it was showing.

"I'm ready to do my part, my lady," he told Margiana as he clanked out onto the balcony.

"I still hold hope you won't have to, my dearest Haroun," Margiana said. "And my eternal love and gratitude are yours whether you do or not."

He nodded, fighting back a tear, and strode up to join her at the balcony.

A ridge of black smoke was rising all along the city's limits off to the west. The wind was blowing it their way to some degree, but it was also strong enough to break it up quickly, keeping the skies clear overhead.

Both of them stared off at that smoke band.

"Word is there's a great beast in with the rest," Haroun said. "Warning you in advance that I might not be the match for it that I once was, and again my apologies."

Margiana turned to him, showing something most unexpected: a glimmer of hope flashed in her eyes, and she might almost have been smiling.

"One different from the rest?" she said, and Haroun nodded. His brow furrowed at the sight of her near-smile so she quickly added, "Often such are leaders."

"Leaders?"

"Yes," Margiana said. "And my Sinbad always said – *says* – that dependence on leaders is an enemy's greatest flaw."

Haroun didn't respond. Margiana slowly turned from him to gaze upon the distant destruction.

Her grim smile was growing. Sinbad had rubbed off on her over the decades; more, it seemed, than even she had realized to this point. And she remembered something old, words she'd heard from a mysterious oracle so long ago.

"Like a race," she said under her breath, but Haroun heard every word.

"My lady?"

"This battle is not lost, Haroun. Not until in fact it's won."

Chapter Thirty-Three

Sinbad's mirror-enabled return to the temple top couldn't have come at a more crucial moment.

The sixty foot high wall of furiously foaming and tumbling debris-laden ocean water loomed over his back as he stepped through the mirror portal. He looked down at his men, Heracles, Jason and his crew and saw all their shocked faces staring up at him.

"What?" he said, still oblivious to the incoming liquid devastation. Then he turned. "Oh."

The tidal wave hit.

But it didn't.

With no time whatsoever all Sinbad had time to do was brace himself. But the potentially deadly surge of water never touched him. Not a drop of it.

He and the rest heard the deafening rush of the water suddenly cut off, and when they all opened their eyes they did so to a most bizarre sight.

The water was rushing past them, to either side as well as over their heads. But they weren't being touched. A dome-like bubble of air was containing them, shielding them from the relentlessly ongoing ocean-driven surge. Some of the men looked up and saw that the water depth over the peak of the dome was increasing with each passing second.

Before anyone even spoke most of them had noticed

that it was getting darker around them as the crater-spanning lake continued to deepen. Surface debris was no longer bumping off the hemispheric "shell" that was keeping them all safe because there was already plenty of depth over the dome's peak to allow it to pass by in the clear.

One by one they all got to their feet; that is except for Sinbad (since he hadn't left them.)

Out of nothing Vrona stood right in front of him, nude and dazzling. And smiling, but that's not what everyone other than Sinbad noticed right away.

"You forced my hand," she said to Sinbad. "You knew I would save you. How?"

"Because you know I'm here to do the right thing," he said, smiling back. "And whether you serve neutrality or not I know it is in your nature to do the same."

"In doing so I have abandoned my duties," Vrona said. "My powers are fading now. Soon this protection I have created will fail, and the waters will crash down on us all. I will be no more immune to them than you."

Sinbad's brow furrowed as he looked into her eyes.

"What of your nature?" he said. "Will it not protect you from your native element?"

"I have no native element now. I am one of you. A human."

Sinbad merely stared at her, stunned to a rare state of speechlessness.

"Does that mean you can't get us out of here then?" Heracles said, swaggering up. He took off his one treasured item – his Nemean Lion-skin cloak – and gently draped it over her shuddering, gooseflesh-covered shoulders. "Because I'm not all that fond of swimming."

Vrona shook her head. "My act of defiance was my last here," she said. "For as long as it lasts we are safe. But that will not be long, and the water grows ever deeper over our heads."

Indeed the gloom about them had reached a twilight-like level…and was deepening.

Sinbad looked around, pausing only momentarily to scrutinize Jason in a way he never had before. But his counterpart, likewise examining their rapidly dimming surroundings, didn't notice.

"The edges," the Chimera's captain finally said. "Move out to the edges. Here in the center the water will slam down upon us, but near the edges we may be able to ride out the magic's failure and then swim to the surface."

"And then what?" Belaricus said, his eyes ablaze. "Dogpaddle until we're eaten by sea serpents?"

Sinbad shook his head. "One problem at a time," he said. "Let's just try to survive this first."

As no better ideas seemed to be forthcoming they did just that, with Sinbad and Heracles flanking Vrona in the final circle they all assumed.

"How much longer do we have, you reckon?" Heracles said.

"Not much, I'm sure," Vrona said, shaking her head slowly. She turned to the equally curious Sinbad at her other side and explained. "My connection to the powers that I stewarded ended swiftly and absolutely. In fact it cou…"

The dome collapsed all at once. All within its expiring confines were shoved forward by the force of the water at their backs, but before most of them hammered bodily down onto the temple top the water engulfed them and saved them from the jarring impact.

And then all was pressure, and swirling, and darkness.

Sinbad had no idea where Vrona or anyone else had gone. All he knew was that his lungs were instantly aching, he was well beneath the surface and needed to orient himself the right way and drive up there before he gasped out what little air he'd managed to take in before the water slammed into him and swallowed him alive in its crushing, all-engulfing maw.

He did just, his saltwater-impaired vision blurrily

seeking the direction of greater light, his legs and feet pulsing with nervous energy eager to burst forth to save his pain-riddled lungs.

He guessed at the light in the end and pushed that way with all his might.

As he kicked and thrust in what he desperately hoped was an upward drive he rued not doing as he'd wanted to – grabbing and hanging onto Vrona's hand – before the bubble had collapsed. IF he were to live – a big if at the moment, all things considered – he couldn't help but think it could well be with the haunting knowledge that his gentlemanly and respectful "hands off" behavior might have doomed the woman who'd just saved his life.

But that would end up as the Fates ruled, he realized, and there was little to be gained obsessing about it.

At the moment those same supremely powerful and utterly mysterious entities were setting his priorities, and crowning that extremely short list was the simple word "air."

Chapter Thirty-Four

Sinbad burst through to the surface coughing out water he'd inhaled just before feeling the blustery winds again. Around him the roller coaster waves were filled with debris and men, some of the latter clinging to larger pieces of the former.

The waves were too tall to allow him much of a view of his surroundings, he quickly realized. Before he had time to call to anyone he could in fact see – only a handful, it appeared, Orpheus closest at hand – a piercing scream rent the air.

Raoul was floundering in the water, splashing around madly as Sinbad twisted himself about to face his crewman. To Sinbad's dismay he saw about forty feet separating them, and as Raoul came up the vicious-looking constrictor wrapped about him raised its head and struck powerfully, burying its fangs into Raoul's neck. Raoul's screaming became a shriek that was quickly muffled as both he and the foot-thick serpent disappeared under the waves.

Sinbad made to move that way, but before he'd given two solid kicks another yell stopped him.

A crocodile – a massive one – was pulling Belaricus under in its mighty jaws.

He was too far away too, Sinbad instantly realized. In a single moment one of his men and one of Jason's had

234

already been taken by the dislodged monsters floating around in this frothy inland sea.

Vrona was nowhere to be seen, nor was Rashid, but then again only a few were from where Sinbad bobbed.

"Look!" Orpheus, one of those few, yelled.

Sinbad turned and saw the bard staring off and pointing. Others had seen Orpheus' outthrust arm and pointing finger and were looking that way too.

The Argo was cruising towards them.

Flanking it, looking patchy but sailing true, was the Chimera.

Even Sinbad had almost given up hope, but the sight of the two vessels coming their way – at what appeared to be almost unnatural speed, in fact – immediately restored his flagging faith.

He studied the ships as others did the same; the ones, that is, that weren't fighting or fending off some floating or barely submerged menace or another.

A sort of Sargasso of clutter had formed around the spot over the temple, much of that alive and dangerous it seemed, but neither ship slowed in the slightest as their prows hit the edge of it.

The ships really *were* moving fast.

They slashed effortlessly through the mess, knocking thick palm tree trunks aside with ease.

Sinbad saw Maruk at the Chimera's front rail. The ship's second mate, temporarily in command, was gesturing wildly...but not at them. In fact he almost had his back turned to the floating survivors because he was wrapped up in trying to get the rest of the Chimera's crew to slow the ship down. Patchwork sails were tilting this way and that, billowing and collapsing as the ship's crew feverishly worked their tethers.

The Argo had been in the lead, but it fell back as its crew did a little better job with their admittedly more intact sails and arrested the ship's impressive momentum.

Maruk turned around to survey the survivor-dotted

mess ahead. His eyes locked with Sinbad's.

"Captain!" he yelled. "Get back! We're having trouble slowing down!"

Sinbad was already thrusting himself backwards with simultaneous squid-like strokes of all four limbs by then, pushing to get clear of the Chimera's path with all he had. Orpheus was doing the same in the opposite direction.

Both of them made it out of the way none too soon. The ship drifted into the space the two men had just vacated as the crews of both ships tossed ropes and ladders overboard.

***

Over the next few minutes those aboard the ships that weren't helping others aboard took to bows and arrows to fend off the snakes, crocodiles and other swamp menaces that milled about menacing those in the water. Within about ten minutes everyone had been brought aboard.

Rashid looked extremely gloomy as Atlas' gauntlet easily hauled him up over the rail and onto the deck with his burden. Sinbad turned and saw him bringing Vrona's limp form aboard and rushed immediately over to them.

Sinbad caught Vrona as Rashid was setting her down.

He checked her pulse. He frowned. He leaned down and laid his head gently against her chest.

A tear streaked down his cheek.

Rashid stood over them, looking helpless and drained.

"I saw her floating," he said. "I grabbed her. Is she…?"

Sinbad looked up at his first mate. He shook his head slowly, looking into Rashid's eyes.

"She's gone," he said. "Because I didn't hold onto her."

Sinbad took her to his cabin and laid her on his bed. Then he came back out, emerging from the cabin's gloom to the sight of Jason boarding his ship.

He bowed.

Sinbad returned the gesture. When he rose from his bow he saw Heracles coming aboard as well.

Sinbad's brow furrowed.

"We have much to talk about," he said to Jason in low voice as Heracles headed their way.

"And little time," Jason said, nodding. "The Argo's crew stands at your command, as does its captain."

He bowed again.

"The Argo and Chimera are great vessels," Sinbad said. "But they can't get to Aderadad in time to prevent its destruction."

Jason nodded. Heracles strode up and gave Sinbad a faint smile and sharp nod.

"You have a plan?" Heracles said. "Tell me you do."

"Something of one," Sinbad said, his smile every bit as thin as the demigod's. "Aderadad needs an army. We're going to deliver that army, although regardless of its effectiveness none will ever boast of its great numbers."

Chapter Thirty-Five

Despite the figurative lateness of the hour the ships set off together for Aderadad. Jason's map – Pentelus' map, rather – looked to guide them well. Aboard the Chimera Sinbad's hand-picked team checked over their weaponry.

Heracles had again lost and somehow recovered his cloak, which he claimed was bound to him by spirit and couldn't have been truly lost anyway. Beyond that he had no other significant possessions, so with help from a couple of the more carpentry-oriented members of both crews a section of broken mast soon became a nicely contoured club that only he (and Rashid, courtesy of Atlas' glove) could hope to wield.

Sinbad had his scimitar and a small but tough shield that had been one of Belaricus' spares. And he had one more item with him, one he was keeping concealed inside a purple silk belt pouch.

Jason had his gladius, his shield and a pair of daggers on a belt.

Rashid had both his favorite scimitar and that glove, but even so he looked as uncertain as usual.

"*This* is your army," he said to his captain. "Four of us?"

"Five," said Orpheus, striding up to the rest with Prometheus' Flame in his gauntleted hand. Seeing Jason regard him uncertainly, he smiled and raised the unlit torch. "I think I know how to use this."

"You *think*?" Rashid said.

"He means he does," Jason said, faintly smiling. "Right?"

Orpheus shrugged.

"In this case it means exactly what I said," he told the quartet. "Were I to test my knowledge here one or perhaps both of our vessels might well end up charred coral sculptures weeping silently on the ocean floor for all eternity."

"For the sake of Lord Oranos, bard," Heracles said, "spare the flowery prose."

"The Flame of Prometheus could incinerate the Argo and Chimera in the blink of an eye."

For a long moment they all looked back and forth between each other and the beautiful (and hardly threatening-looking without its fire) torch.

"There," Heracles said at last. "You could have just said *that*."

"No offense," Jason said to Orpheus. "I know you have sound fighting skills. But perhaps you should instruct me instead of trying to face these monsters yourself."

"You're joking, surely," the musician said. "Heracles destroyed my beloved pipes. My hands are free. I can surely tote this in one hand and wield a worthy blade in another." He looked around and saw that no one was objecting. "Anyone happen to have a worthy blade, by the way?"

"I'm sure we can find you one," Jason said. "And I thank you. But are you certain you cannot...well, pass the torch?"

"The Flame can only be wielded by the thoroughly knowledgeable," Orpheus said, "and even then only at great risk. Sinbad's city is already under attack. Every moment we spend..."

Jason raised a hand swiftly but gently, cutting him off.

"Enough," he said. "You're right. But you will be

risking your life as never before."

"And if I don't," the bard said soberly, "I will be doing my calling a great disservice. Someone must be there to record the events."

"Yes," Jason said. "But they must also survive to relate them."

Orpheus shrugged, looking stoic. "The Muses guide me," he said, and he tilted his face skyward. "Apollo, their father, will see me through this if I remain true to myself. And should I fail – well, I'll finally be with my beloved Eurydice again."

"Good," Sinbad said, flashing a roguish grin. "So at least YOU are covered."

Jason and Orpheus chuckled softly. Rashid notably did not.

Heracles might have been smiling, maybe not; either way he had that special gleam in his eye, the one that had returned about the time the Chimera's splintered mast skewered "pagan god" Molo and cut that powerful if hardly immortal entity's return to power almost laughably short.

"How many are there, did you say?" Heracles said, his gaze locking with Sinbad's. "Roughly, I mean."

Sinbad shrugged. "Hundreds, perhaps more."

Heracles grinned. "Good," he shot back. "Don't want this to be *too* lopsided."

"For the sake of my people, my city and my mother," Sinbad said. "Please don't hold back."

Heracles rose to tower over him and hefted the mighty club to get a good look at its business end.

"No worries there," he said. "I'm fit for another go at whoever's fool enough to try me."

He withdrew far enough to whiff the club around in front of him, testing its feel once again.

"Heracles with a club," Orpheus said, watching him. "Wouldn't want to be his opponent."

"So," Jason said, looking to Sinbad. "All we need now

is this mystical transportation of which you spoke."

"Hopefully we've been watched all along," Sinbad said, nodding. "If so we shall have it soon."

Several brows furrowed around him.

"Hopefully?" Rashid said.

"Watched," Heracles said, glancing around. "Not again?"

"Yes, on and off." Sinbad smiled. "Watched in a good way. Via prior agreement."

Sinbad was staring into Jason's eyes. Jason nodded, his jaw set.

"Much is to be done," the Argo's captain said, his gaze as unflinchingly steely as that of his counterpart. "We have been called to serve today, not in the name of any so-called god but in the name of life itself."

"Aye," Sinbad said. "We five must hold the city of Aderadad against the invaders until the Argo and Chimera arrive."

"I still don't understand that part," Rashid said. "Not that the Chimera was looking its best anyway but to lash that ridiculously ornate device to the prow ...well, it borders on disrespect. There, I said it."

Sinbad showed him a patient little smile.

"You just have no eye for modern art," he said. "You'd lose all for dignity?"

Rashid thought about it a moment. "For the record, captain," he finally said, "I don't like your logic. I agree with it, mind you. I just don't *like* it."

"I understand completely; were I in your sandals I might argue as well."

"Maruk is to captain the ship then?"

"He did well enough rescuing us," Sinbad said, nodding. "Assign Ahmad to first mate duty. He handled himself well on Kryptos."

Rashid nodded. "It will be done," he said, and with a quick bow to his captain he was off.

As Jason and Orpheus were looking over Prometheus'

Flame Heracles went over to Rashid.

"I don't like owing any man anything," he said, looming over the much less massive mortal. "But in this case I do. Stick close to me and hopefully I can pay it back shortly. I have no desire whatsoever to end up owing you a quest anything like this one."

Rashid gave a rare smile.

"You owe me nothing," he said. "Knowing you would have undoubtedly done the same."

Heracles' deep guffaw vibrated the Chimera's deck planking.

"Son," he said, looking genuinely tickled, "you saw me try to kill Jason. Don't assume too…"

He didn't get to finish because a cloaked figure, hood covering all its features, materialized right beside him. Proving a demigod could indeed be startled Heracles caught Rashid's diverting gaze and sudden wariness and turned to see the black-clad newcomer standing solemnly nearly at his elbow. He withdrew and looked the modestly sized entity up and down.

"What's this?" the demigod said. "Don't tell me your sorceress decided to take us all on here by herself!"

He tilted back, raising his new club, but Sinbad intervened.

"Wait!" he said, doing so forcefully enough to curb Heracles' aggression, if perhaps only for the moment. Seeing the demigod turn his equal parts suspicious and angry visage his way, Sinbad quickly explained. "Yes, this IS a wielder of great and powerful magic," he said, and even as he did so he was taking note of the odd looks Jason was giving the new arrival. "One whose help we must have if we are to save Aderadad."

Heracles' suspicions appeared to be lessened, if indeed not quite eliminated, and he backed off.

The stranger's face remained well hidden in the shadows beneath the hood-like cowl, and for a long moment continued to engage Jason in a face-to-no-face stare-down. Eventually it turned its back on the Argo's captain and addressed the air with a gender-free voice that sounded like a chorus of wailing souls.

Hecate's Mirror manifested in front of her. The visitor looked into it and the reflective surface gave way to a terrifying image: On the other side of the mirror Medea's monsters ran rampant, gleefully setting fires, throwing heavy objects and knocking over anything that couldn't be picked up and hurled. Two of the great, hideous beasts were working on either side of a gaslight lamppost of fairly heavy metallic construct; despite its initial soundness it was now rocking like a loose baby tooth as the brutes pushed and pulled on it.

Rashid approached the rest, eyeing and keeping well clear of the mysterious stranger in their midst. Wedging into the mirror's audience between Sinbad and Orpheus he got a good look as those two monster warriors managed to snap the lamppost off at its base. Even as it fell heavily atop one, momentarily flattening and trapping it on the flagstones, the broken gas line ignited almost directly beneath the other; its thick, coarse hair set ablaze it reeled back and staggered off like a torch, howling maniacally but doing little to extinguish itself.

As it moved out of sight beyond the left edge of the mirror Rashid spoke up.

"Well," he said, seeing the half-crushed but defiantly aggressive first monster struggling to get out from under the fallen lamppost, "at least they're not geniuses too."

Chapter Thirty-Six

The five men had to pass through single file. Taking final preparatory deep breaths they all set themselves, weapons ready, and the other four waited for Sinbad to signal each's turn to go.

"The blade first," Jason said to Orpheus. "Remember."

"Weapon of last resort," Orpheus said without letting the Flame move from where he held it beside his waist. "Absolutely."

"Total destruction. Everything in its path. Right?"

"Right."

"Do me a favor, old chap," Heracles said. "Make sure where I am and point it another way."

Orpheus nodded. "Don't run off too far then," he said with a smile. "Keep in sight."

Heracles returned the nod with a deeper, utterly sincere one of his own.

"All right," Sinbad said. "Ready?"

To a man they signaled that they indeed were.

"Lead with me?" Heracles said.

"Not a chance," Jason said. "Not while we're still at sea."

"This isn't your ship," Heracles shot back.

Jason shook his head. "Doesn't matter," he said. "We're still at sea."

"Jason goes first," Sinbad said, "says this ship's

captain."

Jason nodded. And he went first.

"Heracles now," Sinbad said, and the demigod stepped up to the mirror.

He had to turn sideways and expel all his wind much like Medea's monsters had, and even then he still had to squeeze through as they did, but he made it. Sinbad sent Rashid next.

"You're last," he said to Orpheus. "So you can hold back and keep track of where the rest of us are in case you have to let that loose on your enemies."

Orpheus nodded. "May the Fates guide us all," he said.

Sinbad grinned. "I get the feeling that happens regardless," he said, and he turned and went through the portal.

***

Heracles, Jason and Rashid were all back to back and fully engaged with at least three times as many monsters as Sinbad came through. Spinning about quickly he saw another closing in on him. The fact that Sinbad had just materialized out of thin air didn't seem to bother the onrushing beast at all. Sinbad judged his opponent quickly and decided to hold his ground until the last instant and then leap to one side to avoid being run down. The beast was a little more agile than he'd expected, its outstretched claws slashing his tunic and his upper left arm through it, but for the most part it missed him. And as it was trying to slow and pivot Sinbad seized his opportunity.

His scimitar flashed.

The monster's head wasn't quite severed; a thick flap of dense hide still held it on, so instead of dropping off cleanly it flopped down on the thing's own chest. The body actually managed another step or two, the thing's snout bouncing repeatedly off its solar plexus, before it finally pitched forward and quite literally fell on its head.

Sinbad hurried over to join his badly outnumbered friends. Taking down a couple of monsters from behind with powerful thrusts, he quickly carved himself a way in to his allies. Once he had a clear path he hustled in, wedged between Rashid and Jason and turned around, stained blade flashing over his head.

Orpheus still hadn't come through.

The three men and their demigod comrade battled away, taking down one monstrous warrior after the next. The great bodies of Medea's creatures were piling up on each other in short order.

"If this keeps up we'll be buried in bodies," Heracles said. "I'm going to find a little more room."

He sent two brutes flying with successive swings to clear his path and then strode out away from the rest. Taking the enemy on solo, with only that fiercely tough cloak to protect his back, Heracles set about doing his best to destroy the invading army all by himself.

The three mortals weren't quite so brazenly bold. They stayed back to back to back, fending off if not exactly taking out the crush of warrior beasts pressing in on them on all sides.

"We can only do this so long," Rashid said after landing a solid uppercut with the glove and sending a beast flying off through the air. "We are but men...I mean other than Heracles."

"Even he can't keep it up forever," Jason said.

"Perhaps we should have entertained other potential approaches first," Rashid said.

"Believe, my friends," Sinbad said. "Victory may seem distant but it may be closer than you..."

The monster he was fighting managed to get a solid swipe into him, shredding his shirt and opening long gashes across the width of his chest. He pulled back, wincing as they grew crimson, and recovered his wits just in time to fend off its next attack.

"You were saying, Captain?" Rashid said.

Sinbad didn't have time to respond. Like the others he only had time to deflect and parry at that point.

Meanwhile Heracles had come up with a different game plan entirely. Having hefted one of the fallen monsters by its thick ankles he had taken to slinging it around in circles, bashing it into its onrushing comrades and sending them tumbling away. He'd taken out three attackers right off the bat; others, maniacal but not completely stupid, were currently being held at bay by their limp comrade's whooshing passes.

Heracles knew one trick about spinning but he hadn't recalled it until it was too late. He had spied a silver spire in the distance and was trying to fix his eyes on it and follow it but that was proving quite difficult.

"Not good," he muttered to himself as the gleaming spire kept passing through his field of vision at different slants, none of them close to horizontal. "Not good at all."

Giving up, he threw the monster more or less blindly at the blurred panorama of encircling foes. The creature took two or three of them out, but the rest were free to rush in at the demigod. He reached down for his club but was too disoriented; his huge hand grasped at thin air, missing to either side of the club's non-business end with successive lunges.

The monsters fell upon him bodily, raking at the Nemean Lion hide.

The skin protected Heracles for the most part, if but barely, and allowed him to bend into a deep crouch without being shredded to bits in the process. He felt weight quickly piling atop him. The creatures weren't able to claw him much, perhaps, but burying him alive and thus suffocating him instead was soon looking like a viable alternative to taking the demigod out with their claws and teeth.

For a moment – a long, terrifying one – it truly seemed

like they might actually defeat him in such a manner.

Steadying himself the best he could beneath the ever-deepening pile, twisting and rocking to keep the grasping claws from reaching beneath his cloak any more than they already were, Heracles fought the ponderous, ever-increasing weight atop his back and managed to take in a deep breath.

He didn't hold it long. Exhaling as he went, he used his incredibly powerful legs to drive himself up against – and through – the pile of grasping, pummeling beasts. His opponents went flying off in all directions.

For a moment Heracles stood alone, upright albeit teetering a bit.

Then more monsters rushed in on him.

Chapter Thirty-Seven

Heracles grabbed his club; barreling off with it whistling and slamming, he somehow managed to knock back enough of the monsters to plow a path to his allies.

"Back so soon?" Sinbad said, flashing a maniacally determined grin ever so briefly at the demigod as the latter threw himself back into the ranks of his assault team.

"Didn't work out," Heracles growled. "Plus you looked like you needed help."

"No, we were fine." This time Sinbad quipped without a glance because he was far too busy to risk one. "Except in the sense that we all need help."

"Well, at last he finally says it," Rashid put in from behind their backs. "And exactly who is left to provide it, since you thought we could handle the..."

KA-THOOM!

The ground itself had split open not thirty yards away from the embattled quartet. Crevices in the pavement itself – some of them up to six inches wide – spread out in all directions from the center of the thunderous quake-like detonation.

Atlas stood tall at that center, his golden sandals set to

either side of the star-like hole that his manifestation appeared to have created.

He looked around and quickly spied the core of the action.

"All right," he growled, striding boldly forward, showing no concern at all for the creatures around him. "Time to get my glove ba…"

Two of the monsters blindsided him simultaneously from the right, knocking the titan off his feet and sending him crashing to the flagstones, which shattered like windowpanes from the impact.

He didn't stand, he simply floated to his feet. The thick necks of his attackers twisted in his huge hands but had no chance of pulling free.

Atlas smashed their heads together. Their dark, viscous blood splattered his tunic but fell back off it and puddled up around his sandals. He dropped their limp bodies.

More creatures were coming at him, apparently undaunted by his display of supernatural power.

"I did *not* come here for *this*," he said, looking extremely annoyed.

He knocked the head clean off the next one in with an angry swipe of his single gauntlet. An oddly lucky shot, the head streaked away almost horizontally and caught another incoming enemy square in its hideously drooling, fang-filled mug. The second creature staggered back, teetered and finally dropped when its legs finally got the message that its head was out cold.

Admiring his two-for-one shot, a little smirk replaced the titan's scowl. He shrugged.

Another monster came at him. He sent it flying without even looking its way.

"I didn't come here for it," he said. "But as long as I'm here …"

***

Even with the titan fighting – alongside them, against a common enemy, that is, albeit obviously not on *their* side – it seemed quite obvious they weren't going to win in the end. Medea's monster army was simply too large… refreshments had to struggle over their fallen allies to get at the defenders, but these seemed endless as well as endlessly enthusiastic. Demigod, titan, three fast-wearying mortal men…their time quite obviously was running out.

Everyone had taken a claw hit by then at least, if not more. All of them were bloody, although Heracles' wounds (and Atlas' as he fought his way in toward the humans and demigod) were healing so much faster that their blood was more dry than fresh.

Dozens of beasts lay unconscious and dead all around, many in a thick ring around the quartet, but as many remained on their feet and striving to get at the enemies in their midst. The entire army, it seemed, had found this pocket of legitimate resistance and was striving to eradicate it at all costs. And costs were high indeed, but that didn't seem to matter to Medea's diminishing but still ferocious legions.

They kept coming in, slashing away, and generally taking return hits that drove them back or killed them for their efforts.

"When do OUR reinforcements arrive?" Rashid said, joking but hardly mirthful.

Incredibly, something unexpected did arrive in the next moment. Not relief as such, but a diversion certainly… one big enough to instantaneously rearrange the urban battlefield.

First a thunderous rumble, a crash-like noise, shook the buildings all around the melee.

Then, as almost all combatants gave at least momentary pause to glance around, two huge creatures, tangled together in mortal combat, came tumbling over the roof of a three story building and crashed to the ground.

The nature of both creatures was hard to make out at first because even after they hit they didn't stop. They rolled together, snarling, biting, wrestling for supremacy...and scattering the battle scene as even Medea's monsters showed common sense by getting out of the way of the immense combatants.

Some of the twisting, struggling flesh that steamrolled through the battle scene was covered in leathery hide that was thick and reddish black; giant bat-like wings of the same hues but much more membranous texture were in the two-giant scrum as well, folded like rolled up curtains on either side of a muscular humanoid torso. The rest of the tumbling tangle had opalescent, mother-of-pearl-like scales and was somewhat serpentine rather than manlike in its enormous build; it too had wings, and these were likewise folded such that the two-behemoth wrestling match was free to continue to roll.

The combatants lost their last bit of crash momentum upon colliding with a large public market building that collapsed atop them, momentarily half-burying both in its rubble. From the cloud of dust the two great figures quickly rose, however, and they were no longer entangled.

The red-black demon lunged forward, swiping a huge clawed hand at the head of the pearlescent dragon, but the latter was fast enough to avoid it. The dragon's long neck, coiling back to dodge the blow, thrust the long, crocodilian – yet somehow elegant – head in at its opponent.

The sharp teeth found their mark; striking and quickly recoiling, they came away with a mouthful of flesh ripped away from just under the demon's left collarbone.

The giant demon screamed, all of its five head-circling eyes momentarily bulging in their sockets.

Recovering quickly nevertheless it immediately attacked again, and this time its other claw found its mark and raked shield-sized scales away in broad slashes across the upper end of the dragon's torso, just missing slashing its throat. The impact felled the dragon, leaving the building-sized demon momentarily alone and towering over it.

The demon looked like it was about to fall on its opponent, ready to slash it to death.

But it didn't get the chance.

One of Medea's monsters came flying up into its face from below, shrieking in terror all the way like a whistling Eastern bottle rocket. The impact killed the monster, which had been flung by Heracles, and sent the giant demon staggering backwards holding its flattened nose.

Atlas saw the limp monster fall back to Earth and turned to the demigod that had thrown it. Heracles caught his gaze.

"Ha!" Atlas boomed. "Ha-HA! I LIKE that!"

He glanced around. No monster was near enough, though, so he went looking for one. He quickly found two instead but that hardly daunted him. Kicking the first one in away laterally, sending it flopping over and over across the flagstones when it finally came down, he stepped aside as the second one charged in right in the first's tracks and – aiming for just the right angle – punched it hard, aiming up at the spot high overhead where the demonic giant was rubbing its bloody nose.

A remarkable shot, one worthy of a titan, delivered the flying monster right into the back of the demon's hand, imparting all of its considerable momentum into that hand – which in turn, in an unparalleled moment of comic absurdity, slammed right into the demon's battered face.

The immense being staggered back again, black blood staining its nearly as dark sternum.

The giant demon howled, shattering almost every fragile crystal and glass structure in a quarter mile radius.

Bellowing one last roar of defiance at Heracles, Atlas and the others, it turned its back on them and spread its wings. Heracles managed to ding it in the back of the head one more time as it took off, making it dip but not quite bringing it down as well as shutting that creepy eye on the back of the demon's head.

All about the defenders the monsters were running, but most of them were no longer on the attack. They were just running, the way it looked.

The reason for their exodus presented itself in the form of the rise of the opalescent dragon.

Heracles saw the beast turn their way, its rainbow irises flashing, golden blood streaking down its chest scales. A monster was running past him so he lunged out, grabbed it and went into slinging it around himself in obvious preparation for another heave-ho.

"No!"

The cry had come from Sinbad. Heracles aborted his windup with obvious reluctance and turned toward the Chimera's captain while the monster wiggled helplessly in his iron grip, trying to twist free.

"What do you mean?" Heracles hollered back at Sinbad. "Why not?"

"Because," Sinbad said, "I'm pretty sure that's my mother."

Chapter Thirty-Eight

Heracles dropped both his jaw and the warrior brute. The latter picked itself up. Heracles barely noticed as it thrust its chest wide beside him, momentarily ready to take him on despite his obvious power advantage. The monster roared, challenging Heracles, but the demigod appeared seriously distracted by the damaged pearl-scaled dragon looming over the scene.

Seizing its moment the beast lunged at Heracles – only to meet an incapacitating fist slammed into its face at the end of Heracles' abruptly outthrust arm. The demigod had been paying attention after all, stunned as he still looked to be by Sinbad's declaration.

The dragon appeared to have suffered multiple injuries. Sinbad was staring up at it with rare worry in his eyes. The dragon saw this, roared and flew off…heading straight toward his mother's tower at the center of Aderadad.

Sinbad was probably lucky none of the monsters running this way and that were interested in him at that moment, since he lowered his scimitar and followed the dragon's departure with little regard for what was happening around him.

A hard pull on his shoulder shook him out of his near trance.

"This isn't over," Jason said, his blue eyes burning into

Sinbad's brown ones. "But we have to go."

Sinbad nodded sharply. "Aye," he said.

Glancing about, he saw Heracles and Rashid in relatively close proximity to one another. Rashid was taking on one of Medea's brutes while Heracles was jogging around nearby looking for action. The demigod looked peppy and ready for more, but Rashid – still obviously quite mortal despite the glove – appeared pretty worn down. Sinbad caught Heracles' attention with a holler and sent him over to help his first mate.

Atlas was well away from those two and thoroughly enjoying throwing monsters. As soon as he'd get hold of one he'd fling it, and he was tossing them anywhere and everywhere, all the while booming out deep, joyous laughter. Even Heracles seemed sober by comparison, a truly rare moment.

Sinbad watched as Heracles ran up and simply booted Rashid's opponent, who shot away like a missile from the somewhat blindside hit and, smashing into a thick column, broke its base into large chunks of rubble and brought the stone marquee of a public building down on top of the creature.

Heracles and Rashid exchanged grins, Sinbad saw, but the moment ended quickly as more beasts came running at them both. They went back to back.

Atlas had just sent an opponent flailing and shrieking off over the top of a two story building when he caught a glint of his stolen glove. Refocusing, he stomped off that way. Sinbad saw him striding toward his first mate and nearly shouted, but caught himself and waited to see what would happen; after all, Heracles was there too.

Rashid saw the titan coming. He watched as Atlas came up, grabbed both of his opponents from behind, clamping onto their broad shoulders, and slammed their heads together. He saw the titan fling them apart and watched as both went tumbling away.

Rashid's eyes grew wide as Atlas strode right up to

him. "I'm guessing you want your glove back."

Atlas rolled his big, scary blue eyes. "Depends," he said. "Do you want me to go back to holding up the heavens or should I just let it all keep coming down on you? You'll have a day or two either..."

Two beasts – not the ones Atlas had just hammered, they were both out for the count – jumped onto the titan's back at once. Claws did their best to rake his face but, with no little effort, Atlas managed to violently shrug them away.

"All right," he said, and to Rashid's obvious surprise he fell in alongside both the Chimera's first mate and Heracles, spinning about to make their back to back defensive strategy into a triangle. "First things first. Let's finish whatever this is."

Seeing what he'd desperately hoped would happen – that is, no harm to Rashid – Sinbad turned to Jason, who was at that moment engaging not one but two of the monsters. Finishing off the one he'd been fending off for the past few seconds with a remarkable multi-move flourish, Sinbad ran over to even out the odds for his fellow captain.

As he helped Jason take down the pair of brutes Sinbad cast another glance over at Heracles, Atlas and his weary-looking but steady first mate. He bit his lip, knowing he had to decide right then.

"I'm ready when you are," he told Jason as the latter was finishing off his opponent. "I can do little to help Rashid that a demigod and a titan can't."

"I'm not so sure of that," Jason said, turning and watching Sinbad knock off his enemy. "They don't have your mind. But still, it is time. Do what you must."

"Aye," Sinbad said. "May the Fates guide us."

He did something odd then: he looked up to the pensive, cloud-filled skies, searching... searching...

And then, despite the ongoing pandemonium in which he and Jason were immersed, he sheathed his scimitar and raised both hands, fingers spread wide, up to the heavens.

In the next moment Jason beheld a strange sight. A hand – decidedly feminine – appeared to manifest out of thin air. Fingertips became fingers became a hand, followed by a wrist, as though they were emerging from behind some unseen cloak of invisibility hanging in midair next to Sinbad.

Sinbad incanted something and Hecate's mirror appeared around the hand, which withdrew abruptly a split second later. He turned to Jason.

"Let's go," he said.

Jason followed him through the portal. Mere seconds later the mirror vanished, puzzling a monster that had rushed up to it with intent to "smash new thing."

The battle went on as Heracles, Atlas and Rashid stood strong against the slowly dissolving forces that only an hour or so before had been the mightiest army the world had ever known.

Chapter Thirty-Nine

Sheer, unadulterated shock played across Sinbad's face. Not only was Medea there in Circe's lair...so was the deadliest sorceress on Earth herself. Medea had quickly retreated, withdrawing her hand once the mirror had been summoned by Sinbad and drawing back even with her grandmother, who most jarringly looked a lot younger than her haggard, world-weary granddaughter.

Sinbad went for his blade. Jason already had his out, but of course he had even more to ponder than his fellow captain.

"A waste of time, Captain," Circe said as Medea was incanting the mirror back to that side of the portal. "You can do nothing here that I do not allow. So welcome. I believe you know my granddaughter by now, although perhaps not nearly so well as Jason."

Jason's eyes, predictably, were locked on Medea's... and hers on his. But both were saying nothing.

"What is it you want," Sinbad said. "What point is there to the extermination of entire cultures?"

"It's not an extermination, it's a reclaiming of my deity's realm...of her power...on her behalf."

"With all due respect, which may that be?"

"In my granddaughter's realm she is known as Hecate, Queen of Darkness."

The name snagged on Sinbad's sharp memory.

Scimitar still for the moment, he nodded back over his shoulder. "Isn't that the name of the owner of that relic?" he said.

"It is ours, yes. And we thank you for helping us retrieve it for her despite yourselves."

"Interesting …"

Circe's brow furrowed when Sinbad didn't say anything else.

"Interesting in what sense?"

"Oh, it's nothing," Sinbad said, shrugging his shoulders and smiling. "Just that you've been pretty careless with it, don't you think?"

"What do you mean? Those brutes of Medea's couldn't have harmed it. Nothing can."

"No, but it could fall in the wrong hands. Imagine how many others might have that password right now, how many I may have told to be watchful for sorceresses appearing out of the void. You might want to start considering how to reclaim the device from them…and the deadly ambushes I have told them to construct."

Circe and Medea were both staring at him. Circe, at least, looked a little surprised. She was certainly listening, anyway, so Sinbad went on.

"That's right. From now on, when you think my men – and Jason's – aren't paying attention, aren't ready for you to show up, you'll be wrong. Everyone will be watching for you. And eventually everyone will take a shot at getting your deity's precious item from you. You'll be watching out for it now for all eternity. I told everyone to pass the summoning phrase around, and you know what? I'll bet those can't be changed too easily. Oh, and with the kind of traps I told them to set – arrows and the like – I'm thinking you'll have to be really quick just to survive a try at reclaiming it once I'm gone…once the siege to take the mirror has begun."

Circe's triumphant smile was slowly fading, but it was still a defiant sneer.

"You're bluffing," she said. "You didn't have time."

"I had time to write a note and send it circulating around. That doesn't take much time."

Down to a smirk at that, and visibly cracking.

"Well then perhaps I'll just destroy you now," Circe said through her perfect teeth.

Sinbad gave a short bow. "If that is your wish," he said. "For your sake I hope that appeases your deity for the eventual loss of her most valuable relic. Either way your army – your deity's as well, I presume – is all but finished. And it's not a fool's wager to predict you may soon be scrambling just to save yourselves. Now I could call off the mirror siege. And I will if you come to your senses. But without such words on your behalf ...?

Circe was obviously fighting herself, rage vs. rationality. Seeing that Jason's eyes remained locked on Medea she turned to her protégé as well.

"Between us," she said, "how did we not see the risk in giving him the incantation?"

Medea didn't answer. Sinbad did.

"You were too concerned with winning. You gambled too much because you had already played your hand. Sorcerers are known for intellect far more than wisdom. That's why Aderadad has so many dead ones."

Circe's eyes became slits as she turned back to Sinbad.

"I don't know much of your deity, I'll admit," he went on. "Most of the ones I've encountered aren't very tolerant of repeat mistakes. They like their people to get the job done. And while you've made a big mess, killing thousands, leveling cities, I hope that was your entire objective because if it were something larger – world conquest, say – well, you've put a lot into a failing proposition."

"Silence, you fool!"

"He's right."

Circe turned her venomous glare on Medea.

"What...how...how could you *say* that?"

"I failed our Lady once before," Medea said. "I deserted her…for him." She glanced over at Jason.

"Right," Sinbad said. "And why would a high priestess and sorceress serving the deity who watched over her country betray the trust of both a nation and a goddess?"

"Because I loved him."

"And that was the only reason? Not that it can't be the only one, but was it?"

"I…I don't know." Medea was shaking her head and not looking at anyone in particular. "Something happened after we arrived in Thessaly. Not right away. But soon."

"We arrived to great celebration," Jason said, and all eyes went to him. "But Pelias did not step down, not even when I told him of his son's treachery. Our nation was split, with those whose favors he'd earned holding enough strength to keep sway. He took the Golden Fleece and put it to his uses."

"Jason could do nothing," Medea said. "So I did." She went on in a dark, self-loathing tone. "Pelias was a monster. A nation was at stake, and I – fallen priestess that I was – begged for a reprieve. And my powers returned. Hecate was giving me a second chance. Grandmother came to me, guided by Hecate, and we devised a plan."

"A plan I did not oppose upon hearing of it," Jason said in an equally grim voice.

"You only heard of it after the deed was done," Medea said, "with Pelias lying butchered in his own home."

"Pelias was a pig of a man," Circe said. "He was properly executed, not murdered."

"I wonder if his daughters agree with you," Jason said. "They killed themselves after you convinced them their father could add decades to his life by allowing them to cut him into pieces and place him in a reassembling potion."

Circe let out a gleeful little giggle. "That was funny, and no loss. Monsters beget monsters. Didn't Acastus try to kill you?"

"He did. His sisters didn't."

"You'd have preferred they had more time?"

"It wasn't my decision to make. I fight only the armed, and only when no other choice exists."

"A true hero," Circe said. "Who abandoned his wife to go off and find a younger one when wanderlust hit."

"It was over between myself and Medea. I left because I'd allowed that murder, and because of that I no longer deserved to be called king. Truth be told I'd never wanted to be a ruler anyway, but my moral center was gone once I covered up the truth about Pelias. I gave the throne to Medea and left to seek my fortunes."

"Creusa's dress was beautiful, wasn't it?" Circe said, and laughed madly.

Jason's fists were clenching, and the one around the hilt of his gladius was shaking.

"My blade cannot right the wrongs that have been done," he said. "It won't bring back my – *our* – children, whom my wife poisoned in her grief. And it won't return the countless innocent lives that were sacrificed in my place when your hideous army began its accursed scourge.

"You gave me the map," he said to Circe. "You were Pentelus. You came to me in my frustration and offered the one miracle you knew would tempt me. You said I could turn back time, that I could undo all the destruction, all the loss that our theft of the Fleece precipitated in the end."

It was her turn to bow.

"A fair game, wouldn't you say?" she said. "I'd let you do it too – the device is right over there, in fact – but it's your job to defy the gods, not mine. I'm keeping it safely out of your hands."

"It doesn't matter anymore," Jason said. "I realize nothing can be changed. It all had to happen. I simply don't know...where to go now. Destroy me. I've lost everything already."

"Destroy you?" Circe said. "No, not while I can keep you around for entertainment."

"What was it you wanted in the temple?" Sinbad said.

"Are you dim?" the sorceress shot back right away. "The mirror, of course. My Lady – *our* Lady's greatest symbol and relic."

"Is that so?"

Sinbad's smile was faint but Circe couldn't miss it.

"Why would I lie?"

"Perhaps you wouldn't, perhaps I'm stalling for time," Sinbad said, and he watched as the sorceress raised her hands before her chest, fingertips growing rigid and pointing right at him. "It's just that it seems odd to me that you're not getting a pat on the back for all your triumphant work."

Circe relaxed short of assuming full battle pose, huffed her exasperation out...and let him go on.

"I mean yes," he said. "You've sacrificed a big, expensive-looking army to get it. Pretty high budget maneuver. Still, if it's that big a deal...I don't know, I'd just think you'd have some kind of message from your beloved goddess by now. A sign. A cosmic thumb's up, so to speak. But perhaps your deity is not the type to go for such things. Bootstrap philosopher, maybe, or just shy."

Circe recoiled slightly, giving the Chimera's captain the same look she might have had he just offered her something distasteful.

"Goddesses do not send messages on a whim," she said, but her ensuing shrug came off hesitant and rigid and not half as convincing as she'd no doubt have preferred. "What is important is that Zeus no longer has my Lady's relic under lock and key. It's mine to use as her faithful servant."

"Actually it's a lot of people's to use, as I said before."

Circe's ire re-lit instantaneously. She glared.

"You I *will* destroy. Jason can be Medea's toy. You

neither of us has a use for."

"Again, as you will. It will do you little good but perhaps it will be gratifying."

"Hecate is aware of my work," Circe said. "Unlike my granddaughter I have never flagged. I have always been my Lady's faithful servant.

Both Sinbad and Jason saw the look Medea shot her mentor, but Circe apparently didn't.

"Where I'm from servants generally show more humility," Sinbad said. "I must confess my curiosity is piqued by the thought of a lazy 'god' whose servants are allowed both frequent mistakes and inexplicable arrogance."

"Filth," Circe hissed. "Maybe I WILL keep you alive. Perhaps as a tentacled jelly of some kind."

She raised her arms again and set them rigid.

"Hecate is a fool!" Sinbad shouted, and his voice echoed off the cavern walls far out in the darkness. "Her powers are a joke. Here, in her greatest and most prized servant's sanctuary, I call her a puny and worthless being to her servant's face!"

Circe's eyes were nearly boiling. Her fingers and her lips were vibrating like bowstrings.

"How dare you?!"

"How dare I indeed," Sinbad said. "It seems your deity will bear any insults without response, even in her holiest of Earthly places."

Circe had to battle herself but held off turning the Chimera's captain into something that couldn't answer her questions.

"What do you mean?"

"I would not walk into a djinn's lair, or that of one of his valued servants, and expect to be able to get away with insulting it or calling it out. This is your temple? Yet I may profane your deity? To me that rings hollow. Something is amiss."

"Amiss?" Medea said.

"You worship a titan," Jason said. "Their time is gone. Zeus controls the power of the heavens now, he and his brothers and sisters and children."

"Hecate still has power on this world," Circe declared as though saying it forcefully made it true.

"Perhaps," Sinbad said. "But on my first visit here I saw something. A golden apple."

"Melanion's Golden Apple," Circe said, shrugging it off. "The first of a series used against Atalanta to win a race with marriage at stake. A souvenir, more than anything."

Sinbad shook his head. "Perhaps," he said. "But we know of the golden apple as well, and in our legends the golden apple is a dire temptation, meant to bring about disagreement, dissension, conflict ..."

"Discordia," Jason said.

"Exactly," Sinbad said.

"No, I mean the goddess."

Thunder rumbled throughout the darkened lair. The distant apple – a true relic, one of the most powerful of all – came alive and glowed like the sun, dispersing the darkness and illuminating the huge cavern's arching, stalactite-studded natural roof and extremes. The floor shook.

Held in place atop their pedestals, Circe's collection vibrated but remained steady.

Discordia's avatar manifested in a brilliant flash and with a hideous cackle that showed the true ugliness behind her flashy beauty. Dressed in a true anachronism of an outfit that she'd taken from another time – far into the future – the leather clad vixen showed a lot of skin as she strutted about.

"Hey, it's me...Hecate: all hail the powers of chaos!" she said cheerfully. "Do as I say! Bow down before me! And so forth."

Circe looked both embarrassed and appalled. "You dare to insult a..."

"A what, honey, a god? Doubt it seriously. A titan. Nothing nearly so dangerous. The easterner's right. My parents are gods, and that's what flows in my blood. I'm no Heracles, my mortal-tainted half-brother. I'm just as powerful as Mom and Dad, and I get around a lot more."

Chapter Forty

"Oh by the way," Discordia's avatar said as she moved around them all in a wide circle, "this has really been fun to watch."

As she passed in front of them the pedestals and their occupants were half-visible through her form, which was obviously not completely material. She was like a half-phantom, a sexy one with fishnet nylons and pushed-up cleavage under a sharp, v-shaped chin over which short, spiky black hair jutted out in every direction. Her eyes were glassy, black and soulless.

She turned her gaze on Medea. "Your grandmother has been the source of your problems all along. You obviously hadn't figured that out yet so I thought I might as well make sure you got the point. Hardly matters, really, but since you've unwittingly done such fine work on my behalf and been at least as fine a dupe as your grandmother I thought I'd give you a little reward, as it were. Enlightenment. You're welcome."

Circe launched a pair of vicious energy bolts at the avatar but they went right through it, doing no damage. One of them smashed a columnar pedestal, however, and brought whatever it had been holding crashing to the tiles with it.

"You're going to wreck your place," Discordia said, flashing a wicked grin. "But feel free." She hadn't broken stride one bit. "I must say thank you to both of you ladies, though. A sincere one. I could not have done a better job of destruction had mother bade Hephaestus make me a hundred rolling war machines. I can practically hear Harmonia weeping...can you hear that?" She was cocking her head and grinning. "And talk about ramifications for the future. Thessaly attacked one nation after another. And with a force so imposing that the nations in their path broke pacts and abandoned their brethren. Chaos, enmity, suspicion, fear...rebuilding should be a nice, long, painful process. And all of it gives me more than just a rush...much, much more. It gives me...power."

The apparition paused, turned and smiled. Circe was issuing curses, powerful yet impotent.

"I'm an image, you fool. I cannot be harmed. I'm just here to gloat. And watch you kill each other."

"Gloat if you will," Sinbad said. "If we cannot fight you, our true foe, we will not fight each other."

"You will if I tell you to."

Most abruptly the entity became even more vaporous. And in the next moment, in little more than the blink of a startled eye, Discordia's avatar funneled itself in a sort of plasma-like form and went straight into Jason.

The Argo's captain's body convulsed momentarily. Jason clutched himself tightly, fighting the influx of dark power. He dropped to his knees, groaning, his body apparently wracking itself in an unwinnable struggle.

Medea did something quite unexpected: she rushed over to him.

He rose up as she closed in, the gladius in his hand once again, and ran her through.

His eyes registered the helpless horror of the body's trapped owner even as the controlling force kept his face locked into a maniacal grin.

Medea gasped, her eyes dimmed and Discordia lowered Jason's arm to allow her to slide off the blade and slump to the floor.

Circe was aghast. And off guard.

Sinbad seized what he knew would likely be his only chance, however slight it might indeed prove to be. He rushed at the distracted sorceress. She didn't react until the last moment, and that wasn't quite in time to prevent Sinbad from tackling her. They went down together and he made sure her head hit the ground hard enough to stun her or – better yet – knock her unconscious.

He only accomplished the former, but that was good enough for his purposes. He jumped up off her as the possessed Jason came hurtling after him, and only via a quick tumble-and-grab roll did he manage to come up with his scimitar in time to block a potentially deadly swing from Jason's gladius.

Swords clanged in the great cavern, still lit by the golden apple's radiance.

"I could destroy you now through magic," Jason said, his voice his own but the words obviously not. "But this is far more entertaining. I hope I slip up and you kill him, actually. You're more…fun."

"I appreciate your sense of fair play," Sinbad said, parrying a vicious flurry of high-low-in-out-thrusts with quick and flawless deflections.

"Oh, I don't have one of those," Discordia-controlled Jason said. "As long as I'm enjoying myself, the whole immortality/can't be touched thing makes this just a show for me. I am curious as to how it will end."

"As am I, I must admit." The fair match continued, blade ringing against blade, with Sinbad doing his best to be subtle and indirect in his maneuvering of the contest towards one particular spot. "So you'll play dirty tricks, then?"

"If I'm losing, perhaps."

"I see."

CLANG! Hiiiissss… CLANG! CLANG! CHING! Whoooosssshhh… CLANG!!

"You sound disappointed," Discordia Jason said.

CLANG! TING! Hiiiissss… CLANG!

"No, not so much that …"

CLANG! SHING!

"Then what?"

CLANG! Whoooosssshhh!"

"I just like to know all the rules."

CLAAANNNGGG!

Sinbad had been saving up his strength, preparing a particularly hard swing for just the right moment. This was it. Now or never. Telegraphing his intention deliberately, he made sure Jason/Discordia would be able to block it…and then, delivering all the force he could muster, he threw his weight into the blow as well.

Pushed slightly onto the back edges of his heels, Jason/Discordia teetered.

Sinbad struck.

Chapter Forty-One

The scimitar found its mark.

But it had not been aimed at flesh. Instead it hit the golden apple dead center: the relic seemed to detonate, emitting a blinding "death flash" as it crushed inward from the mighty blow that the Chimera's captain had landed on it. Along with this came a shock wave that hammered the bodies of both combatants – even as an agonized female scream rang out into the ether.

The brilliance made the darkness that followed all that much more intense.

Silence fell as well. Some light remained, that generated by the still-active mirror: a dim and pale glow to be sure but enough at least to illuminate the spot where it still stood. Not far from it Circe was getting to her feet, staggering and wiping blood from the corner of her mouth. She spoke and soft magical light illuminated the chamber from end to end at her command.

She saw two bodies in the distance, about ten yards to either side of a pedestal upon which sat a caved-in (but still quite beautifully shimmering) golden apple. Steadying herself, she grinned with vengeful determination and headed off that way.

Sinbad was stirring slightly, Jason wasn't, so Circe passed by the latter to attend to the former.

He didn't seem to register her approach, lying as he

was such that he was facing away from her with his left cheek on the tiles. He was twitching more than exhibiting any deliberate motion.

Circe drew to within ten feet or so, decided that was close enough, and raised her hands to position in preparation for a quick magical rearrangement of Sinbad's anatomy.

"Ready to go to Hades?" she growled.

He rolled over, displaying a most surprising smile.

"Ladies first," he said.

Lying on his side he thrust both arms out toward her: one was holding Mnemosyne's phial, the other was pulling out its stopper.

Circe howled like a demon as she was sucked into the bottle.

Sinbad quickly capped it.

He got to his feet, shoved the phial into his shirt and, shaking off what cobwebs still remained in his head from the stunning blast, he hustled over to Jason.

"Still out," he said to himself, kneeling at Jason's side and checking his pulse. "Good."

With his tackle of Circe he'd pulled a sneaky move, one the sorceress in her haste and anger hadn't even noticed. Reaching back inside his shirt, he pulled out the necklace and the final remaining teleport crystal.

He was about to crush the crystal when a faint but distinct golden glow caught his eye.

***

Haroun helped the critically injured Margiana to a sofa once she'd transformed back into herself.

"I did...what...I could..." she said.

"Please be still my lady," Haroun said. "Save your strength."

"It doesn't...doesn't...matter," Margiana said as Haroun gently set her down. "Aderadad may survive

273

now. My son is here, and he has brought…powerful allies to our aid. I couldn't…destroy her…the invader's lea… leader. But we…drove her…"

She slipped away.

Haroun tried to revive her but she was too far gone.

He wept at her side while the otherwise silent upper reaches of Aderadad's central palace echoed with the distant sounds of combat and destruction.

***

So grieved was Haroun that he had his face down between his sleeves where he crouched beside his deceased liege (and friend of several decades) and thus didn't see Sinbad step through.

The Golden Fleece lay in the easterner's arms.

Sinbad saw his mother and Haroun and hurried over to them, but his footfalls were too quiet for Haroun to hear over his own sobs. Sinbad moved up close, saw that his mother was lifeless and just stood there for a second, stunned and wordless.

Haroun must have finally heard or sensed something, for he turned and saw the son of the man who'd saved him from a life as a wastrel looking down upon him.

Once he'd registered the fact that Sinbad was actually there – it took a few seconds – he glanced back at Margiana's face, then turned back to look up at Sinbad, shaking his head.

"It is indeed beyond hope to see you here," he said. "But you're too late."

"Perhaps not," Sinbad said, and ignoring Haroun's puzzled expression he gestured him aside.

Sinbad knelt, holding the robe over his mother's body.

"I do not know how it works," he said, staring at Margiana's face. "We can only hope it does."

He lay the Fleece, a stunning shag of twined golden hair, carefully over his mother's body. Then he drew back and watched, Haroun standing at his side.

"If there's an incantation or something that I must do I fear I do not know it," Sinbad said when nothing happened right away. "And I dare not free the only person who would know…"

He stopped because the Fleece had begun to glow. The golden fibers radiated wondrously rich light that somehow made the visually dazzling into the simply amazing. Incredibly, the deep slash just beneath Margiana's neck knitted itself back together. The blood that had stained down from the wound vanished as hot breath clears the steam from chilled glass, much as though it had sunk right back down through her skin.

Margiana stirred.

She opened her eyes. The Fleece ceased glowing.

"Sinbad," she said, looking through still-foggy eyes into her son's.

But he knew she didn't mean him, because she called him by his given name – Ali.

"No Mother, it is I…Son of Sinbad."

Margiana's eyes cleared. She smiled. "No son," she said. "I mean you. Your father is right: you deserve the title."

Their reunion celebration was sweet, although by necessity fairly brief.

"I need to get back to Rashid and the others," he said. "And I had hoped to hear Orpheus' playing by now. His absence gives me concern for the Chimera. But even so I cannot control all fronts." He pulled the phial from his shirt and handed it to his mother, whose strength was fully returned, all wounds healed. "Take this," he said. "By all means keep the stopper in. I can think of no more secure place for it…and *her*."

Margiana lifted the phial up before her eyes and she and Haroun both stared at the quite angry sorceress inside it.

"Keep the Fleece as well. I don't want anyone else

getting their hands on either."

"Who else is involved?" Haroun said.

"A powerful being with great skills in dark magic. In the west they call them gods. They are much like our djinn, and more than a match for any mortal's magical skills. With respect, Mother."

Margiana smiled warmly.

"Really?" Haroun said.

"She made short work of that sorceress' disciple and – quite by accident, I'm sure – gave me a chance to trap her mistress. I was fortunate enough to vanquish the goddess by damaging a sacred object of hers but if she's as powerful as she seems then I doubt the shriek I heard as she disappeared was from fear of eternal destruction. We can only hope that she isn't angry enough to come looking for trouble here, but if she is…"

"If anyone besides you appears here out of the ether," Margiana said, gently cutting her son off, "they'll get more welcome than they would ever want."

"NO. Even if I appear. Do not trust that I am who I say. The sorceress in that phial was masquerading as a scholar named Pentelus. And you yourself can become a dragon."

"Not often."

"You've done enough for Aderadad, Mother. You've already died for it once today. Be on guard now here and let me finish what you have begun."

Chapter Forty-Two

After a hug from his mother and a handshake from Haroun, who promised to guard her back as always, Sinbad turned and went back out to the balcony...to the spot where he'd appeared. He called for the mirror.

It appeared. He closed his eyes and the scene in the mirror – the interior of Circe's museum-like central chamber, with Medea lying motionless in a dark pool in the foreground – shifted. Heracles, Atlas and Rashid were still at it, fighting in the midst of an almost ludicrously tall ring of fallen monster bodies (and parts.) Rashid had taken a bad slash across the bicep that had apparently rendered his weapon arm useless, Sinbad saw with dismay. But his certainly nearly exhausted first mate was still going at it ferociously with the gloved arm regardless of how tired he indeed looked, and besides that Heracles and Atlas apparently knew he needed more cover fighting one-armed because they were all now wedged in even more closely together.

"Hang on just a little longer, old friend," Sinbad said, his eyes open and watching the scene through the mirror. "That you are still fighting tells me we have even more vital issues elsewhere."

He shut his eyes again and changed the mirror link to reveal a scene aboard the Chimera.

The deck was manned from stem to stern, he saw.

But not with men.

The creatures had deep blue skin, human-shaped bodies and demonically angular faces. Nearly man sized, they had horns and bat-like wings and looked like extremely thin and wiry humans as their larger-than-man-sized claw feet struggled to deal with the deck planking.

Sinbad saw three of his crewmen lying motionless on the deck amidst the prowling group of creatures. The intruders weren't steering the ship or manning anything: rather they were just strutting awkwardly about here and there, jumping and flapping and repositioning themselves every time one of them crowded another. Their actions appeared more animal than intelligent.

A cluster of five of them were gathered around a ripped-open crate of food supplies including dates, nuts and the like. They seemed to be omnivores, Sinbad saw: one was chasing a rat around the deck in the foreground.

Sinbad's view was narrow and didn't allow him to confirm whether the Argo was still sailing along with the Chimera or not. All he could really see were about two dozen bat-winged, gargoyle-featured invaders loitering around between the prow of the ship (his point of view) and his cabin in the stern – where at the moment two of the things were clawing at his brand new door, so far without getting it open. Three others formed the remaining "cluster" on the deck: these were bent over trying to pry open the main hatch.

He couldn't even see behind him, where his crew had been installing the calliope.

He quickly noticed something: clear or nearly clear passages were opening here and there, now and again, between the portal's locale and the two creatures working at his cabin door.

He glanced back and saw that Margiana and Haroun had moved up behind him.

"The Fleece," he said, beckoning for Haroun to hand it to him, which he did right away. He looked to his mother as he took it. "Father would take this risk."

"He takes any risk," Margiana said. Her smile was oddly bright, more earnest and pain-free than her son had seen it in…years. "I'll explain…*when you return.*"

He matched her grin. She moved up to him, tilted her head up and kissed his cheek.

"Haroun, do you have a fairly heavy coin with you?" Sinbad said, holding his mother's hands.

Indeed Haroun did have one, and he passed that along as well. Sinbad took it as he was adjusting the Fleece over his shoulder.

Then, turning to the mirror, the Chimera's captain set himself, took a deep breath…and rolled the coin through the portal. He'd made sure to roll it off his fingertip in hopes that it would hit and roll down the Chimera's deck, and he'd put a good amount of force into the toss to make sure it went as far as possible.

That's exactly what happened. Bouncing once, wobbling frighteningly, the coin eventually righted itself and rolled right down the center of the deck on its edge.

With the exception of the three clusters – the trio at the main hatch, the pair prying at his cabin door and the four or five fighting each other over cashews – the rest of the things locked onto the coin as it rolled right through their midst.

As it was rolling Sinbad went into action. He leapt through the portal, grip tight on the Fleece. Drawing his scimitar as his sandals came down on the deck, he sprinted wordlessly through the midst of the monsters. He set his blade out before him even as his ears were bombarded by a nearly deafening chorus of eagle-like shrieks. Had more been on his mind, were he not so aware and focused, the horrible cacophony would likely have scattered it from his thoughts like straw in a stiff wind.

But he had only one goal, and but two of the creatures blocking the path to it. And as he raced in on them he saw that they were only just noticing something was up behind their backs.

The effect was nearly comical as Sinbad met them both turning around. He ran the one on the left through at where a heart would have been in the human thorax the creature's somewhat resembled, and whether a fatal blow or not that one dropped before it even had time to register the hit.

Sinbad pulled back, jerking the blade clear to let the creature fall, and moving with accuracy and what strength reserves he had left he brought the scimitar up just in time to fend off the other one's sweeping claws. One talon did manage to rake his cheek anyway, but had he not deflected the full blow it would easily have torn his throat out. And even as the others continued their high-pitched howling and raced in on him the Chimera's captain feigned a swing and then kicked the other creature solidly in the chest. It fell back, flapping its wings, and with only a couple of seconds before the rest were on him Sinbad *dropped his scimitar.*

He'd done it deliberately, needing the free hand to pull the emergency cabin key down from its form-fitting slot atop the door frame and slip it into the keyhole. He turned the key and felt the click.

The creatures were on him.

He stepped aside and flung the door open wide, slamming it into the three that were leading the rush toward him on his right. Another four were crushing in on his left.

The door was bouncing back his way as the creatures behind it squawked and staggered.

Sinbad rued not being able to grab his weapon but realized that move would have likely been his ruin. All he had time to do, he knew in the instant he had left, was catch the edge of the door as he backed inside so that he could pull it closed behind him.

And he couldn't even quite manage that.

All four of his would-be assailants couldn't fit through that gap, as he'd figured. Only two of them were close enough to keep him from closing the door, with the other two nearly climbing up their allies' backs to get their pieces of the action.

Four claws raked at him in a flourish.

He withdrew far enough to dodge three of them, but the fourth struck with an actual plan.

He felt searing pain as talons raked across his hand.

Sinbad held on somehow. His ripped mitt already sheeted in blood, he pulled with all he had left.

The creatures pulled back. They couldn't reach him, but he couldn't close the door either. And his hand was vulnerable to more mangling. He slipped it up and down randomly, absorbing splinters but preserving his fingers.

As his strength ran out he changed tactics. He threw himself bodily into the door, driving several of the winged horrors back while unavoidably exposing himself to the pair at the abruptly widening gap itself. Hearing thudding beyond the door coupled with the surprised squawks of tangled creatures, Sinbad focused his attacks on the pair rushing at him through the widened gap.

He drove his boot into the chest of the one in front and sent it flying back, where it collided with the other and blocked its advance...if indeed only for a moment.

Withdrawing as the wailing monster fell back, Sinbad snatched the door and pulled hard. To his great relief it shut without resistance and he immediately barred it with the nearby barricade board, letting the Fleece slip to the floor. Even if they figured out the key he'd been forced to leave in its hole on the other side of the door they wouldn't be able to get the door open with that heavy timber in place.

From the sound of it they were going to bypass keys and boards and just rip until they got into him.

That would be a little while, he knew: his cabin had been a stronghold before, and rebuilt with plenty of reinforcement after its brief occupation by Molo it would serve as such again...hopefully for at least as long as it took.

Sinbad turned his back on the raking of claws, the muffled pounding and shrieking, and gazed at the elegant, yet pale and motionless, figure that lay across his bed.

Chapter Forty-Three

The Chimera's captain picked up the Golden Fleece and walked over to the side of his bed.

Vrona was obviously dead. Beautiful but ivory white, she lay absolutely still.

Sinbad gazed down at her.

"This can restore life to a mortal," he said. "But you were once more than that. Whether it will work – or how, if it does – I have no way of knowing. But I owe you a life, and I am obliged to try."

He bent over and lay the Fleece across Vrona, making sure to cover her as completely as possible.

Then he rose, stood and watched.

Nothing seemed to be happening. The Fleece was not glowing. Not even after he'd waited for a while as he'd had to when the Fleece had eventually resurrected his mother.

The claws were still raking. Sinbad noticed that his shuttered windows were under assault like the door, but those barricades were likewise hardy defenses so he knew it hardly made things any worse.

What threatened to make them worse – dire, in fact – was that his great gamble didn't seem to be working.

And then it was – or may have been – it was hard to tell.

The Fleece came aglow. Crackling, popping, sparks

shooting here and there. Little spider webs of electricity jumping around all over it.

Sinbad stepped farther back, eyes wide. He grabbed his second favorite scimitar off the wall and raised it towards the firework-like spectacle.

The Fleece was glowing brighter than ever before. Too bright. Radiating like a sun.

Sinbad shielded his eyes with his free hand but the light shone pink through his flesh, so potent was the energy being given off. Soon he was forced into a corner and had dropped the scimitar to add more shielding to his face.

And then the light was gone.

To Sinbad the creatures' assaults had by that point become just so much background noise, so they didn't even register with his mind in the aftermath of the miniature nova that had just gone off in his cabin. His skin felt sunburned, a sensation he'd thought his years at sea had left far behind. Rising slowly from his crouch, his eyes adjusting to the once again minimal cabin light, his boot toe shoved the hilt of his scimitar and he made sure to grab the weapon on the way back up onto his feet.

The Fleece was gone.

Vrona was no longer pale, but she still wasn't moving.

Sinbad hurried over to her.

He took hold of her hand. Warm.

He saw her open her eyes.

She smiled.

Staring into those eyes, Sinbad barely even registered the thunderous roar that arose in the following moment beyond the cabin walls, nor the readily noticeable reeling of the ship to port and then starboard in quick succession. His sea legs kept him well balanced. But he was so entranced by Vrona that he didn't even notice that as the great rumbling subsided it had silenced the creatures' shrieking assaults as well.

"Are you all right?" Sinbad said.

"I'm a bit more than that," Vrona said, "though I am not quite sure yet what I have become."

She floated up off the bed and set herself gently down on her bare feet beside Sinbad.

"Your ship is your own again," she said. "The goddess Discordia sent the harpies to punish you for destroying her relic. Most of your crew escaped and swam over to the other vessel, where they all just bore witness to the true power of the oceans."

"What about Discordia..." Sinbad said. "What's to prevent her from retaliating again?"

"I'm going to Olympus. I will speak with her brother, Ares. A juggernaut of destruction is no war, and if she is not serving her brother's interests – her sire's as well – then I will ask him who indeed she is serving."

"You can go to Olympus?"

Vrona's smile was supernaturally reassured. "I can now."

"I'm not sure what you've become," Sinbad said, "but I think I'm glad we're friends."

***

Though indeed it may have appeared that Sinbad's workload was getting lighter such did not turn out to be the case. At least he got a reward: Vrona gave him a long kiss and then vanished, leaving him in his ozone-filled cabin.

He emerged onto a deck swept clean by a pair of very accurate miniature tidal waves, which Vrona had summoned on either side of the ship and used to rid the Chimera of the harpies.

Splashing through puddles, seeing his three dead crewmen had been washed up against the rails, Sinbad heard a new sound: cheering.

He looked over to his left. About a hundred feet off the port side sat the Argo, its sails rolled and stowed, its port rail lined stem to stern with cheering members of both crews.

Sinbad didn't have time to acknowledge the applause.

"Well, it's been a long day or two."

Sinbad spun around.

Once again he was face to face with Discordia herself, but this time he wasn't facing an avatar.

He was facing six of them.

They strolled the Chimera's deck as Sinbad backed to the port rail, scimitar waving.

"You went over my head?" one of the avatars said. "Dirty play."

"What is it you want now?" Sinbad said. "Your deceptions have laid waste to countries and killed thousands."

"That's what I do," a different avatar said. "Don't you get that we all have roles to play?"

"Like Jason," a third avatar said, dragging one vixen-sharp nail across the idle wheel.

"What has become of him?" Sinbad said. "I left him quite alive."

"Yes, you did," a fourth Discordia said. "Thank you for that. I needed the bartering chip."

The avatars were actually moving to a common plan, one that finally dawned on Sinbad when he noticed that – though not directly approaching it – the handful of "deity clones" were all moving invariably closer to the prow.

"You have nothing left to gain from dealing with me or my crew," he said to the fifth avatar, who was bringing up the rear just behind the smiling but silent sixth. Sinbad addressed the sixth as she passed. "But of course that's not why you're here anyway, is it?"

All six avatars stopped as one, paused and turned.

"That instrument," Sinbad said, and he pointed with his blade toward the battened-on calliope. "That's what you wanted all along."

"It belongs to my sister," the sixth avatar, nearest to

him at that moment, said. "The nature god Pan seduced her and took it from her. I want it back for her."

"Interesting," Sinbad said, "that someone so dedicated to disharmony would want to even touch a device design for harmonious accord."

The Discordias had all been smiling – faint but decidedly smug little half-grins – but as one their faces became dark scowls.

"Perhaps we will destroy you," the fifth avatar said. "No loose ends."

"Do as you will," Sinbad said. "I cannot hope to defeat you. But know well you may be defeating yourself should you triumph here. And as a mere mortal my failure will be minor by comparison."

Discordia – all of them – appeared to think about this for a long moment.

"I guess," she finally said, "I'll just have to take my chances."

As one the half dozen deadly magicians gestured.

And the first thing they had to do in the very next moment was decide whether to let Sinbad have it with their various lethal and deforming spells...or deal with the quite angry avatar of the War God himself.

***

"Brother!" all six avatars of Discordia cried, no two in sync because that would have been against her inherent nature. She looked shocked. "Why have you come?"

Ares looked extremely angry.

"This is not WAR, you fool," he told his sister "deity." "This mortal is right. I expect more of you than this pettiness. You want your sister's relic for your own? How does this serve me?"

"But my lord!" the second avatar said. She was standing next to the calliope. "With this instrument of harmony out of reach of mortals there will be no lasting peace."

"It was already out of reach in my father's temple. You coveted it for your own, to lord its possession over your feeble sister. A waste of time. And now your actions bring me here."

"But why?"

"Because father is mad!"

He flung his gleaming spear at the second avatar: it impaled her through her solar plexus and she and all five of the other avatars gasped. The second avatar disappeared in a flash and the spear was instantly back in Ares' hand.

"Now go," he said in the most deadly tone imaginable.

The other five avatars vanished.

Ares turned to Sinbad.

"I was never here," he said.

Sinbad nodded.

Ares vanished.

Chapter Forty-Four

The Chimera entered Aderadad's harbor waters with Orpheus at the prow, manning the calliope. Great billows of smoke rolled from the city's western perimeter as the ship cut the waters with the Argo trailing several ship lengths behind.

"How close do we have to get?" Makili asked the bard.

"Yeah," Ahmad said, "how far is that thing effective?"

"As far as it can be heard," Orpheus said. His head was wrapped in a bloody bandage since he'd taken a swipe from a harpy claw that had actually knocked him over the rail and sent him off to the Argo (whereas most of the others had jumped ship once it was obvious they couldn't take the harpies.) "I'd like to tell you more but I'm not good at estimating distances anyway."

"We'll just get close," Pollux said. One of a handful of Argo crew helping out on the Chimera, he was up at the prow as well. "You start playing and it will work when it does."

Orpheus nodded.

"Maybe I should start now."

***

Across the city the calliope's notes rang, but they weren't quite potent enough yet to reach the battle scene.

Sinbad had rejoined first his mother and Haroun, then passed through the mirror again to provide much needed relief for Rashid...whom he'd arrived to find barely on his feet.

The battle was hours long by this point and not over by any means, but the casualties were ridiculously lopsided and Rashid, Heracles and Atlas had drawn virtually the entire assault wave to their locale...and thus spared about ninety percent of Aderadad from destruction.

Sinbad raced in from the portal and hastened over to the trio, taking out a pair of Medea's monsters from the back on the way in with a flourish of vicious slashes and thrusts to vital regions.

"Miss me?" he said to the dead-haggard Rashid.

"You owe me," was all Rashid could manage.

"Certainly," Sinbad said. "Allow me to give you a moment's break to refresh yourself," he added, and he moved in, spun about and went to work defending his depleted first mate.

Rashid flopped to the ground at his captain's back, looking half dazed. "Want the glove?" he said.

"HEY!" Atlas yelled, hearing him. "That's not a toy to be passed around."

"Keep it," Sinbad said, chuckling between parrying thrusts at new monster opponents.

"How much longer," Heracles said. "I'm actually getting a little tired myself."

"Not too long," Sinbad shot back. "The ships should be in the harbor now."

"I hear nothing."

"Is your strength flagging?" Sinbad said, shooting Heracles a sharp grin. "I could relieve you too."

"Of course you could. You've been off playing and should be well rested."

"You actually want me to..."

"And let it be known a mortal had to cover for me?"

"I had to ask."

Heracles returned Sinbad's grin. "What about their leader?" the demigod said.

"She's dead," Sinbad said.

"And yet her army persists," Heracles said.

"Perhaps if they knew she was gone?" Rashid said.

"Look in their eyes," Sinbad told them both. "Tell me you see any potential for reason there."

"If that's the case," Heracles said after a moment's contemplation, as blows rained and metal clanged all about, "how exactly do you expect …?"

Music was wafting to their ears now, borne on abruptly shifted winds. Undeniably stirring and inspiring though still faint, it brought with it a distinct sensation: something was coming, and it was powerful and committed.

Medea's brutes didn't pick up on it quite so quickly as Heracles (or Sinbad, Atlas and Rashid) but they had ears, so it happened fairly soon.

The calliope's supernatural chords were ringing out across Aderadad, the Chimera and Argo drawing ever nearer to the core of battle. Around that central commotion – the berserk, nearly mindless monsters still seemed to think they could take the demigod, titan and company – the creatures remained oblivious to the music. But farther back, on other streets, inside burning shops and destruction, the beasts were clearly hearing Orpheus' long-delayed "assault."

Chapter Forty-Five

Fear.

These manufactured monsters weren't even aware such an emotion existed. That is to say, until they heard Pan's Calliope played by a man who'd lost his beloved mate to Hades – twice.

Doom rolled in on that song.

It washed over the monsters, striking this terrible, confusing new emotion into hearts and semi-minds that had no way to handle it.

They ran.

Well, they were already running in general. But not in the same direction, just about every which way as was their custom. Orpheus' dread-inducing anthem organized them quickly into an exodus bound out of Aderadad. There was a general direction to these less centralized invaders once the music sank in, and that was "Away." At utmost speed.

The sight of the fleeing creatures would have been comical had they not been making tracks through the ruins they themselves had wrought of the city's western fringe.

More of them peeled away from the main conflict as the Chimera neared and Orpheus' song grew louder. Powered by forces beyond the ken of most mortal minds, the Calliope was actually resonating the standing structures that remained about the monster body-piled, rubble-strewn battle scene.

At that point even the broad ring of attackers encircling Heracles, Sinbad, Atlas and Rashid were hearing it, and despite their strength of numbers they soon proved just as vulnerable to the song.

"Look at that!" Rashid said, rising to his feet with renewed vigor and pointing at the exodus. "They're running for their lives."

"I wasn't even sure they had a sense of self preservation," Sinbad said.

"Looks like they've got plenty," Heracles said.

Atlas grabbed two beasts before they'd gotten out of reach, and as the rest fled he hurled the pair at them one right after the other. They impacted their brethren and more went down like bowling pins.

Most of them got up, and all who did just kept running.

The driving, haunting music was all around the quartet...but their opponents were gone.

***

For a few long moments all four men just listened to the music, catching their breath (even the titan and demigod were exhausted) as their opponents evacuated the area. Then they celebrated, exchanging handshakes.

The celebration was brief.

"Jason," Heracles said, his smiling fading as he looked to Sinbad. "What of him?"

Sinbad shook his head. "I cannot say. He was unconscious after...the battle with Discordia."

"Discordia?" Heracles' broad, bearded mug grew stormy. "You told me we were fighting witches, not the most treacherous half-sister a hardworking man can have."

"Someone else came and put her in line. With a great golden spear."

"Ares," Heracles said. "My half-brother."

"He seemed a little upset. Apparently he didn't agree with what she thought of as war."

"Yeah, it was a little unbalanced. I blame the design. If they'd been a little smaller but just as strong so more could have gotten at us at once, now THAT might have been a fair tussle."

They all laughed: weary, deep laughter. Even Atlas was smiling.

But his smile faded as he turned to glare at Rashid.

"What?" the Chimera's first mate said. Then he remembered the glove. His shoulders sagged. "Oh yeah," he said glumly. "Guess you want it back."

"Not necessarily," Atlas said. "You take the other and hold up the Heavens for a few millennia if you want. By the way the skies have been falling since you invaded the temple and summoned me for a test. Lucky for Earth the fall is slow, but one of us will have to go back to the Nexus and do the job soon."

"I don't think I'm qualified," Rashid said. He took one last look at the silver glove, which certainly looked as though it was fitted closely around a hand and wrist. "Nice while it lasted," he said, staring at it.

He pulled it off.

Beneath the glove his hand and wrist had completely regrown.

"I don't believe..." Rashid said, marveling at his restored limb and flexing it, bending his fingers.

"The Golden Fleece restores life," Atlas said, jerking the glove out of Rashid's other hand. "Yet THIS surprises you? Enjoy that new one and try not to lose it again too soon."

Atlas stepped back.

"Thank you for helping," Sinbad told him, and he bowed.

Atlas shrugged. "Lucky for you," he said. "I needed the exercise."

He put the glove on, swelled to about a hundred feet in height, became vaporous and drifted off on the wind in a matter of seconds.

"Well, I can imagine a day with an angry titan worse spent," Heracles said.

"We should go," Sinbad said to the demigod and Rashid. "We need to get back to Jason."

***

Sinbad guided them to the portal and they stepped through it to Margiana's terrace.

Orpheus' song was still ringing out in the distance, over in the harbor's western reaches not far from the smoking curtain of half-demolished western Aderadad.

Margiana hugged her son – again (she'd done it upon his return from the Chimera) – welcomed Rashid back with another and then stood smiling as Sinbad introduced her to the demigod.

"We have to get to Jason," Sinbad said.

But no sooner had he spoken than a web of lightning-like energy manifested a few yards across the balcony, an elongated oval of sheer bluish white power that heralded the arrival of ...

"Father!"

Heracles looked stunned.

"Hello, my son. It has been a long time."

"Forgive my ignorance," Margiana said, bowing respectfully. "You are akin to a djinn?"

The newcomer laughed and the skies rumbled.

"I suppose you could say that, my dear," he said. "Although it's highly unlikely any of them have my level of responsibility."

He turned to Sinbad.

"You are not of my realm," he said as Sinbad bowed. "Pity. You should be. We could use more such as you."

He watched Sinbad bow even more deeply.

"Lord Zeus…" Heracles said. "…Father…you bring word of Jason?"

"I do, my son. Jason's circumstance, as you know, has become…unique. His children, his wives…are in Elysium, and to reward him for his heroic deeds I gave him the opportunity to join them there while waving the customary entry fee of death."

"So his days of captaining the Argo are done?" Rashid said.

"He refused me. He defied me, and hardly for the first time."

"Where is he?"

"He said he wanted to atone for his mistakes. He wants to captain the Argo until he's done so." Zeus looked around at them all. "I could hardly deny him the opportunity."

The deity smiled, including a little extra warmth for Margiana.

"I suppose since this is a case of the mortals in my realm invading yours, I owe you a little something as a peace offering."

"That's all right," Margiana said. "I wouldn't expect…"

"Your husband is alive," Zeus said. "Where, I cannot say. I'm telling you more than I should, in fact."

Sinbad's jaw was hanging as loosely as his mother's.

"I can't tell you how to get to him," he said, turning to Sinbad. "But I have little doubt a sharp fellow like you will figure it out eventually. You certainly have plenty of help, considering that on the balance it seems fairly obvious that Jason now owes *you* a favor or two."

Ever the fan of spectacle in such circumstances, Zeus graciously bowed, rose…and was struck by a blinding bolt of lightning. The flash faded and the deity was gone.

"Pretty powerful djinn," Rashid said, staring at the flash burn on the balcony tiles.

Zeus' final words on the matter came gently, drifting

through on the breeze.
  "I'm not a djinn …"

Epilogue

Aderadad Harbor shimmered in the morning sunlight. A steady and bracing breeze brought the smell of delicious (and, likely, some not so delicious) breakfasts being served in various waterfront restaurants, inns and taverns wafting over the decks of the newly outfitted Chimera.

And across the planks of the Argo as well, for she bobbed just off the Chimera's starboard bow.

A few minutes earlier Rashid and Sinbad had rowed over to the Argo and they were currently standing with Jason, Heracles and Orpheus amidst a circle featuring the rest of the Argonauts.

"If I could have told you the entire story I would have," Jason said as he and Sinbad shook forearms. "I had grown ill...obsessed with the idea of undoing past mistakes. Pentelus – Circe – came along and promised me exactly what I most desired."

"She was used as well," Sinbad said. "That Discordia is one malign djinn."

"I'm afraid she's far worse than that," Jason said. "Although from what I hear none of us should have to worry about her for a while, and you're to thank for that."

"We can hope. And we can guard against her at all times anyway."

"Indeed. We shall strive to be free of discord."

"Not to be negative," Rashid said, "but I foresee two problems here. First off we have no idea where we're going, although I'll concede that's never stopped us before. No, I see the biggest issue being that we are carrying around some items on both of these vessels now that are not meant to be in the hands of mere mortals."

"Not exactly," Sinbad said. "As Orpheus explains it I believe the relics are simply meant to be kept out of the hands of immortals. Nothing about we death-susceptible folk in that at all. Am I wrong?"

Orpheus saw Sinbad addressing him and conceded that it wasn't specifically in the lore, but he certainly didn't seem too thrilled by the prospect of hauling around forbidden treasures.

"Between the two vessels," Rashid said, the traditional worry back in his face, "we are carrying around a severed head with a face that turns flesh to stone, an instrument that can drive away hordes of monsters and a torch we should probably thank our various gods, djinn and/or common senses we didn't have to use."

"Right," Sinbad said. "And until rightful owners come to collect them from us I'd much rather be with them than without them."

He looked around. Most everyone else was nodding, none more vehemently than Jason.

"These don't even belong to the Olympians," the Argo's captain said. "Atlas has his gauntlets back and Orpheus tells us the big man – no offense there, Heracles – is not one for holding grudges...at least as titans go. Immortals may lay claim to these but those are fallen gods, their powers gone. And in the interim I vote that considering we really don't know where we're going, we take everything we think we could ever need...including forbidden relics possibly coveted by vengeful gods. After all, as most here know by now I'm no novice to dealing with their wrath."

"I will trust your wisdom," Sinbad said, smiling. "But

tie up my camel."

The whole crowd laughed.

"We set sail then?" Jason said.

"Aye, to the east beyond the east," Sinbad said.

"And the east past that one!" Rashid said, and more laughter ensued.

"My father sailed that way ten years ago and never returned," Sinbad said. "In all that time I never once considered that he might be dead. And now that I know he is not, I must try to find him."

"Aye," Jason said. "With the Argo at your service."

"And the Chimera beneath your feet," Rashid said. "For better or worse."

"That's reassuring, old friend," Sinbad said, and he patted Rashid on the shoulder. "Otherwise I'd have to swim and I doubt I'd keep up with Jason's ship."

Yet more chuckles.

"These will be unknown seas, filled with great and treacherous dangers," Sinbad said to Jason. "I cannot rightly ask you to follow us into them without full and fair warning. You owe me no debt so great. How my father and his crew survived their journey I do not know, nor where they are, but I must find him. I must find... Sinbad."

Jason thrust out his arm and they shook again, both smiling as were those about them.

"My men and I are pledged to this," he said, and looking around he saw ubiquitous nodding that confirmed his statement. "Although there's one part you've gotten wrong: we're looking for your father. YOU are Sinbad."

Cheers erupted, along with raucously approving laughter and whoops.

Sinbad shook his head. "Hopefully there is room in the world for two of us then," he said, smiling. "I'm keen to find out."

***

He and Rashid headed back to the Chimera a few minutes later, propelled by cheers at their backs as much as the oars they were working. They came up the ladders to more applause, which Rashid quickly hushed with a stern look and wave of his hands.

"This isn't the Argo," he said. Then his grim look cracked into a smile. "But it IS a good day!"

Sinbad left Rashid and the rest and headed into his cabin. Once inside, he verified that Prometheus' Flame was safe and then went over to Hecate's mirror.

He stood in front of it.

He smiled.

"Are you there?"

Vrona stepped through.

They embraced. They kissed, long and deep...and unhurried now that the crisis had passed.

"So, please take this the best possibly way," Sinbad said. "What exactly are you now?"

"They don't have a name for what I've become," Vrona told him with a smile. "I'm a first."

"Perhaps that's why the relics are kept out of the hands of the immortals."

They embraced and kissed again.

"I missed you," Vrona said.

"And I you. I must confess my mind has struggled to focus over thoughts of your accompanying me on this journey."

Vrona drew back a little. Her smile faded.

"I can't go along," she said. "It is difficult to explain but my presence will draw more danger to you than my powers can keep from you."

"Danger is easier to deal with when you're constantly exposed to it," Sinbad said. "Stay."

"It is not that simple," Vrona said, but a faint smile traced across her beautiful face. "Yet."

"Then I must travel alone?"

"You have Rashid and the others. You are not alone."

"It will feel like it during the long nights."

"Perhaps not."

Her enigmatic smile did not come with any more explanation.

"What about the hourglass?" Sinbad said.

"Only Circe can access her lair," Vrona said. "All its contents are safe."

"ALL of them?"

"Yes, including their owner."

"It seems unfair in a way," Sinbad said. "That's true isolation."

"She sponsored the deaths of thousands upon thousands of innocents and ravaged cities."

"Well, when you put it THAT way ...but wasn't all that Discordia's work?"

"Gods do not wreak such terrible destruction. Only those who blindly serve them in disregard of their own humanity can do that."

"You are indeed wise," Sinbad said. "Perhaps it is I who should call you Sinbad."

Vrona smiled with the warmth of the South Seas.

***

Circe stared out from Mnemosyne's phial. Perched atop a pedestal, her powers cut off by the impassable stopper, she could but look upon the half-gloom helplessly, cursing Sinbad and Discordia alike in turns. How long had she been there? Days? Months?

She'd been deceived by a goddess, one that had insulted her deity – and from the looks of it, without reproach. Had Hecate abandoned her? The titan god still held power of some note in Olympus, a virtually unique status. Perhaps Zeus was preventing her from coming to her faithful and powerful servant's rescue: that would make sense, Circe figured, considering his beloved

302

Heracles had become involved in her machinations.

WAIT!

Did something move there in the shadows beyond her other relics? A figure, perhaps?

Yes, Circe realized, squinting into the depths of her lair. Definitely. She hadn't imagined it.

In the next moment the shadow proved itself real enough as it moved in front of her and blocked her view of everything else.

The witch gasped and fell back as a great face materialized on the other side of the phial's crystal walls. The decidedly masculine features grinned.

"Ah," a thunderous voice said. "Exactly who I'd been hoping to find. I think we need to talk."

STAY TUNED FOR THE NEXT ADVENTURE:

SINBAD AT THE END OF THE UNIVERSE

About the Author

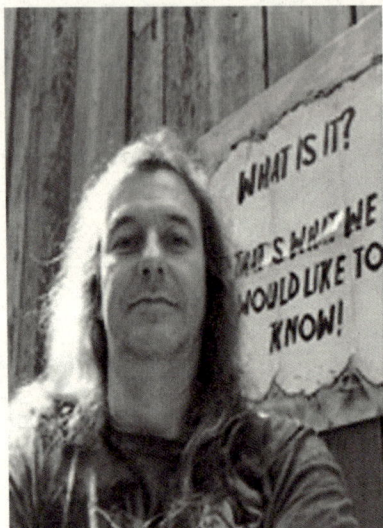

The classic science fiction of the Fifties mirrored our fears; the rock and roll of the Sixties reflected our hopes. Kevin Candela channels both – and a lifelong obsession with all things supernatural – into his work, spinning harrowing yet humorous tales of humanity's ongoing struggle with the weirdness of The Other Side. "I'm into truth," he says. "That's why I write fiction. You can get away with it there." Candela and wife Jackie live in a feline-guarded cave in the mystical Mid-World of Godfrey, Illinois.

(Picture taken by Jason Myers)

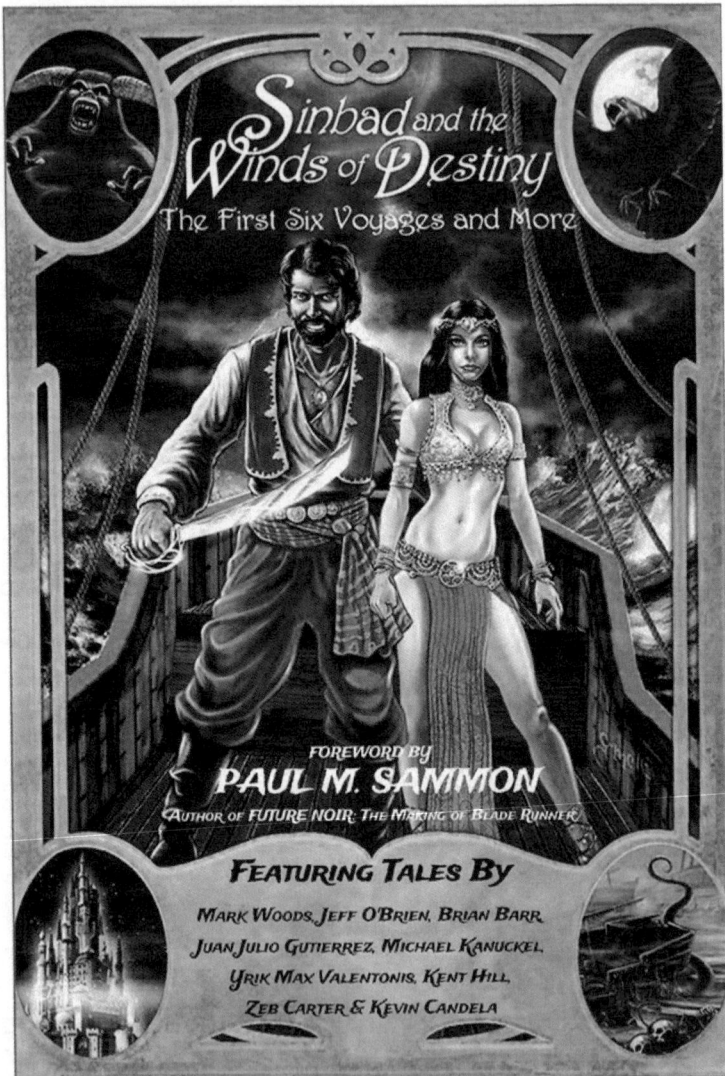

Sinbad and the Winds of Destiny

The First Six Voyages and More

FOREWORD BY

PAUL M. SAMMON

AUTHOR OF FUTURE NOIR: THE MAKING OF BLADE RUNNER

FEATURING TALES BY

MARK WOODS, JEFF O'BRIEN, BRIAN BARR,

JUAN JULIO GUTIERREZ, MICHAEL KANUCKEL,

YRIK MAX VALENTONIS, KENT HILL,

ZEB CARTER & KEVIN CANDELA

INTRODUCTION BY
ERIC LUKE
WRITER OF
EXPLORERS

CINEMA OF AWESOMENESS SERIES

KNP

KEVIN CANDELA

WEEDEATERS
THE COMPLETE ACROPALYPSE

INTRODUCTION BY
RUSSELL MULCAHY
DIRECTOR OF
HIGHLANDER

CINEMA OF AWESOMENESS SERIES

KRP

MICHAEL KANUCKEL

BLACK TAR

INTRODUCTION BY
C. COURTNEY JOYNER
WRITER OF
TRANCERS III &
CLASS OF 1999

CINEMA OF AWESOMENESS SERIES

KJW HILL

HERCULES
WITH A SHOTGUN

Contains crude
Language: Poems by
Kent Hill